Three, Seven, Ace

Three, Seven, Ace

& other stories

Vladimir Tendryakov

Translated from the Russian by
David Alger, Olive Stevens, Paul Falla
with a Foreword by Max Hayward

HARPER & ROW PUBLISHERS
New York, Evanston, San Francisco, London

An abridged version of the story 'Three, Seven, Ace'
appeared in a collection of stories, edited by Max
Hayward and Patricia Blake, published by Pantheon
Books Inc., New York, 1962

THREE, SEVEN, ACE AND OTHER STORIES. English translation
copyright © 1973 by The Harvill Press Ltd and Harper &
Row, Publishers, Inc. All rights reserved. Printed in Great
Britain. No part of this book may be used or reproduced in
any manner whatsoever without written permission except
in the case of brief quotations embodied in critical articles
and reviews. For information address Harper & Row,
Publishers, Inc., 10 East 53rd Street, New York, N.Y.
10022. Published simultaneously in Canada by Fitzhenry
& Whiteside Limited, Toronto.

FIRST EDITION

STANDARD BOOK NUMBER: 01-42422

LIBRARY OF CONGRESS CATALOG CARD NUMBER: 72-8319

The publishers dedicate this volume to the
memory of Alexander Trifonovich Tvardovsky,
Russian man of letters, 1910–1971

Contents

Foreword by Max Hayward   9

Three, Seven, Ace   17
translated by David Alger

Justice   71
translated by Olive Stevens

Creature of a Day   161
translated by Paul Falla

Foreword

The growth in recent years of *samizdat* – literature that circulates in typescript – in the Soviet Union has tended to eclipse the fact that many of the outstanding works of contemporary Russian literature have appeared there in print. It is often not realised in the West that the distinction between *samizdat* and published literature (i.e. that which has received the imprimatur, though not necessarily the wholehearted blessing of editors and censors) is not as rigid as it seems. Books which circulate in *samizdat* were originally, in a number of cases, submitted for publication in the normal way, but were then eventually blocked by overcautious or ill-disposed editors, or through higher intervention on political grounds. Censorship as such plays a minor role: the decision as to what stories, poems or novels appear in print, and in what form, has often, till recently, been a matter of editorial policy. A timid or reactionary editor will insist on more cuts or reject a manuscript altogether, often forcing the author to resort to *samizdat*, while a bolder and more liberal one will fight to publish a work he believes in, taking personal risks if necessary. Quite exceptional in this respect was the late Alexander Tvardovsky who with supreme courage and skill succeeded for over a decade in turning the literary monthly journal *Novy Mir* into something resembling an independent republic of letters, sheltering, succouring and giving refuge to the finest talents in present-day Russian literature.

Vladimir Tendryakov has been fortunate in enjoying the patronage of Tvardovsky who, with an unfailing flair for recognising excellence, published a good deal of his best work at relatively auspicious times during the sixties – including the three stories in this first collection of Tendryakov's work to appear in English. If Tendryakov has never been driven into the position of having to choose between intolerable compromise with his integrity and the ostracised status of a *samizdat* writer, he certainly owes it first and foremost to Tvardovsky who fought his battles for him, as for so many others. But it must also be said that Tendryakov's relatively secure situation in Soviet literature has been helped by the fact that his interest in social and political issues has generally been subordinate to literary and what might be called 'moral' considerations. In other words, he has never emphasised themes or expressed overt opinions which could be seized upon as provocative – much as he has come under fire at times from the *bien-pensant* critics who are an even greater curse in Russian literature than craven editors. As will be seen from the three stories in the present volume, he takes the political and social land-scape very much for granted – it is not something to be either promoted or rejected, attacked or praised, but is simply 'there', like the weather, part of the drearily familiar everyday setting in which life, with its eternal quandaries and discontents, goes on much as everywhere else. If any general point emerges from Tendryakov's work which could be said to conflict with the official viewpoint, it is that a revolution in the social and economic structures hardly affects the universal rules of human behaviour, people's response to circumstances beyond their collective power of regulation. Marx thought you could change man's nature by changing his institutions. A great deal of the best prose work published in the Soviet Union since 1956 (the year of Khrushchev's denunciation of Stalin) has implicitly denied this proposition. That, indeed, is what it has been all about. Tendryakov's achievement is to have done it almost wholly by the bye, without contentiousness or self-defeating emphasis, but in the tradition of classical Russian prose fiction, through the quiet accumulation of telling detail and the incomparable ability to create characters who, while alive, vivid and plausible as individuals, nevertheless strike the reader as typical of their time and place. To this extent Tendryakov is admittedly only one representative of a trend:

with all other younger writers (he was born in 1923) who
made their mark after Stalin's death, he has endeavoured
to restore Russian prose to one of its traditional functions:
as a prism through which everyday life can be viewed with
no other 'distortion' than that introduced by the author's
compassionate involvement in what he sees.

Although Tendryakov has thus pursued the same general
aim as his other contemporaries, such as Kazakov, Nagibin
and Aksyonov – with whom he is often not unjustifiably
bracketed – he is at the same time readily distinguished
from them. The special hallmark of Tendryakov is perhaps
the structure of his stories, which is nearly always on the
same lines: a crisis – usually an accident or a crime – inter-
rupts the normal flow of life and creates a situation in which
the people involved become morally confused, uncertain of
which path to choose when taken unawares by the pressing
need to make a decision. The result is that good people drift
helplessly into situations where they do bad or even evil
things, while bad or ambivalent people may appear good in
the eyes of their neighbours. In *Three, Seven, Ace* the decent
and brave Leshka Malinkin finds himself betraying his
admired boss because he is incapable of solving a moral
equation of a type he has never encountered before; the
pathetic, kind-hearted Nastya in *Creature of a Day* gets so
entangled in a false situation by no means entirely of her
own making that she can find no way out except by committing a monstrous act of cruelty. In *Justice*, the
hunter Simon Teterin, a man of natural integrity who has
always instinctively known the right thing to do in his
simple forest surroundings, suddenly turns into a pre-
varicator, liar and coward. This last story is especially
characteristic of Tendryakov – and it was the one that
raised the most furious outcry among orthodox critics –
because it brings into particularly sharp focus what is
probably his main preoccupation: the disturbance of a
natural 'moral equilibrium' that occurs when people of a
relatively unchanged way of life (i.e. that of the countryside,
for the most part) become enmeshed in the institutions –
administrative, judicial, etc. – of a world devoted to pro-

gress under the universal flag of technology. The bulldozer
is the great leveller in more than one sense: it seems to be
invested with special significance in *Justice*, leading not
only to the destruction of nature but also of the simple
values associated with it. It might be said that this is a
problem all too familiar and overworked in the West, but,
as is often the case, universal issues appear more starkly in
Russian literature, and strike the mind and imagination
with fresh impact. The fact that Soviet writers have had to
fight hard for the – still only grudgingly conceded – right to
treat of such themes at all gives their approach a tension
and 'edge' of a kind rarely maintained when all is per-
missible.

The mood expressed by Tendryakov is undoubtedly
shared by most of his contemporaries (and the younger
generation too) not only in Russia but in the West as well.
The encroachment on the personality in the name of
'progress' takes different forms, under different political
and social systems, but the consequences are similar everywhere. In most Western countries it has come about more
gently, with the gradual spread of 'urban' attitudes and
standards, but in Russia, where the pace was much more
forced and the methods incomparably more brutal, the
feeling among writers and intellectuals that mankind may
be hurtling towards an 'anthropological' disaster is cor-
respondingly keener. The destruction of the natural environment may be as nothing compared to the accompanying
breakdown of moral and spiritual stability, of the cultural
environment – this is the constant apprehension voiced
in the best prose and poetry (notably that of Andrei
Voznesenski) published in Russia today.

Despite his 'moral' preoccupations, however, Tendryakov
is first and foremost a story-teller. Even the best of Russian
prose tends to be static, preferring the slow unfolding of
character, the creation of 'atmosphere' – sometimes with a
great deal of studied digression – to the structured plot
favoured in other literatures. Tendryakov's stories are real
narratives in which the central incident or crisis round
which they are built provides a dramatic focus for the

background detail. Even his superb nature descriptions are
carefully related to the plot and the fate of the characters –
the river in *Three, Seven, Ace* and the forest in *Justice*
not only provide a setting for the events, but play a direct
part in them. Although, like most Soviet prose writers,
Tendryakov is basically an heir to the 'naturalist' tradition
of the nineteenth century (with Turgenev and Chekhov,
perhaps, as his main teachers), his preference for disciplined
narrative with a minimum of incidental detail to obscure
the actual story suggests that he has also learnt something
from Pushkin's insistence on the primacy of action over
mere description. (It is an indication of Pushkin's influence
that the title of the first story, *Three, Seven, Ace*, is taken
from the card sequence in Pushkin's famous tale of com-
pulsive gambling, *The Queen of Spades*.) This concentration
on narrative creates a tension, a feeling of anxious concern
for the outcome – in fact 'suspense', which is by no means
always present in Russian prose.

Yet it is a noteworthy and characteristic feature of
Tendryakov's stories that the final outcome is not revealed
to the reader – it happens, as it were, offstage. At the end of
Three, Seven, Ace and *Creature of a Day* we are left to guess
at the ultimate fate of Dubinin and Nastya. The author
knows and shows them to be innocent (even the poor
Nastya, though she has done a dreadful thing under the
strain of impossible circumstances), but in a familiar
Russian way he is pessimistic about the formal processes of
justice. Once these cases are in the hands of Authority,
truth ceases to be the paramount consideration. This is not
an implied criticism of the Soviet institutions concerned,
but a reflection on the inadequacy of any judicial or investi-
gatory procedure to the unravelling of the tangled strands
in a person's motives and conduct – particularly if he has
lost his bearings in a world of alien or contradictory
standards. In *Justice* we actually follow the formal
judicial process of confusion and obfuscation through to its
end, but this only leaves us even more in doubt as to the
further destiny of Simon Teterin, one of Tendryakov's
most poignant figures.

Like much contemporary Soviet literature, Tendryakov's work – though this is only incidental – has considerable sociological interest. In contrast to the 'classical' Socialist Realist writers of Stalinist times who were fantastically isolated from the realities of the country, the younger writers of Tendryakov's generation have made it their business to convey the quality of life in the vast hinterland beyond the big cities. Tendryakov's stories are set mainly in the remote areas around his birthplace near Vologda, some three hundred miles north east of Moscow, a land of rivers, lakes, marshes and dense coniferous forests – all as described by him with such intensity of feeling that he can stir nostalgia even in a reader who has never been there. As a district Komsomol official for two years at the end of the war in a region further to the east he also clearly gained first-hand knowledge of the workings of the local Party and government administration which controls the destinies of the loggers, hunters and collective farmers who are his main heroes. Partly, no doubt, because of this he is able to draw a most convincing and informative picture of the relations between country people and officialdom – prosecutors, kolkhoz chairmen and the like – as well as of the 'new' men who herald the advent of the bulldozer and all it stands for. The portrait of Dudyrev (in *Justice*), the 'tycoon' who is bringing industry and progress to the backwoods is masterly, as is the picture of the social and 'moral' consequences of this inexorable advance. Since Tendryakov accepts the social structure with detachment for what it is, he probably succeeds in giving a more tangible sense of it than someone bent on defending or attacking it. Over fifty years after the Revolution its once romantically controversial institutions have become, for the vast majority of people in the Soviet Union, humdrum and commonplace, particularly at the provincial level. The shabby incongruities, the hollow rhetoric, the bumbling inefficiency are now the legitimate stuff of literature. Like other younger writers, Tendryakov is even able to exploit the rich comic potential offered by this institutional mellowing – as he shows in the banqueting scene with the local notabilities in *Creature of a Day*.

Tendryakov is a modest, unassuming man who is most at home in the humble places he writes about. He has little interest in the world outside Russia, though he has made brief visits to Western Europe. He is not untypical of a good part of his generation in knowing the irreplaceable virtue of such steadfast provincialism and clings to it, well aware perhaps that it may be the last hope. Added to his native literary culture (acquired, like that of many of his contemporaries, by study at the Gorky Literary Institute in Moscow), it makes him into one of the most distinctive of the handful of 'new wave' writers who, after Stalin, returned Russian prose to its rightful paths. The classical qualities are easily discernible: humility before the life around him, respect for truth, concern for the world at large and – above all – the gift of touching the poor dross of daily existence with meaning and poetry.

Max Hayward

Three, Seven, Ace

Hundreds, perhaps thousands, indeed countless rivers, tributaries and stubborn streams gnaw their way through moulding fallen leaves and dig among the roots of trees, carrying water from the rust-red swamps to the big river. This is why the water is dark and glints with reddish scum. This is why in dirty weather the river takes on its particular leaden colour, a lead not new but aged and weathered.

The river is always in flood. Sandy shallows by its banks are rare. It flows in fanciful loops through wild unpeopled country to the polar seas. And along the river, day and night, a silent procession passes. Day and night timber floats downstream.

Its journey is not easy. The shallows, which every river has, even in full flood, the quiet creeks and even the banks themselves, are all traps. The current is leisurely, the pace is slow. Many of these river pilgrims fall by the wayside. Many logs get sodden, one end sinks, leaving only the shorn top sticking out of the water, but the log crawls stubbornly on, scraping along the bottom until the whole of it is overburdened and it lies down quietly on the river bed. Sluggish eels hide beneath it in the summer; sand and slime silt it over. Other pilgrims float on their way to be trapped at the sorting base and rolled ashore – builder's timber for the saw mill, wood for paper pulp, for pit props, for musical instruments. Graphs and schedules record it all – oblivion for the river bed corpses, new life for those who reach the end.

The northern river flows on, a great artery of floating timber. Every so often its sluggish, morose aspect is transformed into fury – it seethes among the stones, spluttering and flecked with yellow foam. These are the rapids. There are several along the river's length, and the biggest are at Ostrozhye.

2

To be exact there are two rapids – the Big Head and, a couple of hundred yards downstream, the Small Head. The water surges in everlasting agitation over the enormous flooded boulders, its ceaseless roar hangs in the raw, damp air.

Facing the Big Head is a tiny logging camp – five houses in all, counting the small shop which sells bread, sugar and tinned goods.

The forest crowds the huts to the water's edge; there is nothing else but grey sky and seething rapids . . . The only way to the nearest village is by river; every week supplies come by boat.

The man in charge of the camp is called Dubinin. It has thirty-two inhabitants – twenty-five lumbermen, Klasha the shop assistant, Nastya the cleaner, Tikhon the mechanic, three canteen girls and the foreman himself, Dubinin.

The logs drift their separate ways down the stream, they hit and rub against each other, huddle into creeks and settle on the shallows.

Every morning the loggers get in their boats and row away to patrol the river. Logs washed up into the bushes are dislodged and set afloat, creeks and shallows are cleared of timber . . . The only reason these people are here is to see that the endless flow of logs along the stream should never be held up.

3

Dubinin lived in his office. His bed stood beside the rickety desk at which he did his paper-work. Fixed to the wall above it was a telephone with a hoarse, growling bell. As the line was shared by countless other people, it growled every other minute. One ring meant that somebody was trying to get through to the exchange, two were for Krotov, the foreman of another base, three for the lumber camp . . . Some calls were for Gorshkov and Dymchenko, these were foremen at other points on the river . . . Dubinin paid no attention to other people's calls and slept soundly through the growling of the bell. Only if it rang four times did he wake up – then it was for him.

Dubinin was neither tall nor broad-shouldered; he walked with an unhurried swinging gait. The loggers – all tough men whose time was spent in rolling tree-trunks – spoke respectfully about his strength. All of them called him Sasha, though he was their senior in rank and probably in age. His small eyes were drowsy and rather sullen under overhanging brows, his chin, large and firm, sprouted reddish bristles; there was always a cigarette hanging from his drooping lower lip; he wore rubber boots with turned-down tops, a baggy coat of an indefinite colour, his cap was pulled low over the head and, to complete his forbidding appearance, he carried a sheath-knife in his belt. The knife was not a weapon: he used it to clean fish, slice bread, to whittle sticks for fishing rods and cut willows for baskets which he wove himself. Life at the camp was peaceful and friendly, and no one would have thought of going about armed.

On Saturdays the place was by and large deserted. The men put on leather shoes instead of rubber knee-boots, crossed the stream by boat and made off home along silent forest tracks. They all came from nearby villages, Kurenevo, Zakutnoye, Yaremnoye. They returned on Sunday night – fresh from the bathhouse and their wives' embraces, most of them happy enough but a few troubled by family worries. A good many were a little drunk from their week-end jaunt – the base was 'dry' and Klasha, the shop assistant, sold no spirits.

Dubinin too had his home nearby, in Zakutnoye. There he spent one day a week with his wife and children. A visitor at home, he lived with his men.

One of them, Ivan Stupnin, had a younger brother, Tolya, who was known among the men as a bookworm;

when he asked for leave to go and study in town, Dubinin had got him a travelling allowance and given him his own pair of new shoes; afterwards he wrote to him, secretly sent him money and made his elder brother do the same.

'Sasha,' the men said, 'our Sasha's all right . . . He's one of us.'

4

The men lived together in a hut. Twenty-six beds, separated by plywood bedside cupboards, surrounded the huge stove, kept so hot on cold days that you couldn't lean against it without getting burned.

A lumberjack's work is rough. It isn't skill you need to get a grounded, water-logged tree trunk back into the stream and floating on its way – you need a boat-hook, an axe, a good lever and strong muscles. And yet the men had their virtuosos among them.

There was the time when Klasha, the shop assistant, breaking the rule against the sale of alcohol, stocked a case of champagne in her shop. The men bought a bottle between them. Stupnin balanced it on one end of a log on which he stood and, using his boat-hook, punted himself across the river there and back – man and bottle upright – despite the current sucking at his raft and thrusting it towards the rapids. It would have been a risky game for anyone, and Stupnin, though he had made his living by the river all his life, could hardly swim.

He drank the bottle, spitting and spluttering.

'What a business! It's no better than *kvass* except it goes up your nose. Not worth putting on that show for.'

'What a business' was Stupnin's own expression to fit any of his moods – joy, grief, astonishment, contempt.

'The Osheherinsk lock has burst. That'll be a nice job for us.'

'Hell! What a business.'

'It said in the news, they've put another sputnik up. Weighs more than a ton.'

'Fancy that! What a business.'

'A bear has mauled a woman near Kurenevo. They've taken her to hospital. They don't know if she'll live.'

'Well, well, that really is a business.'

There were two other virtuosi beside Stupnin – Yegor Petukhov and Genka Shamayev.

Petukhov had a sharp nose thrusting from a soft, womanish face and a high, womanish, uncertain voice. Dressed, he was undistinguished; he even had a hang-dog look. But without his clothes, you saw his great, broad swelling shoulders, the sculptured chest with its muscles rippling at the slightest movement, the taut biceps rolling under the skin.

Petukhov was famous for his meanness. He always thought they were swindling at the canteen.

'Five roubles for dinner, and what d'you get? – Water.'

'Would you eat your own shit for five roubles?'

'Other people may be rich – I don't print five rouble notes. I have to count every penny.'

As a good lumberman, he made more than the foreman. Everybody knew that he was childless and that his wife, who had a job at the main base, lived on what she earned. The money he had not had time to put in the bank he kept in a suitcase. The suitcase was like a trunk and had a heavy padlock, though not even within the memory of such old inhabitants as Stupnin had anything ever been stolen at the base.

It was a strange sight to see Petukhov standing upright on a log, shoulders slightly hunched and with a bored fastidious face, crossing the river just before the rapids above the Small Head: to see the water pound and sway the log, which his feet gripped fast, while he lazily swung his boat-hook and brought it leisurely down to push at boulders and other logs. Never a miss or a slip until he landed and began at once in his complaining voice:

'All that stuff we've rolled – and how much will they put in the book? I know them . . .'

Shamayev was tall, big-shouldered, with dishevelled hair falling on his brows and a bold, weather-beaten face. The girls in the canteen always made sure to give him the best of the soup. Every evening Shamayev got into his boat, and leaning on the oars, jolted it across the river, where he left it and made off through the woods to a lumber camp four miles or so away, to see Katya, a twenty-five-year-old widow who worked there. It was said that her husband had been a sailor and was drowned at sea the spring before.

Sometimes Shamayev was kept late at work. Then Katya would come down to the bank and stand, muffled in her shawl, waiting for him in the drizzling rain until darkness fell.

Shamayev always came home late. His mates put logs and sticks under his sheets; he threw them out, lay down and slept like the dead.

In the morning the room was filled with braying voices and the jokes were fit to make even a lumberjack blush. Shamayev stretched, cracking his joints and smiled condescendingly, pale-skinned, loose-limbed and pleased with himself.

Stories were told of an old-time lumberman, Terenty Klyap, one of whose feats was to cross the Big Head standing on a log. Shamayev had to try; he sailed straight into the rapids on a weathered stump, but at the first dip he lost his footing and went under. They were sure he would be sucked into the whirlpool and battered to death, but he came ashore barefoot, dripping and furious – his rubber boots had sucked him down and he had had to throw them off.

'It's all lies about Terenty. You can't get through.'

5

All three men were secretly envied by Leshka Malinkin. He was just twenty and had only been working at the base for eighteen months. Fresh from the village, clumsy and round-headed like a schoolboy, he had gone about in fear and trembling of Dubinin. But recently he had begun to fill out a little and tried to walk with the same swinging gait as Dubinin. Nor did he only imitate his walk . . . He also put on Dubinin's tightlipped manner, frowning in the same sullen and meaningful way, and he dreamed, after another year or

two, of going away to study and coming back to be a foreman himself. He already saw the tough loggers listening to
his every word and saying respectfully behind his back:
'He's one of us.' He would rule the base as fairly and firmly
as Sasha. There was no one in the world like Sasha.

Leshka was beginning to feel the strength of his arms. It
astonished and delighted him. If anybody noticed the great
load he had picked up and shouted to someone to help him
in case he strained himself, Leshka, usually placid, would
burst into childish rage:

'Leave me alone. I can manage.'

Every evening, while Shamayev crossed the stream and
vanished into the forest, Leshka took his boat-hook and,
casting careful looks around him, made his way towards the
dam on the other side of the canteen. There, all alone till
nightfall, he would practise balancing himself on logs, to be
as good as Stupnin and Shamayev. He came back to the
hut, drenched up to the waist and dispirited.

One night he was going as usual to the dam, leaping from
boulder to boulder, his boat-hook in his hand. The sun had
set behind the steep wooded bank but the clouds above the
black jagged skyline were still ablaze and the spray from
the Big Head was pink.

Across the river, Shamayev's boat lay half out of the
water, tilted on its side.

Leshka stopped dead and his mouth dropped open in
surprise. Slithering, stumbling, clutching at reeds and
shrubs, a man was climbing down the opposite bank
towards the boat.

Who could it be? Someone from the village or the lumber
camp? No one came out here, to the back of beyond, without good reason.

From the clumsy way the man launched the boat and
fixed the oars into the rowlocks Leshka guessed he was inexperienced with boats and unfamiliar with the river; he
would be swept into the rapids at once. Not that the Big
Head was fatal: it tossed and frightened you but if you went
with the current, using the oars only to right the boat and
keep the stern in the water, it would always carry you

through safely. God forbid that you should fight the current – it lashed out and knocked you under, then you hadn't a chance.

As the boat began to dance about, the stranger rowed in a frenzy of hit and miss.

'Ship your oars!' Leshka shouted. 'Hi, you! Want to kill yourself? I said, ship your oars!'

But the roaring river drowned his voice. The boat was floundering, swept to where the raging breakers played at will.

'Hi! Your oars! Oh, hell!'

The boat swung round, the useless oars fluttering once or twice; a wave patterned with pink foam leaned over it and tossed it, with a dull gleam in the sunset, bottom up.

Leshka, frozen with horror, watched it whirl and spin, then, stumbling over the boulders in his flapping boots, tore back towards the camp.

A boat lay grounded on the bank in front of the canteen; he ran at it, launching it with his weight, fell in over the stern and feverishly sorted out the oars. Leaning on them so that the rowlocks creaked, he rowed towards the Big Head, helped by the current.

The stone dam, the wooded bank with its jagged edge cutting the burning sunset – everything around him swung and swayed, rose and fell. The boat shot into the rapids.

Leshka stopped rowing and peered on every side, almost cricking his neck, but he could see nothing, not even the stranger's boat. Spray blew into his face and drenched his coat, the banks rose and fell, the roar fuddled his brain. He couldn't think and there was nothing to be seen – not even the boat. But no – there it was, its bottom glinting in the sunset. It had swept past the breakers and was floating on towards the Small Head.

Now the watery mountains softened, the stern stopped kicking, spray no longer whipped his face. Within a couple of minutes the Big Head had spat him out. He could use his oars again.

Logs floated past jerkily, as if still unsettled by the shaking they had had. The water round the boat was black, spattered with swirling flecks of yellow foam. An oar came up . . .

The lonely sight of it chilled Leshka's heart. This was all that was left of the man. Deep under the black surface of the log-strewn water the current would be idly rolling his body along. There was nothing to be done. Under his very eyes. Leshka shivered with cold.

Ahead of him the smaller rapids tossed the stranger's boat.

But nearer to, clinging fast to a hump-backed, slippery log, were a sodden sleeve and yellow hand . . .

Leshka tried to shout but his voice died in his throat. He grabbed the oars.

A black, unshaven, rigid face with crazy, staring eyes bleached with terror.

'Let go the log! I'll catch you.'

But the man, his unshaven cheek pillowed on the wood, only stared silently from under the drenched hair plastered on his forehead; his bony hand still clutched the log.

'Let go!' Leshka shouted in tears. 'Let go! There's another lot of rapids coming.'

They were nearing the Small Head, the boat was rocking again. If it spun around they would both drown in the rapids.

Instinctively Leshka, when he launched his boat, had hung on to his boat-hook. He could not have saved the drowning man without it. He pulled the log towards him, angrily hit out at the stranger's right hand and seized him by the hair.

Now the stranger lay in a dead faint, his head resting on Leshka's boot, one leg twisted up under him.

He came to when he was brought ashore and for a long time rolled on the ground, vomiting water.

6

They carried him into the hut and put him on the bed which had been occupied by Leshka's friend, Tolya Stupnin, the one who was away, studying in town.

He lay, with his head thrown back on the pillow, bristly chin pointing at the ceiling, a vein throbbing under the stubble on his Adam's apple; his eyes were closed; his thin, weary arms stretched out along his sides and his fingers curled nervelessly. The room was hot; the blanket covering his legs left his flat, bony chest exposed; on it were tattooed the words 'The years go by but bring no luck'.

The lumbermen crowded round, exchanging low-voiced comments.

'Must have been inside. Look what he's got written there: "No luck".'

'Well, he's been lucky this time. If it hadn't been for Leshka he'd be feeding the fish by now.'

'All the same he must be tough, coming out of that alive.'

'Not the first time he's been in trouble, I bet . . .'

Petukhov said in a worried voice:

'Looks like a shady character. I hope he won't pay us back by . . . well . . . cleaning us out.'

'Don't worry – he's not after your money right now. You needn't lose any sleep tonight.'

Across the room, Leshka was telling his story in a hushed, mysterious voice, for the umpteenth time:

'So I see him being carried off, and I start yelling, but there's too much noise from the rapids.'

With his hands deep in his pockets, his chin tucked into his chest, and his cap pulled down over his eyes, Dubinin stood looking at his uninvited guest; the scrawny neck, the weary arms stretched out, the cheap wet shoes flung under the bed, and the tattooed inscription. Dubinin chewed the cigarette which had gone out between his lips as he gazed at the stranger, and the more he looked the sorrier he felt for him.

If you met a man like that on the road, you'd pass him by without a second glance. Had he any family? Had he anyone who really cared for him in the whole world? If it hadn't been for the log he'd managed to hang on to, he'd be gone, vanished, leaving no name, nobody who would be even vaguely sorry – nothing. There he was, the man who had cheated death, lying on a strange bed, surrounded by strangers who stared at him with unceremonious compassion.

Dubinin tore his eyes away from the tattooed inscription on the scraggy chest.

'Which of you took his clothes off? Did he have papers on him?'

'Yes. They're all wet. We put them on the stove to dry. Fifteen roubles in his pocket – that was all the money he had.'

'Let me have it.'

Dubinin carefully took the sodden papers, shouldered his way through the crowd and went out.

7

Before becoming foreman, Dubinin had been an ordinary lumberjack. His modest life was neither crowded with events nor overshadowed by tragedies: he had not even been at the Front. He had never got into the habit of reading; he had never drawn on books for noble aspirations or lofty thoughts; he did not know (or knew only vaguely at second hand) that there were people in the world who, for the sake of others, endured torture, braved the stake and made their voices heard through prison walls to future generations.

He had been a lumberman, and he had become a foreman – that was all.

There had been some trouble sixteen years ago.

The stony shallows near the sombre Lobovsk reach had been blocked by a couple of logs, wedged between the boulders, and the rest of the timber which the current had piled up.

The place was not too dangerous and had not been blocked for long. So, instead of going himself, Dubinin, who was then acting for the foreman, sent three other lads to clear the shallows. 'They'll manage, they won't do anything silly . . .' One of them was Yasha Sorokin, a boy of seventeen with high cheekbones and widely-set blue eyes. The timber collapsed and crushed both his legs . . .

Dubinin took him to the hospital by boat. Yasha cried all the way, not only because he was in pain, but because his father had been killed at the Front and his two small sisters (the elder only ten) were left to be supported by his ailing mother. Who would help her now that he, the only breadwinner, was a cripple?

Dubinin cursed himself silently. He had backed out, he had sent somebody else in his place – 'They'll manage.' – and now this . . . What should he do now? Take on the whole family – aged mother, two small girls and crippled boy – and have them round his neck for the rest of his life? With a wife and son of his own, could he take them on as well? What was he to do?

No one else thought of blaming him for the accident. Things like that happened, they couldn't be helped. People were sympathetic, and mild in their reproaches, so that in the end he even convinced himself he was innocent – he had nothing on his conscience: accidents couldn't be helped.

One day they had all been out clearing a log-jam near the village of Kostoz. At noon they boiled fish soup and un-packed bread, salt, potatoes and hard-boiled eggs. The food was spread out on a handkerchief on the grass. A little girl, barefoot, with tousled, faded hair, her scraggy body showing through her tattered dress, hung about staring spellbound at the food.

'Want some?' Dubinin asked. 'Here, take it, don't be frightened.'

He held out a piece of bread, an egg and a couple of cold potatoes; he looked at her and froze . . . Out of the grubby, drawn face with its flat cheekbones and its button of a nose, widely-set blue eyes stared out at him . . .

The child clutched the food to her filthy dress – her hands, dark, thin, grasping, like the claws of some little woodland animal – rushed off to the village without a word of thanks. Dubinin gazed after her.

The lumbermen, sitting in a circle, ate and talked about the war – how it had taken all the men, so that the women had to manage all the work alone and hungry children were a common sight.

The river sparkled in the sun, the rich smell of soup rose into the air, feathery willows bowed over the stream. And in the dazzling light, the satisfying smell, the willows bending over rafts of water-lily leaves, there was a sense of indestructible tranquillity, of the soundness and solidity of life. Yet at this very moment, somewhere, mines were tearing up the tortured earth, stench and smoke billowed over burnt-out houses, and unburied dead lay scattered in the fields. Somewhere, far away ... But here, in the village at his back, children were hungry.

Dubinin put his spoon down, got up, took all the bread out of his bag and without a word strode off to the village. At the first cottage he came to he asked if Yasha Sorokin lived anywhere near and was directed to a solid, prosperous-looking house.

He had expected to work like a slave, day in day out, to feed two families, but what he found he had to do was fight. He fought the regional assistance board and the *kolkhoz** for help for Yasha and a pension for the widow of a soldier killed on active service, but most of all he fought Yasha himself.

'Scared, are you? Want to pay me conscience money. Well, your money won't buy me back my legs ...'

Unexpected and unasked, the man who was to blame for Yasha's misfortune, the man who had spoiled his life, had walked in and put himself at his mercy. But whatever he did, however humbly he apologised, there would be no forgiveness.

'Hand it over, bastard. Give all the money you've got. There's nothing left for me in life, but at least I'll have some fun before I die.'

One day Dubinin took him by the scruff of his neck:

'You little runt! You're used to being treated like a dog, you can't take it if anybody's kind to you. Well, here's my last word – I'll have your sisters to live in my house. I'll treat them as my daughters. As for you, you can get to hell, you can do what you like.'

* A collective farm.

At this, the cripple changed his tune and agreed to leave the kolkhoz and do a course in book-keeping.

It was one thing to work for your living and your own happiness – to have a roof over your head, a full belly, a warm stove and a loving wife – and to enjoy your comfort and guard it against other people's envy. But now Dubinin discovered something else in life. To protect the weak, to comfort the despairing, to help those who had fallen by the wayside, feeling that you were strong and generous and capable of giving joy to others – this too was happiness.

By now Sorokin had long been working as a ledger clerk in the kolkhoz; he was married and had two children. His sisters had grown up and left the village – one was married, the other training to be a nurse.

Dubinin's life was his round of daily tasks – making sure that the work was fairly shared and justly paid, that the food in the canteen was nourishing, the hut clean and the sheets changed every week . . .

The five houses wedged between the forest and the noisy rapids were a small part of the huge world. The people in it worked, and worked hard, but it was a happy place in its own way. The man who walked about it with a swinging step, reserved and taciturn, was its law-giver.

Back in his office, he spread the stranger's sodden papers on his desk. Some were hopelessly illegible, but the identity card had fared better. A man who had an identity card was within the law.

Using the tip of his knife, Dubinin separated the wet sheets and read: 'Bushuyev, Nikolay Petrovich, born 1919.' The back page was stamped; the ink had run but it was still possible to make out that the owner of the card had been tried, condemned and served his term.

He had cheated death; now he lay with a look of deathly weariness on a strange bed, surrounded by strangers. He must have had a tangled and comfortless past. At some time, in his early youth, he must have made a grab at happiness. The kind of happiness for which you pay your money and you take your choice. His fingers, reaching for the money, had got caught in someone's pocket, and he was

sent where he belonged. Perhaps they even let him off the
first time, but happiness eluded him. He had to go on
looking, looking . . . Years went by and brought no luck.

8

Next morning, after the men had left, Dubinin looked into
the hut. The bed on which the uninvited guest had slept
was made.

'Early bird,' thought Dubinin. 'Gone already. On his way,
is he? Well, I've got his identity card. He won't go far.' He
walked back unhurriedly.

The house in which he had his office was the only two
storey house at the base. The office was on the ground floor,
next to a room shared by the mechanic, Tikhon, and his
wife Nastya, the cleaner. Above it was the recreation room
with its desk, its bookshelf and its table covered with a
faded red cloth. Here the men gathered in the evenings to
play dominoes and listen to the wireless.

As he passed the stairs Dubinin heard a man singing in a
low voice and playing a guitar:

> Why do some men have such luck,
> All their dreams fulfilled,
> While others' lives are just a wreck,
> Joy and laughter killed . . .

Dubinin went up. The stranger sat, still unshaved but
wearing a clean shirt borrowed from someone with broader
shoulders than his own, its collar pitifully loose around his
stringy neck; he was nursing the guitar which had hung
unused over the desk for years.

> Why do some avoid
> The cruel blows of fate . . .

At the sight of the foreman he stood up hastily.

'A very good morning, boss,' he barked with a show of
jocularity.

A narrow face, evasive eyes: the smile bared a gap
between the small, tight teeth.

Dubinin lowered himself into a chair.

'Sit down, Bushuyev. That's your name, is it? We'll have a talk.'

'That's right, Nikolay Petrovich Bushuyev in person. I was making for Tormenga, further down the river, but here I am, landed on you by accident. Sorry I didn't let you know in advance so I could be met . . .'

'Stop fooling. Where have you come from?'

'I had a job at the lumber camp . . .'

'Ran away?'

'The boss is a bastard. Doesn't treat you like a human being. Once you've been inside, he says, you're a crook, a criminal, a has-been. We didn't get along.'

'That really all?'

'Why should I mess up my life again for a swine like him? Better get away from temptation . . . I had a couple of hundred owing to me, I didn't even take that.'

'What were you in for?'

'They say there was a good reason. I don't argue with them, they should know.'

'Murder?'

'God forbid!'

'Stealing?'

'Don't let's go into the details, Chief. What I will say is, I've turned over a new leaf.'

'Sure?'

'Believe it or not. It's a long time since I was twenty. I don't somehow feel like playing cops and robbers any more.'

'Where are you from? Why did you take on this job instead of going home?'

'My home's under my hat.'

'And you never miss it?'

Bushuyev lowered his eyelids over his oddly light, glistening eyes and for a second his pale, bristly face grew still, closed, expressionless. Dubinin's chance question had stripped it of its assumed cheerfulness.

'What's the good?' he said after a moment. 'I know what it's like to go home with empty pockets.'

'I've been told that people work – where you were – and

take their earnings with them when they come out.'

'I had a bit, but I lost it at cards to a man in the train . . .'

Dubinin, stolid in his chair, his coat unbuttoned, cap pulled low over his head, watched his visitor with his usual placid, rather gloomy air.

'And where will you go now?' he asked.

'Tormenga . . . There's bound to be work loading timber there.'

'Are you trained for anything?'

'Jack-of-all-trades, that's me. Chopped timber, dug foundations, dug up stumps . . .'

'So you're not trained . . .' Dubinin shifted in his chair and turned aside. 'How about this,' he said, looking past his guest. 'You can stay here . . . You'll have to work, like everyone else. A lumberjack makes a couple of thousand a month on an average. You've got no family, you'll spend about five hundred on your food and clothes. By the end of a year you'll have saved up fifteen to eighteen thousand. After that – if you like it you stay on, if you don't you go where you like. I'm doing this for your own good, because I'm sorry for you. I'm not begging you to stay and I'm not forcing you, so don't imagine I am.'

'Why should I want to go? I don't mind, it's all the same to me where I fill in time.'

Dubinin struck the table with his hand clenched into a small fist – it was covered with red hairs and heavy, like a stone from the river bed.

'Fill in time? No, my friend, you'll have to work. You don't get paid for filling in time. And don't imagine you can get away with anything. This is the back of beyond, the police are a long way off, we make our own rules. You've seen our boys? They'll know how to take care of you. And there's nowhere to run to – there's nothing but marsh and forest all around, even the village people don't like to go too far in. There are only three ways out – one to the lumber camp, where I don't suppose they'll make you very welcome, one to the village where you'd stick out like a sore thumb, and the third is down the river past the other bases. All I have to do is lift the receiver and you'll be held till

further notice. So get that into your skull – don't try any
tricks. If I take you on, it's because I'm not afraid of you –
you can't do much here. That's how it is.'

Dubinin got up.

9

Bushuyev slept in the hut on Tolya Stupnin's bed. Every
morning he walked down to the boats with the rest of the
men, an axe stuck into his belt and a boat-hook in his hand.
When Dubinin asked the boys what his work was like they
shrugged their shoulders: 'He just pokes about.'

Leshka Malinkin slept in the bed next to Bushuyev's, and
worked in the same gang with him. You cannot be indifferent towards a man for whom you have done something
important, not to say heroic. He managed to be next to
him at work, to teach him, help him, shift the logs Bushuyev
found too heavy for him.

The guitar, which had been bought out of money officially
allotted for cultural purposes and which had hung in the
recreation room for so long, was moved into the hut and
here Bushuyev, lolling on his bed in the evenings, would
strum away, singing of love betrayed, crimes of passion and
the sorrows of captivity:

> A dandy in a satin tie
> May be kissing you by the gate . . .

The men were not too choosy; they shook their heads if
the song was sad, laughed if it seemed funny, and there was
always someone to slap Bushuyev's shoulder with a hefty,
grateful hand:

'Wherever did you learn all that, you son of a bitch . . .'

Dubinin would come and listen too, sitting and smoking
silently, but it seemed an approving silence.

When Bushuyev tired of the guitar and flung it down,
Leshka stretched a timid hand towards it. He would take a
long time making himself comfortable on the bed, then, his
head bowed low over the strings, he plucked them cautiously
with his stiff, clumsy fingers, but all that came from the

guitar were timid, disconnected sounds. Putting it respectfully aside Leshka shrugged his shoulders and said in honest
surprise:

'Well I never! There's nothing to it, but it makes your
back ache!'

As usual, every night Shamayev rowed his boat across
the stream and vanished in the woods. As usual, Petukhov
dug about inside his suitcase, locked the heavy padlock,
settled on his bed and discussed his future plaintively:

'I'll stick here a bit longer, but not much longer. I'm sick
of messing about on the river, I'll leave you to it. I'll buy a
house in the town, I'll have a kitchen garden and a hot-
house. I'll get a job as well, just in case. Might be a night
watchman. That's not a bad job for an old man . . .'

They either paid him no attention or grunted idly:

'There he goes; he's off again . . . Stop nattering . . .'

As always on Sundays, the men scattered to their villages
leaving the settlement deserted and dreary. Bushuyev
killed time with Tikhon. Tikhon always had a bottle put
away for such occasions.

Tikhon was short and narrow-shouldered, with a
wrinkled, weather-beaten face and a drooping nose; he was
never satisfied. He swore angrily at everything – the
weather, the river, the base where he'd been stuck for the
last five years.

'You see, pal,' he confided to Bushuyev, grabbing him
by the lapel. 'I'm a trained mechanic, I've looked after
combine-harvesters and tractors . . . What the hell am I
doing in this lousy dump? A real dump, that's what it is.
Just look around – nothing but trees and trees and you see
the sky like it was through an air hole.'

At such moments Bushuyev was gloomy and silent. He
watched the windows weeping tears of rain, listened to the
ceaseless, steady weight of sound from the Big Head, and
sighed:

'Y-Yes. Even prison was more cheerful than this.'

Sometimes, whether because of the vodka he had drunk
or just because a momentary mood of frankness came upon
him, he would reminisce:

'I'm from the Kursk region. We get a lot of sun there, and it's all fields, no forest to speak of. I can hardly remember my village. It's only here the thought of it gets me down every now and then.'

Suddenly he would add:

'If I can't stick it I'll quit. Five years I've waited for freedom . . . Call this freedom.'

10

One evening he took down the guitar, plucked at the strings and damped them straight away.

'To hell with it . . . I've sung and played enough in my time . . .'

He swore obscenely, took a tattered pack of cards out of his pocket, shuffled it expertly and offered it to Leshka Malinkin:

'Have a game? – Just for fun.'

Leshka wriggled in embarrassment.

'I don't know how to play.'

'I'll teach you. Beginners are lucky. Don't be scared, I won't fleece you. Here, I'll start the bank with a rouble. You can stake ten kopecks if you like.'

Afterwards nobody could tell how Bushuyev happened to have had a pack of cards. When they brought him in out of the rapids there was nothing in his pockets except sodden documents and fifteen roubles in small notes.

Bushuyev made himself at home on Leshka's bed and patiently taught him.

'Don't you get excited, boy. Cards don't like you if you get excited. Want to try another? All right. Here it is. Look at that, you've won again. I told you you'd be lucky to start with.'

Leshka held good cards and grew pink with excitement. Stupnin stood close by; he blinked his yellow-fringed eyelids and shook his head.

'It's a wicked business. How much have you got in the bank? Only eighty kopecks! Well all right, I'll have a card – just out of curiosity, like.'

He took it, looked at it doubtfully and drawled:

'What a business! Give me two more. Fancy that! Well, deal away, take yours . . . My trick!'

Others from the nearby beds joined the players and surrounded them. Petukhov watched the cards, his lips pursed.

'Ten kopecks here, ten kopecks there, before you know where you are, you've lost a rouble. It's years since I've touched a card.'

'Better keep away now,' Bushuyev agreed. 'Cards don't take to misers.'

Towards ten o'clock they finished the last bank and counted the winnings: Leshka had won twenty roubles. Stupnin and the rest had won and lost trifling sums. Bushuyev paid.

'Luck is a great thing, friends.' His strangely bright eyes peered into Leshka's face. He added with a faint leer: 'Only don't imagine you can keep up with me, sonny boy. I could strip you to the bone. See this?'

He showed Leshka a card. Leshka, excited by success and embarrassed by having had to take Bushuyev's money, nodded shyly: 'I see it.'

'Remember what it was. Sure you remember it? I haven't looked at it, see? Put it back in the pack. Now shuffle! Get on with it, sonny boy! Goodness, you've got hands like rakes. Finished shuffling! Now cut. Cut again . . . Now give me the pack . . .'

Bushuyev flicked over the cards – his small quick hands had flat white nails and still bore the marks where he had grazed them while being swept over the rapids. He narrowed one eye mockingly.

'Is this it?'

Leshka's mouth fell open in surprise.

'That's it.'

All the onlookers grinned and wagged their heads.

'A real expert!'

'There you are,' Bushuyev closed the session. 'I can see right through them. Better be careful.'

11

Nonetheless, the very next evening five of them settled down to a game of cards on Bushuyev's bed – just to kill time; besides Bushuyev himself there were Leshka, Stupnin and two others – a lanky youth called Kozlov and the red-headed Savateyev. Curious onlookers crowded round, including Petukhov, who always got worked up when he saw money changing hands.

The stakes were small. Now one man, now another got his pennyworth of luck. Leshka was winning steadily again. He took the bank. Petukhov grunted:

'Some people are born lucky.'

Stupnin sighed:

'What a business . . . Well, you can play for kopecks if you like, I'm going the whole hog. Fortune favours the bold as they say.'

Little by little the stakes rose, until not only rouble and ten-rouble notes rustled on the crinkled eiderdown, but twenty-fives and even hundreds.

Leshka was winning, so was Stupnin. From time to time Bushuyev calmly took more money from his pocket and flung it down with a careless gesture.

'What's that? Call this a game? I remember games, my children, when there was ten thousand in the bank.'

Others joined in. It was after pay-day, everyone had money and they all felt they could let themselves go a little and have some fun.

Only Petukhov, his lips pursed primly, watched the cards, followed every movement of the players' hands as they stuffed their winnings in their pockets, and shook his head in disapproval, though he never left their side. No one took any notice of him.

When Stupnin, flushed and jubilant, grabbed the bank in his huge paw, Petukhov gave Leshka a nudge.

'Move over a bit. My legs aren't made of iron.'

'You don't mean you want to take a hand?' asked Bushuyev.

'So what? Think I'm not as good as you?'

'You'll lose your shirt. Cards don't take to misers.'

Petukhov still hesitated and just sat there watching, biting his lips. At last he could stand it no longer.

'Throw me a card.'

Bushuyev, baring the gap in his teeth, leered in Petukhov's face.

'Let's see your money.'

Petukhov lost his temper.

'Listen who's talking, the crook! Who'd trust a jailbird like you!'

'What are you shoving into the game for, if you don't trust me?'

'Deal me a hand. I've got more money than a jailbird like you. If I lose, I'll pay.'

'Show your money or keep out.'

'To hell with your game!'

Petukhov got up, went over to his bed and lay down.

'What d'you want to hurt his feelings for?' said Stupnin reproachfully. 'We don't do the dirty on each other here. If he loses he'll pay up.'

'Don't you believe it, brother. He'd sooner choke. I know these characters. It gets them, being up North. But it's easy to knock the stuffing out of them.'

'I'd knock the stuffing out of you if I didn't mind getting my hands dirty,' muttered Petukhov, his head on his pillow.

'What are you waiting for then? With fists like that, what are you scared of?'

'That's enough, fellows. Watch it, you've taken one too many,' said Stupnin, dealing out a new hand.

'So I have, blast your eyes.'

The game went on and the voices sounded in turn restrained, expectant, alert, surprised. The bank-notes rustled. Petukhov got off his bed, pulled his suitcase out and undid the lock.

Straightening his shoulders, with a sour, contemptuous look on his face, he came back.

'Here, you bastard, here's the money. Now deal me a hand.'

Bushuyev gave a short laugh.

'That's a lot of money you've got there! Hoping that five-rouble note will rake you in a fortune?'

'Just you go on grinning. I'll stake what I want. Let's have the cards.'

'Staking the lot?'

'I'm staking one rouble.'

'Why bother to get change? – You'll lose the lot anyway.'

'I'm staking a rouble,' Petukhov repeated with stubborn anger.

'Well, well, that's quite a skirtful from a careful girl like you.'

Bushuyev dealt nimbly.

Petukhov's card disappeared into his huge red hand with its broken finger nails; his eyes were riveted on it, his lips were pursed as though he was about to whistle in surprise. Bushuyev smiled his mocking smile, blinking his deceptively transparent eyes and showing the gap in his strong teeth.

As soon as Petukhov sat down the game changed. Until now the players had joked, sniggered, exchanged idle comments and not minded when they lost; although the stakes had risen you could still feel that they were playing for fun. With the entry of Petukhov the stakes rose no higher, on the contrary they fell, but the jokes ceased at once and suddenly everyone was grave, not looking at the crumpled notes but shooting them sidelong, shamefaced glances.

Bushuyev was still smiling complacently, but every now and then he bit his lower lip, and at such moments his lean, drawn face had something sharp and rapacious about it, like the look of a cat ready to spring at a sparrow.

Petukhov, his shoulders hunched and strained, held the bank, but somehow he soon lost it. Bushuyev, raking in the pile of crumpled notes, threw him a glance.

'Out you get. Your five roubles are gone.'

But the five roubles Petukhov had started with had gone imperceptibly and the loss was somehow painless. He was left only with a feeling of having missed his chance.

Snorting crossly, Petukhov got up.

'Wait a bit. Don't start without me.'

Once again he dragged out his suitcase, clicked the lock and put another note on the bed. Stupnin grinned all over his face.

'What a business! Here he comes thrusting another five roubles in the face of the poor, that's what it is.'

Bushuyev said nothing, just shuffled the cards and threw a hundred roubles on the bed.

'Who's got guts? I'll stake the lot.'

Now it began to look like real gambling. One of the men who was standing said:

'Come on, fellows, let's push the bed into the middle of the room so we can all sit down.'

'Why shift the furniture? We'll sit on the floor.'

'That's an idea. We're not in our Sunday best, a little dirt won't do no harm.'

12

They sat in a circle, some leaning back against the stove, others cross-legged in the gangway. There was not a man lying on his bed; more than half were gambling. The bank grew bigger. Crumpled ten, twenty-five and fifty-rouble notes came out of coat and trouser pockets.

'That's it,' called Bushuyev.

A sigh went round the room, the players shifted, straightening their stiff backs. This was the last round. Unless the bank was split, Bushuyev would get a pile of money.

Petukhov had been lucky so far. He had snatched fives and tens out of the bank and not missed once. Now he had a beautiful card, the ace of hearts, lying in his sweaty palm. Even if he only got a queen or a jack he ought to do all right. And suppose he got a ten or another ace! It was a good hand all right.

Petukhov gazed at the heap of notes – yellow roubles, greenish fifties – a dazzling heap in which the hundreds stood out by their size and magnificent colours.

Bushuyev dealt, biting his lip, his eyes narrowed, his hands as always quickly flicking out the cards. That heap of money and those hands! Deft hands with freshly grazed

knuckles, long fingers that looked chopped short at their
flat white nails. Who could know this man whose hands
inspired so little confidence? A man who might be capable of
anything. A real crook who had been in jail – probably for
swindling.

What a lot of money he had round him on the floor . . .
And Petukhov held a beautiful card, the ace of hearts. For
the fifth time he had drawn a red suit. Four times he had
won. There hadn't been a miss. If only his luck held . . .

That lovely heap of money! He sat so close to it, it made
him shiver as if he had a fever. Everyone was eyeing it . . .
And what a good card he had drawn!

'How much?' Bushuyev asked him abruptly, his eyes cold
between their thin, fair lashes, no longer mocking, but
hostile now, it seemed to Petukhov.

'How much in the bank?' he asked tonelessly, the card in
the palm of his hand damp with sweat.

'Want the lot?'

'It's none of your business. How much is there, I'm asking
you?'

'I haven't counted.'

'Count it.'

'Leshka,' Bushuyev nodded carelessly. 'See what the
bank's worth. I don't seem to remember.'

Leshka frowning, kneeling upright, counted clumsily,
taking the money from the pile note by note and putting it
down.

Everyone else was silent. Petukhov wiped his sweating
face with his sleeve.

'Seven hundred and forty-five roubles.'

Petukhov passed his sleeve over his face again and
mumbled through dry lips:

'The lot.'

'Who are you trying to fool?' A muscle quivered in
Bushuyev's cheek. 'You put down seven hundred and
forty-five roubles right here in this corner where everyone
can see it, then I'll believe you.'

'I'll put it down all right. What d'you mean?' Petukhov
countered, his voice quavering slightly.

'Well, do it then. Don't hold up the game. Get out your trunk.' For once Bushuyev's eyes were wide open.

Petukhov knew he must get up. That was what Bushuyev expected, so did the other men in the room, as they looked on silently with bated breath. 'Well . . .'

He got up heavily. His legs were numb and hard to move, he had pins and needles in his feet. He was crushing the card in his sweaty hand. It was a beauty all right. But no one card was enough by itself. Suppose he drew only a six now? Bushuyev had boasted he could see right through the cards. But were the cards all right? Nobody had had a proper look at them.

He crossed over to his bed, dragged out the suitcase, felt the heavy, well-made lock, the small steel clasp gripped by solid rings. He had riveted the rings on himself. All desire to go on gambling had left him at the first touch of the padlock. But now the suitcase was open and his hand groped under the clothes to where several bundles, all his earnings for the past three months, lay discreetly hidden in a corner. He had been meaning for a long time to make a trip to town one Sunday and pay it into the bank, but here it still was – five thousand in hundred-rouble notes and about three hundred in small change. Now he must take one thousand out and count seven hundred and forty-five! And all for whom? For that jailbird! He had earned it with his own sweat and blood! He never gave a penny to his wife, he never ate in the canteen. And now seven hundred and forty-five roubles for this scum!

'All right.' He turned his head stiffly without looking up. 'To hell with you. I'll stake fifty roubles.'

'That's more like it,' Bushuyev drawled mockingly. 'You just meant to give us a fright.'

Petukhov thought he heard a note of relief in Bushuyev's voice – maybe he had been worried too – in case he lost everything in the bank? But now that pile of money would all go to Bushuyev, while all Petukhov could hope for was fifty roubles. A measly fifty roubles. The rest would be squandered on drink and high living by that crook. And he had such a beautiful card in his hand.

The suitcase was open. His hands groped through the clothes for the bundle of notes.

'Come on. Hurry up. What are you waiting for?' Bushuyev egged him on.

'All right – I'll go for the lot!' Petukhov suddenly blurted out in a trembling voice. 'There's the money, you bastard.'

Petukhov took out his wrapped-up savings, peeled off a thousand and slammed the suitcase shut. Then he spent a long time looking for the ace of hearts which he had dropped behind it.

And while he was looking his confidence ebbed away. The lot . . .

Now he had the card in one hand (a good card – come on, God, help me, help me!); and in the other – a bundle of hundreds. Money he had sweated for, toiled for, skimped and saved – gone hungry for.

'See, you louse? Believe me now?'

'Sure' – Bushuyev's answer was terse and deadly earnest – 'Sit down.'

Everybody was hushed. From all sides wide-eyed stares converged expectantly on the middle of the room. But Petukhov now felt an agony of despair. What did he think he was doing? Bushuyev would make mincemeat of him. He no longer had that leer on his face – he was now dead serious for a change.

Bushuyev had already flicked him a card. He took it. Should he back out? Too late. Once he had taken a card, there was no backing out – it wouldn't only be Bushuyev who would mind.

The king of diamonds.

Bushuyev's eyes narrowed on the sights.

'Another?'

The whole circle could be heard breathing.

'Let me get my own,' Petukhov said hoarsely.

His fat clumsy fingers drew a card from the pack. Please, God, please! Petukhov could not see. Sweat ran from his brow, stinging his eyes.

'Well?' Bushuyev asked, leaning forward.

The third card was an ace – a bust.

Bushuyev laid his narrow, almost refined, hand on Petukhov's money. Without a word he pushed it over to his own pile.

'Here's your change,' he threw Petukhov a few notes.

Petukhov obediently took them.

Genka Shamayev, back from his usual jaunt across the river, for the first time found the hut awake. They were all seated on the floor under the light in a fog of tobacco smoke.

Shamayev went to his own bunk and pulled back the blanket.

'I see you're really at it. You'll get it if Sasha finds out.'

Nobody paid him any attention. Petukhov went on to lose the rest of his thousand.

13

Next morning was dark and overcast. The clouds were clutching at the tops of the fir-trees along the water's edge and a fine drizzle was coming down. As they came out of the warm stuffy hut, their belts buckled round their jackets and waterproof capes, the men could not help shivering. Sleep was still in their faces; there was no talking. As always in the morning the noise of the water at Big Head seemed louder and more insistent.

Head bent, eyes downcast, Petukhov went out with the others towards the boats. His face had become puffy overnight – his step was leaden, he dragged his boat-hook behind him.

Bushuyev was standing by the boats where the rest of the men shuffled around waiting for the latecomers. An old waterproof borrowed from the lanky Khariton billowed out over his jacket. And though Bushuyev was to all appearances just like the others, with his axe stuck in his belt and his hook in his hand, he managed somehow to look as if he was not serious and didn't really mean business.

Petukhov, his head still bent down, edged towards him, poked at the ground with his boot, and said guiltily:

'Listen, mate, it wasn't . . . it was a bit of a joke last

night – very funny – I know I sort of asked for it – listen,
give me my money back and let's forget it.'

Bushuyev's face twisted into a sneer, his eyes became like
slits.

'You're joking, fellow. Rivers don't go backward.'

'Listen here, give it back, I said. Or else . . .' Petukhov
closed in threateningly.

'Hold on now. Clear off!' Bushuyev squared up.

'Lousy bastard. I'll smash your face in!' Petukhov raised
his boat-hook. Bushuyev leaped back and grabbed his axe.

'Come on, hand it over. I'll split your thick skull open.'

Shamayev turned round to them – he was a stocky figure
in his short coat and thigh-length rubber boots; a dry tuft of
hair stuck out from under his forage cap.

'Stop fooling around, or I'll give both of you a walloping.'
Striding over to Petukhov, he grabbed the hook. 'Serves you
right, you fool – you'll keep your nose out of it next time.
Get in the boat.'

Petukhov calmed down and did as he was told.

Until now life at the camp had been quiet and monotonous; days followed nights with no alarms, no excite-
ments. Even the distractions were monotonous – listening
to the radio and a game or two of dominoes. Such entertain-
ment as this did not stave off sleep for long. And in the
morning – it was back to the boats, and the logs, then home
again for the evening meal and so on endlessly.

But this was really something new – a solid ring of people
sitting on the floor, tense faces, excited shining eyes,
clipped words, money, piles of notes growing or shrinking,
money going from one pocket to another, the fever of near
success, the bitter taste of disappointment . . . not to
mention Petukhov digging into his suitcase! It was really
something – and a damn sight more entertaining than
dominoes at bedtime!

The next night the whole hut gathered in a circle, some
to play, others to watch enthralled from the sidelines.
Only two didn't take part: Shamayev, and Petukhov, who
lay fully dressed, face down on his bunk.

The stakes rose straight away. Stifled exclamations

reached his ears. He lay clenching his fists in hate. He couldn't touch Bushuyev now – all the others would stand up for him. The thousand was gone – he wouldn't get it back.

But every word that came to his ears was agonising.

'Pass.'

'Let's have another.'

'Damn – there goes the bank.'

Even the short tense silences were agonising. Here were people winning money, while he, wronged and forgotten, lay alone. It never entered anyone's head to feel sorry for him. What if he tried again? But no risky stuff this time – play it clever, careful, cautious. He'd get his money back again. He'd gone bust on big stakes – better stick to smaller ones.

Petukhov slid from his bunk, carefully pulled out his suitcase, got the money, took out a hundred-rouble note.

He roughly shouldered the others aside, banking on their sympathy for a loser.

'Move over!'

He sat down, trying not to meet anyone's eyes, and took a card.

14

Dubinin was in the habit of laying bait at the end of the stone dam behind the camp. He went to check his lines each evening, and now he was returning with a bucket full of splashing perch.

He walked straight along the dam, striding on the great boulders. It was a stone barrier almost the height of two men, stretching a quarter of a kilometre from the canteen to where it sloped down at an angle into the tempestuous river.

Up till two years ago Dubinin's section had been more difficult than anywhere else on the river. The force of the water at Big Head drove the timber on to a stony shoal and there, several times each summer, great blockages piled up. At peak flow you had to work twelve hours a day. By autumn the loggers were at the end of their rope. This was why they had decided to build a dam to keep the logs off the shoals.

It was made of huge porous boulders piled on top of each other: there was an untold number of these in the wall. They had been laid in the winter by twenty or so people with the help of simple wooden levers, ropes and one wretched horse. Thousands of tons of stone. That meant that each pair of hands had lifted and carried hundreds of tons.

Dubinin had manhandled boulders with the rest of them, his hands numbed through his waterproof gauntlets by the intense cold. As he stepped now from stone to stone he thought that if all their work on the dam during his six years here were miraculously converted into a vertical pile of stone, then it would make a mountain with snowy peaks lost in the clouds. But the men were by now just as used to the dam as to the ceaseless noise of the Big Head and took it for granted. Dubinin was possessed by a vague sort of pride for his charges: 'They're a hard-working lot, you've got to admit – they earn their keep, all right.'

At the end of the dam a cobbled slope ran up to the canteen wall. Behind a corner of the canteen Dubinin could see a lighted window in the hut. It was pretty late but they still hadn't turned in.

His feeling of pride and quiet confidence – that everything was all right, that life was fine – now vanished completely. 'They're at the cards again.'

This dead beat, this scum was lording it over a score of grown, healthy, thinking, self-respecting men. And for him, Dubinin the foreman, the most powerful man on the site, whose every word was listened to, it wasn't so easy just to say 'That's it, boys – stop the nonsense.'

Dubinin could make the men haul boulders in biting frost – that was necessary. He could order them – they weren't exactly teetotallers – not to drink on the site. That too, was necessary. It was in that one word 'necessary' that Dubinin's whole strength lay. But try taking away their cards – they'd be up in arms, straight away. 'Who do you think we are – your slaves? How do you like that –"Now,

now, boys – no cards." Does the work suffer? No. Well then
don't stick your nose in.'

But it wouldn't end there. Wherever there were cards,
drinking and trouble were not far away. 'All right, let it
go on. When trouble comes I'll be there; that's when I'll
call stop. And then they'll have to listen to me!'

A boat nosed into the bank. Shamayev jumped out,
hauled the boat on to the pebbles and sprang up on to the
dam.

'Crystal-gazing?' he asked, also fixing his eyes on the
lighted window.

'Just sizing things up.'

'He'll skin the boys and then beat it, the son of a bitch.'
Dubinin was silent.

'Sasha, let me have a go. I'll get the money from him
and throw him out into the bargain.'

'Plenty of time for that.'

Shamayev brought his face closer to Dubinin's.

'Why are you so soft on him? Other people are paying for
his luck. No point in pulling fellows like him out of the
water – better hit them over the head and push them back
in again!'

'You'd have to do it to a lot of people at that rate. I
know of much better fellows than Bushuyev who swindle
other people.'

'What are you getting at? Who do you mean?'

'Well, there's you for one . . .'

'Me?'

'Yes you – leading that girl on this past month. You fool
around with her and then push off. You get all the fun, she
gets the tears. So there – don't be so rough on other people.'

Shamayev straightened up. His eyes shone in the darkness.

'You're sticking your nose in where you're not asked.'

Clattering down the rocks he ran off the dam. Dubinin
stayed behind a while and then unhurriedly started down
himself.

15

Tobacco smoke hung in layers above the figures huddled on
the floor. Many of them shot fearful glances at Bushuyev: it
was not possible to bring off such wins without swindling –
he couldn't fool them, they'd fix him. The joking had
stopped, the laughter had vanished, in the thick smoking
air something evil was gathering and everyone was waiting
for it to break.

Bushuyev squatted by the money, his vest hanging loose.
Every so often he stuffed some of the money into his pockets,
but the pile at his knees soon grew again. When Bushuyev
got up and went for a drink all heads turned to follow him,
ten pairs of eyes suspiciously followed his every move.
Bushuyev leisurely filled an aluminium mug with water
from the tank, drank thirstily, returned to his place and
squatted down again.

Petukhov shuffled the pack with trembling hands; an
unaccustomed desperation on his face, his eyes red. His
suitcase had been pushed right out into the middle of the
room. It was open and one could see the crumpled clothes
inside. Petukhov was staking his last few roubles.

'The lot.' Bushuyev called relentlessly, as he had already
so often that evening.

The lot. Petukhov's head sunk into his shoulders, his
hands shook. He threw out a card. Bushuyev calmly took
it over, gave it a fleeting look and reached out for the pack.

'Let me take it myself.'

Petukhov's hands trembled. So did the pack as he picked
his card, so did his lips.

Someone behind Bushuyev shouted in an angry voice:
'He's made it!'

Petukhov abruptly flung the cards to the floor, lunged
across the scattered money at Bushuyev and shouted:

'You're cheating, I'll strangle you, you bastard.'

Bushuyev sprang to his feet. Lurching clumsily to his feet
among the huddled bunch of dumbfounded figures, his face
purple, baring his teeth like a wild animal, Petukhov
roared:

"I'll slaughter you, smash you to bits, you swine!'

Now upright, heavy and clumsy, he charged towards
Bushuyev, whose narrow shoulders were enveloped in his
flapping shirt – he had him cornered, now he would squash
him, crush him, cripple him. But Bushuyev nimbly ducked
out of the way and then dived at Petukhov. A short butt
with his head brought Petukhov heavily to the floor.

It all happened quickly – nobody had time to take it in.
Nobody had managed to grab Petukhov, or hold back
Bushuyev.

Bushuyev leaped to his bunk, flung off the mattress and
turned round with an axe in his hands.

In the sudden silence the muffled roar of the waters at the
Big Head pressed through the windows.

Till then all they had felt towards Bushuyev was distance,
an intense one for sure, kindled by vague misgivings, but
the moment they saw the axe in his hand they understood
that he was their enemy. He recognised it too – not for
nothing had he kept this axe hidden in his bunk.

'Now' – Bushuyev brandished the axe – 'anyone who likes
to . . . I've nothing to lose . . .'

His white shirt hung outside his trousers, his sharp collar
bones stood out under the open collar. His long neck was
scraggy as a chicken's leg; his bright eyes stared blankly in
his pallid, black-bristled face.

It was one against all the rest. There was not one of those
men who was not stronger than him. There was a whole
crowd of them, more than a score. And what if he did have
an axe? There were axes in the corridor – it would have been
easy enough to dash through the door and pick them up.

The noise of the rapids seeped through the tightly closed
windows. Nobody moved. They just stood, shifting their
feet uneasily, and looked at Bushuyev. Fists were out of the
question. In the twinkling of an eye the axe would be up and
there was no doubt that this man wouldn't think twice
about bringing it down on the first head that came his way.
No conscience, no law, would restrain him. Even Petukhov,
mad with hate and despair, hesitated to grab an axe and
brain him. More than a score of hefty men stood bewildered

before this one weak, narrow-chested runt of a man. They stood in silence. The noise of the river went on.

Petukhov stirred on the floor, raised himself on his hands and began to get slowly to his feet. They all watched him closely. So did Bushuyev, sharply, coldly, warily.

Petukhov staggered over to his bunk and flopped down on it. The others stirred. The tension relaxed, but the wariness and caution were there still. They looked furtively at Bushuyev. Nobody spoke.

Bushuyev then sat down on his bunk, dropped on to the pillow, put his axe by his side, casually took out a cigarette, lit up, leaned back and puffed smoke to the ceiling. All the others went to their bunks as well.

The door opened and Shamayev ducked his head to come in. He cast a sour look at the bunks, tripped, picked up a padlock – a big strong door padlock – and threw it on top of the disarrayed clothes in Petukhov's suitcase.

'You might at least clear the money up off the floor,' he growled, pulling off his jacket.

The money lay mixed with the cards scattered by the stove. Nobody moved to pick it up.

16

For the past few days Leshka had gone around in a daze— the piles of money, the stakes won and lost, the people breathing hard down the back of his neck as they watched him play. He found it vaguely disturbing and frightening. He would have been only too glad to get out of it, but he hadn't the strength of will. He was worried about what Dubinin would think, too. He was getting out of his depth. His heart sank as he wondered how it would end. And now all this – Petukhov's hoarse cry of rage, the scuffle with Bushuyev who was lying there on his bunk, axe in hand.

Leshka shared the hatred which the others felt for this stranger. He had expected Stupnin and Petukhov, who were both strong men and never reckoned to be afraid of anything, to go for Bushuyev and pin him down. But no one did. They had all stood, as bewildered as himself. The sight of this man with his narrow glinting eyes was terrifying. They cowered before him.

Leshka went apprehensively to his bunk which was next to the one where Bushuyev was sprawled smoking. He started hurriedly to undress. If only he could get his head down quickly, turn his back on Bushuyev and forget him. Scarcely had his head touched the pillow, however, when he felt something hard bulging up through the pillow-case. He thrust his hand inside but Bushuyev's intent stare made him turn.

'You,' Bushuyev hissed, scarcely audibly, 'go outside.'

Leshka stared open-mouthed, not understanding.

'Go outside, I said. As if you were going for a piss. Wait for me there. Go on.'

Bushuyev casually turned back, letting the smoke drift to the ceiling. Leshka was still at a loss.

'Get out!' Bushuyev hissed again through a cloud of smoke. Leshka didn't dare disobey. He got into his rubber boots and holding up his pants he made for the door. Nobody paid any attention.

The moon behind the forest was almost full. From the dark river came the muffled detached noise of rushing water. Leshka started to wait in the shadow of the wall, shivering from the night cold in his underclothes, trying to stop his teeth chattering and looking around every minute. He felt as if eyes were somewhere watching suspiciously. He strained his ears to listen through the noise of the water for the sound of approaching footsteps.

He had a long time to wait. The moon, large and plump, but with a thin sliver cut from one side, lit the deserted yard and the cistern in the middle. A dim light shone from the office window. Sasha was still awake. Suppose he ran over and told him what Bushuyev was up to? He'd soon put a stop to it.

But Leshka just went on standing in the cold, shivered, and couldn't bring himself to move.

There was a slight creak on the wooden steps in front of the hut and Bushuyev appeared with his shirt outside his trousers, gripping his axe. With his free hand he grabbed

Leshka by the chest, dragging him forward and breathing into his face with a stench of tobacco. He whispered hoarsely:

'There's ten thousand under your pillow. Take it home to your village on Saturday. Stay there till I come and see you. Maybe not too soon – but I'll be along all right. You're from Yaremnoye, third house on the right. I know all about you, see? Double-cross me and you're good as dead. If you do it right, you get two thousand to play around with. Get it, babyface? It will never enter their heads that you've got the money. They can search me as much as they like.'

Bushuyev spat through the gap in his teeth.

'Get going.'

Leshka's teeth chattered.

'Give the money back,' he begged, 'the boys are pretty wild about it.'

'Don't you tell me what to do.'

'Th-then go away now – take your money and go away.'

'Listen, you snivelling little runt, how can I go away without my papers? Dubinin's got them. Now push off, or the others will start getting ideas. And remember, one squeak out of you and I'll kill you.'

17

Leshka went back to the homely warmth of the hut. Some of the men were already peacefully snoring. Shamayev was smoking and thinking. The money was still on the floor.

Petukhov lay face down on his bunk, still dressed and with his boots on. At the sound of the door he quivered and jerked up his head. His eyes were wild, the lids red and swollen.

'Were you there? Did you see him?' he asked hoarsely.

'Who?' asked Leshka, his voice wavering.

'Who! Who! Don't pretend you don't know. You went out. He went after you. You're in with him.'

'You're out of your mind,' interrupted Shamayev. 'It's all because of that money. You'll be accusing me next. You lie down, Leshka.'

Leshka's knees were shaking. He dragged his feet over to
the bunk and crawled under the blanket. The moment his
head touched the pillow he felt the money again. For a
second he felt like jumping up and shouting: 'Here's the
money, boys! He stuck it in my pillow!' They trusted
him. To double-cross his own mates! But Bushuyev had
threatened 'One squeak out of you and you're dead.'
And he would kill him, too, without thinking twice about
it.

Leshka lay curled up. He couldn't get warm and went on
shivering as before.

Petukhov said in a whining voice:

'He'll clear out – get across the river with our money;
we'll never see him again.'

'He's not got his trousers. How could he get away like
that? Everybody would notice,' Shamayev interposed
lazily. 'You'll see tomorrow.'

'Why doesn't he come back then? He's hiding the money.'

'He'll give it back. We'll make him.'

Somebody raised his head:

'That's enough fellows – we have to get up at seven.'

Stupnin sighed from his corner:

'What a business.'

The hut was silent. Petukhov's bunk creaked.

Leshka's ear was pressed on the money under the pillow.
He lay still, no longer feverish but gripped by a strange,
confused, aching sensation. It was not so long since the bunk,
which now waited for Bushuyev had been occupied by
Tolya Stupnin. He had often talked to Leshka about what
he read in books. He told him about big towns, colleges,
educated people, aeroplanes big enough to take up everybody on the site. Listening to Stupnin, he thought the
outside world must be like a fairy story – full of kind and
mighty people. Now for the first time it dawned on him that
the world also had its Bushuyevs. How could he reconcile
the world of Stupnin's stories with this black-hearted man?
The big wide world was certainly bewildering and hard to
understand.

Leshka lay with his eyes shut tight, feeling infinitely

small, helpless and stupid in the midst of the ocean of life
which surrounded the small island he knew – the tiny camp
skirting the river. It was his first disillusionment, his first
dismay, his first fear, the first naïve realisation of a childhood which had gone on too long.

Petukhov could not calm down. He stumbled over towards Bushuyev's bunk, angrily felt the jacket hanging
above it, picked up the pillow, thumped it, raised the
mattress.

'He's after the money.' Leshka froze. 'Now he'll tell me
to get up.' The money pressed on his temple through the
pillow. 'What shall I do? Tell him? What about Bushuyev?
What can they do to him? If they beat him up and throw
him out – he'll still be alive and kicking. And he even knows
my village, and the house I live in. He'll track me down
wherever I go.'

He lay still with the money pressing on his temple.
Petukhov, who was tearing Bushuyev's bed apart, was a
changed man. He used to be no different from the others –
even though he was a bit meaner. But now he had a fierce,
dogged look about him and his eyes were bloodshot. If
Petukhov found out that he was lying on the money he
might hurl himself on him and strangle him. Leshka suddenly found him strange and baffling. And yet they had
lived side by side for over a year.

Leshka held his breath under the blanket and watched as
Petukhov finished tearing at the bunk; at last he cursed and
went away.

18

Dubinin cleaned the fish, wrapped it up in nettles and stood
the bucket outside the door, where it was cool; then, without
taking off his coat, he sat down in his office and tried to
think; as usual, the telephone kept croaking out its hoarse
signals for other people who shared the line.

He thought of Bushuyev as he had lain on the bunk, just
after he had been pulled out of the river, his face green and
stubbly, his sharp knees jutting up through the eiderdown,

his thin arms stretched out by his sides, the tattooed inscription on his chest . . .

So he was down on his luck, the son of a bitch! And we gave him a helping hand . . . But that just wasn't good enough for him and he has to start grabbing our money: anything for the easy life. But the trouble is there are always people in your way – it's not like fighting wild animals – that's why Bushuyev can't make it: 'The years go by but bring no luck.'

The water boomed on, the telephone rang shrilly on the wall. Dubinin got up.

The first time he had met Bushuyev he had told him that it was hard to leave the district. But was it? Instead of walking or rowing he could take the outboard. It was always near the bank and Tikhon never took the motor out. If he started in the evening, he could clear all the other logging camps on the river by morning. Once he got down to Tormenga he wouldn't be easy to find among all the hundreds of workers there – and he could get out of there by rail or road . . . He'd have a good laugh about it afterwards – the way he hoodwinked those half-wits up the river!

Silent and mysterious, the wooded slope rose above the river, separating the small settlement from the rest of the world. The river was black, except in midstream where the moonlight seethed and thrashed about together with the current to which it was captive.

Dubinin took the motor out of the boat, put it on the bank and stood for a long time among the boulders, looking at the moonlight feverishly trembling on the stream, listening to the roaring rapids and the patter of spray on the sides of the boat.

What could he do? Reason with him? He was no good at talking. Just throw him out? Or leave him to the others to deal with? That would be to act as selfishly as Bushuyev himself . . .

Dubinin shouldered the heavy motor and, watching his own shadow crawl over the stones, he climbed the slope towards the dim light of his office window.

Some ten yards before he got to it he saw a shadow flit

across the window. Whoever could it be at this late hour?

Bent slightly under the weight of the motor, he cautiously approached.

Humped over the desk, Bushuyev was going through the drawers. His axe lay on top of the desk.

What was he doing? What did he want? Suddenly Dubinin realised – his identity papers.

They weren't in the desk. They were in the rucksack hanging on the wall next to the telephone, just behind Bushuyev's back. He hadn't noticed it.

Dubinin must have made a careless step – Bushuyev glanced round sharply at the window – his face went rigid, and his eyes darted like those of a hunted beast.

19

They met in the dark porch.

'It's you, Sasha? I was just coming to see you.' There was not a trace of fear or embarrassment in Bushuyev's voice.

Dubinin grabbed him by the arm and pulled him outside. 'Come on.'

'Where?'

Dubinin did not answer.

The bare yard looked even more deserted by moonlight. Half way to the bunkhouse, the old iron cistern loomed black in front of them. From the light in the hut windows – though it was long past midnight – not to mention the discovery of Bushuyev in his office with the axe under his arm, Dubinin could see all too clearly that something had happened and that it was time for him to act.

Bushuyev stopped before they reached the cistern.

'Where are you taking me?'

'Come on. Don't talk.'

'Wait a bit . . . Do you want me to give back the money? . . . Well, why not say so?' His voice was peaceable.

'You'll give it back. But first we'll have a talk with the boys.'

'It will be easier to talk if I put the money in front of them – they'll be in a better mood.'

'You'll put the money in front of them all right.'

'But I've hidden it.' Still held by the arm, Bushuyev looked back. 'Come on, I'll show you.'

Dubinin slowed down, then made up his mind.

'Lead the way.'

Bushuyev took him in the direction of the river, away from the canteen and the hostel, towards the dam.

'Remember, Sasha,' he went on in the same peaceful voice, 'how you asked me if I wanted to go home? I haven't been home for seventeen years, not since the beginning of the war. Well, I keep turning it over in my mind: why not go back, marry a girl with a house of her own. Any girl will take you if you have money. Why shouldn't I live like everybody else? I'm sick of drifting, and I don't want a guard with a gun at my back any more.'

'You should have done some honest work and then gone home. We'd have given you a good send-off.'

'And apart from that – I'm sick of these forests of yours. Living here isn't freedom and it's too wet and cloudy for me – to hell with it. At home we have wide open spaces, and it's warm. I didn't want to fleece your fellows – the fools just asked for it. None of them could resist it. I'm sick of the sight of this lousy river and all the nitwits who live in this dump . . .'

'All right, smart alec, that's enough talking. Where did you hide the money?'

'Wait a bit. We're a bit hasty today, aren't we? I don't feel like hurrying.'

'Come on.'

'Don't rush me.' Bushuyev tore his arm out of Dubinin's grasp and faced him, his white shirt hanging outside his trousers; because of the gum boots he was wearing, the lower part of him was big and clumsy, but his shoulders were narrow, and his neck was thin.

Behind him the boulders and wooden piles of the dam stretched back into the transparent moonlit shadow. The noise of the Big Head was close, you could feel its damp breath.

Bushuyev shifted his grip on the axe.

'You wanted to talk with a lot of people around, but I'd rather do it like this – it's more intimate. Much better with nobody around, isn't it?' Bushuyev looked at the foreman mockingly.

'Where's the money, you son of a bitch?' Dubinin made a step towards him.

'Get back you. What's all this about money?'

'Don't think you can frighten me with your axe.'

'Now, now, mister foreman, don't get worked up. Let's have a quiet talk. You tell me where my papers are and let me go without any fuss, and I won't touch you.'

'Drop your axe!' Dubinin clenched his fists.

But Bushuyev raised his axe and hissed back:

'Bare fists, is it? Tired of life, are you? I'll split your skull and throw you in the river. There's plenty of room in there. Give me back my papers, you swine. They're not in your office, so you must have them on you. Give them back, you bastard!' Dubinin leaped back, bent down and tried to pick up a stone.

'So that's it, is it!' Bushuyev advanced on him. 'Carrying a knife, are you? I'm not frightened. Just you try anything, and you'll see!'

Dubinin had completely forgotten the sheath-knife in his belt. He pulled it out . . . But a knife is not much more use than fists against a man with an axe. With the knife in his hand, Dubinin backed towards the river, anxious lest he stumble on the stones and fall down.

His foot slipped on the slimy pebbles – the river was at his back, there was nowhere to retreat.

'You're done for now! Give me those papers or else . . .'

Dubinin threw himself forward. He just had time to swerve and cover his head with his hands. The axe must have been blunt – it caught his sleeve and slit it from wrist to elbow. His arm went numb and useless to his side.

Bushuyev's face, contorted into a wild-eyed leer, was close upon him. Once again the axe swung up. Dubinin threw himself underneath it – if he could get in close enough the axe would not be dangerous – he tried to clasp Bushuyev's body to him but his shattered arm would not obey.

Bushuyev twisted sideways, still holding the axe above Dubinin's head.

Without another thought, frightened only of the raised axe coming down, Dubinin struck Bushuyev with his knife – he struck him in the chest again and again.

The axe fell with a dull ring on the stones. Bushuyev stiffened, stretched out his neck, and fell back without a sound.

Apart from the roar of the rapids there was not a sound. The huge boulders, piled one on top of the other, reared above. Bushuyev lay, his legs stretched out, his white shirt flapping around him, the blunt toes of his rubber boots sticking up. The water roared on . . .

Dubinin looked at his knife. Dark stains showed on the blade which shone in the moonlight. He threw it down. He stumbled towards Bushuyev, bent over him and suddenly jerked back . . . Bushuyev's eyes were open, his neck was throbbing convulsively, a black stream of blood flowed from his mouth and he was still breathing in fits and starts. Dubinin bent down again and tried to raise his head but his fingers felt something sticky on the back of the head. Bushuyev's fall had only seemed soft and noiseless – in fact his skull had smashed against the stones. A dark oily stain was spreading on his shirt . . . Dubinin straightened himself up.

He went back home. The tops of his rubber boots scraped against each other, the sand squelched under his feet and the moon looked down . . .

Back in his office Dubinin picked up the telephone. The line that only a short while ago had seethed with other people's conversation was now frighteningly still. His left hand was helpless. He had to tuck the receiver under his chin in order to crank the handle with his right hand.

A man called Osipov, whom he did not know, was on duty at the regional militia post.

'Dubinin of the Fifth River District speaking . . . D-U-B-I-N-I-N. I've just killed a man . . . Yes, me . . . There's nothing to tell, you'll see for yourselves . . . Send the boat for you tomorrow morning? All right . . .'

He hung up, sat down on his chair, and gingerly put his wounded arm on his lap.

20

Around eleven the next day, Tikhon, the mechanic, fetched three people by boat – the Prosecutor, a woman doctor, and the district militia officer.

All the inhabitants of the small settlement stood waiting for them in a silent crowd; they followed them to the dam where Bushuyev's body still lay on the stones beside the water.

The doctor, middle-aged and with a faded homely face, cut Bushuyev's shirt from hem to collar, examined his wounds, carefully feeling his chest with her fingertips, lifted his head and looked at the broken skull. The Prosecutor picked up the knife and frowned at it, and asked the militia man to take charge of the axe.

Back in the office, the doctor undid her coat, pushed her shawl back from her hair on to her shoulders, sat down at Dubinin's desk and busied herself with her forms. Calm radiated from her industrious figure, filling the room which was half office, half bachelor dwelling. Looking at her, Dubinin felt as though what had happened was not so frightening after all.

The Prosecutor was young – his large gristly ears propped up his cap and underneath it his face was round and full-cheeked with a heart-shaped mouth. His manner with Dubinin was coldly polite.

'You knew about the winnings of the deceased?'

'Yes.'

'And had you no idea where the deceased kept the money?'

'If I had, I wouldn't have gone with him to look for it.'

As Dubinin answered he guessed what was in the Prosecutor's mind and was appalled – he suspected him of having killed Bushuyev for his money. He almost lost his temper and shouted: 'Who do you think you are, you young puppy?' Then he realised: when he was the Prosecutor's age, he had had no more intelligence or charity. The Prosecutor had been sent out to bring in the criminal. And since Dubinin was the criminal, the Prosecutor, even as he got into the boat, had made up his mind. No shouting, no argument would dissuade him; there was nothing for it but to endure.

Dubinin answered briefly and obediently.

'We'll question the others and look for the money,' declared the Prosecutor. 'If we don't find it, I'm sorry to say that I'll be obliged to arrest you. Please sit in the porch and don't go away without my permission.'

Dubinin went out of the hut.

Bushuyev's body was brought to the door of the office. He lay beside the porch, his chin pointing at the sky, his blood-stained shirt cut open to expose his flat chest with its inscription: 'The years go by but bring no luck.'

21

The conversation with Bushuyev, the business with the money, and then, in the early morning, all this shouting and talk about murder had left Leshka completely dazed. He felt like sobbing, like tearing his hair, or crying for his mother. He could understand nothing. It was all too much for him.

All night the money had lain under his pillow. That terrible money! He longed to shout: 'Here it is, take the cursed stuff away from me!'

But what would happen if he did? Petukhov would be on him straight away like a ton of bricks. 'There I was looking for it, and you were lying on it right next to me all the time!' And not only Petukhov – they would all go for him and say he had got together with Bushuyev, that he had sold out his friends for money . . .

And what about Sasha? The very idea that he could be called a murderer! He did not dare say the word aloud, he hardly dared think it – it made his blood run cold. What must Sasha be feeling now? And it was all his, Leshka's, fault. He had pulled Bushuyev out of the water (if only he

had known!); and last night he hadn't had the nerve to run
and tell Sasha all about it . . . Now there was this money . . .
If Sasha ever got to know of it . . .

Sasha would turn his back on him, they would all turn
their backs on him, they would drive him out of the district,
in the village they would call him a thief. Bushuyev's
threats were nothing compared to that. It was all frightening, and confusing. What was he to do?

Tidying his bunk, Leshka got the money from the
pillow-case. No one noticed. The money was tied up in a
dirty handkerchief. Leshka started stuffing it into his
pockets but the pockets bulged and he felt still more
frightened – anyone could see it now. Leshka went to the
wooden lavatory outside and undid the bundle. He divided
the money into two bundles and stuffed them into the top
of his gum boots, one in each leg.

He went with the others to see the Prosecutor, and then
to visit the scene of the murder; not for a single moment, as
he stood beside the office porch, did he stop wondering what
he was to do. Should he hide the money among the stones
and later on pretend he had found it? Or better still, arrange
for someone else to find it – say Petukhov? But the very
thought that he would have to hide it like a thief made him
shake all over as though he had a fever. He felt like throwing
it into the river and forgetting all about it.

The men gathered in the hut, and now for the first time
he heard someone say out loud: 'They suspect Sasha.'
Leshka felt faint. He sat hiding his face, trying not to look
at the boots where the money was hidden. Somehow he had
never thought that Sasha could be accused. He was blaming
himself enough as it was, and now, on top of it all, there was
this suspicion that Sasha had committed murder for the
money. What was all this? He must tell everything, he must
produce the money, he must save Sasha . . .

The militia man came in. He asked them all to stay where
they were; the first man he summoned to the office to be
questioned by the Prosecutor was Shamayev.

Leshka was summoned immediately after Petukhov and
this alarmed him. Petukhov did not trust him, and Lord

knows what he might have said to the Prosecutor. The
Prosecutor would already be suspicious, and when he saw
the money . . . Just try and get out of that one!

'I'll tell him anyway, I don't care . . .' Leshka kept re-
peating to himself, stepping carefully in his boots stuffed
with thousand-rouble notes.

Near the porch the body of Bushuyev lay in its blood-
stained shirt. Dubinin sat on the doorstep and next to him,
leaning against the door-post was the militia man.

Dubinin sat erect, looking sideways at the roaring waters
of the Big Head and holding his wounded arm. To Leshka
at this moment he appeared small and lonely. Sasha was no
longer the foreman, he was as helpless as himself.

22

The master of the lumber camp was now this stranger with
the shiny peak to his cap, bright buttons on his jacket and,
underneath the cap, eyes which looked calm and cold.

His first words to Leshka were frightening: that he must
speak nothing but the truth, otherwise he would be held
responsible under the criminal code . . . There was something about statutes. What code? What statutes? Leshka
did not know, but it all sounded very terrible to him. All he
wanted was to be understood, to be pitied and forgiven.

The eyes looked steadily from under the shining peak.
The man would never believe him. He would say that he
had been in with Bushuyev. And suppose even Sasha didn't
believe him? How could Leshka prove he was telling the
truth, when Bushuyev was the only one who had known it?
For the first time he was sorry that Bushuyev was dead and
gone so that even the man with the shining peak couldn't
make him talk and tell the truth.

The Prosecutor wouldn't believe him . . . Nor would
Sasha and the others. When the Prosecutor asked him if he
knew where Bushuyev could have hidden the money he
answered:

'I don't know.'

Once again he walked past Dubinin, past the militia

officer and past Bushuyev's corpse with the chin jutting up at the sky. He passed them with his head bowed. He stepped as cautiously as before, conscious at every moment of the money hidden inside his boots, and turned not towards the dining-room but down to the river. He walked on, afraid to look back, expecting someone to shout: 'Hey you! Where are you off to?' But no one called . . .

23

One after the other Dubinin's friends walked past – those he had lived with, those he had lived for. They threw him a pitying, puzzled glance and hastily looked away. One after the other they went into the office and came out again.

The silent militia officer stood at his back; on the ground nearby was the man he had killed with his own hands.

He wasn't guilty. He couldn't have done anything else. And when he turned and looked at the logs diving over the Big Head, at the steep wooded bank, at the low, peaceful clouds, he believed that he wasn't guilty. But he couldn't help looking down at the waxen chest, the lolling head, the blood-stained, tattered shirt, the stiffened yellow hand on the trodden grass.

Yes, he had done it in self-defence, he had had nothing but his knife against a man armed with an axe, and if he hadn't killed him, he would be lying there by the porch himself . . . But all the same, there was the corpse in front of him – the rusty blood-stains on the shirt, the clenched hand – there could be no excuse for killing a man.

The Big Head seethed, flinging the logs about, the sombre firs and pines climbed the steep bank towards the sky – it was low and still holding out the promise of a brief shower. Bushuyev would never see it. One stab with a knife and the world had ended for him.

A stab with a knife. A story as old as life – one man quarrelling with another. Hundreds, thousands of years ago Bushuyevs like him had raised axes or knives against their fellow-men, forcing them to do likewise. Was this an ever-

lasting curse, would it really never be possible to be rid
of it?

Dubinin sat hunched in the porch looking at the wooded
banks, the stream, the sky. Everything was familiar to him,
he had seen the river and the banks every day. The poor soil
was full of stones, but life nevertheless sprouted from every
crack. Weeds had insolently grown up on the trampled,
iron-hard path, as though to say: 'Here we are, we're alive
and kicking.' And next to them lay the bloodless, stiffened
clenched hand . . .

Dubinin just sat there, his face stony. His friends stepped
past him and lowered their eyes.

24

Tikhon, the mechanic, who usually cursed his fate before
every journey, now only fussed and sighed: 'Oh Lord,
Lord . . .'

The engine wouldn't start.

'Oh Lord, Lord . . .'

Finally the engine spluttered. The Prosecutor, the doctor,
and the militia man climbed into the boat.

The men stood on the shore in a silent crowd. Dubinin
nodded to them as though to say: 'Don't worry. Everything
will be all right.'

'Sasha,' Shamayev stepped forward, 'I just want to say
. . . Hold it, Tikhon, don't push off . . . If we have to turn
the earth upside-down, we'll prove that you're innocent.'

'Everything will be all right,' Sasha said.

'And remember what you said to me the other day –
about Katya? Well, you needn't have worried . . . When this
business is over, we'll dance at my wedding.'

'Well, I'm sorry I said anything if that's the case . . .'

Leaving a puff of bluish smoke drifting above the water,
the boat turned into mid-stream and began to bob up and
down on the Big Head, plunging into a trough of waves, or
creating them with its bow jerked skywards; it passed the
Small Head and vanished. No one said a word.

Silently, looking down at their feet, they all went back to

the hut and silently dispersed to their bunks.

All except Petukhov that is – he roamed the river bank, turning up stones in the gathering dusk, peering under bushes, still hoping to find the money.

Shamayev was the first to speak.

'That's what comes of gambling . . .'

'All right, don't rub it in. It's bad enough without.'

'Better try and think how we can get Sasha out of this mess.'

'The hell of it is the money. If we could find that, he'd be proved innocent straight away.'

'Suppose we have a collection among ourselves and say we found it?'

'That's right – we could. It wasn't marked.'

'That's no good. They'd be sure to find out. We'd only make things worse.'

'You're all trying to be too clever. The money must still be around somewhere – Bushuyev can't have taken it with him! We'll turn the whole place upside-down. We'll look under every stone and take the hut apart until we find it!'

Suddenly there was a sound of muffled sobbing. They all raised their heads. It was Leshka, crying into his pillow.

The Big Head roared outside. Leshka sobbed openly, without restraint. The rest were silent, they looked at each other. Only Stupnin said:

'Well, what a business.'

Under the title *Troika, semiorka, tuz* this story first appeared in *Novy Mir* 3, 1960, pp. 3-31.

Justice

A rickety bridge made of planks had been thrown across the brackish forest stream. With their tails between their legs, the dogs carefully made their way along the wooden boards. The one in the lead was short, stocky, with a dirty yellow coat; she kept stopping and looking round in a mournful way. Her owner, the old bear hunter Simon Teterin, gazed at her with deep interest.

'Look, she's afraid, the bitch,' he thought in surprise. 'Kalinka, afraid. Who would have thought it? Come on, old girl, come on. What's the matter?'

'Unfamiliar surroundings,' pronounced the first-aid man, Mityagin, rather portentously.

'What's unfamiliar about them? If she falls in, what does it matter? She's swum across bigger streams than this. She's swallowed enough water in her dog's life. She must be crazy . . .'

The third hunter merely turned his eyes silently from the dog to its owner.

They put down their guns carefully, stacking them against the trunk of a great uprooted birch tree, and settled down on grass that had the day's warmth in it. The dogs, having negotiated the bridge, ran up boisterously, tongues out, and lay down by Teterin's heavy boots.

These dogs, Kalinka and Malinka, mother and daughter, were not in the least like each other. The daughter, Malinka, was bigger than her mother, with a darker coat, and looked more solid, older. Up till now it had seemed strange that the bear hunter should praise only the scrawny, plain-looking Kalinka, with the untidy tufts of hair along her spine. Now that both dogs were lying side by side, it was obvious that in the cut of Kalinka's long, narrow jaw,

with the damp protruding tongue, with the yellow teeth and
the blackened gums, there was a pitiless cruelty, a sort of
cold rapacity, which one sometimes observes with surprise
on the face of a great pike; her eyes, narrowed by the skin
which had been pulled back tightly to the ears, watched the
hunters' faces in utter indifference, and there was no hint
of the usual canine affection in them. It would not have
occurred to a passer-by to stretch out an idle hand to this
dry, elongated head with its sleek forehead, and give it a
friendly pat. An unpleasant character, but a strong one.
One felt she would not run away from a wolf, nor hesitate to
hurl herself against a bear. The sleek, big-boned Malinka, in
contrast to her mother, seemed a guileless creature, full of
goodwill.

Two birch trees towered over the forest clearing. A
mighty, gnarled one shut out the sky over the heads of the
hunters with its leaves and branches. The other, down by
the stream, was surrounded by tall bushes half way up the
trunk. The hollow trunk, of enormous girth, was festooned
with strips of rough bark. The branches, gnarled and
twisted like great bony arms, were bare. Perhaps this was
the mother of the other great birch tree, a worthy matriarch.
Decades ago its roots had stopped sending life-giving juices
up the trunk, but the tree had obstinately continued
standing, and, though dead, had not fallen.

The sun had scarcely touched the tops of the fir forest.
There was a smell of mushrooms and rotting needles. In the
warm air was something heavy and peaceful, like the sleepy
feeling after a full dinner. The huge branches of the fir trees
sagged limply; not a leaf stirred on the birch silhouetted
against the sky. There was complete silence but for the
soothing murmur of water in the willow bushes by the
stream, and the whine of mosquitoes in the air.

The hunters, sprawled lazily on the forest track which
was completely overgrown with soft grass, felt a sort of
vague intoxicating freedom. There were no worries, there
was nothing to think about, they were simply alive, feeling
the sun's rays on their faces, breathing in the smell of
mushrooms, and they were the equals of these austere firs,

particles of untouched nature dissolving in her without a trace. Only the mosquitoes annoyed them, and their nerves were slightly roused by the thought of the great venture ahead of them – a bear hunt at night. It was not for nothing that the well-greased barrels of the rifles glinted under the birch trees.

2

The villages, hamlets, fields, meadows and pastures of the district of Gustoi Bor were all surrounded by forest. Roads made their way timidly from village to village, stagnant streams of dark water wound through the forest in the depths of which marshy lakes shone like black mirrors. Human life was engulfed in a sea of fir trees. Even the hunters – and there were quite a few of them in these parts – felt that they were visitors in the forest, and did not venture far from the roads. The only one who could say that he knew the forest was Simon Teterin, the most famous of the local hunters. He had spent all his life there. By the shores of gloomy lakes, in the depths of the forest, he had built huts of pinewood for himself. There were many of these huts (known to the village people as 'Teterin's huts') round about. Wherever Simon happened to be, on a winter's night crackling with frost, or in a downpour of autumn rain, he would make his way to his nearest hut, light a fire, dry himself, cook something and feel at home.

If Simon Teterin, in a manner of speaking, was ruler of the forest, the man lying opposite him was intent, sooner or later, on destroying his kingdom. Konstantin Dudyrev was the man's name.

Only a year ago there was nothing to distinguish the little village of Dymki from the other villages in the district. Its dark log huts looked down from the river bank on to a backwater covered with water-lilies, there was only one street, and the road which went through was muddy in rainy weather, dusty when dry. As in every other village, the cocks crowed in the mornings, and at sunset the cows returned from pasture. Who could have imagined the extraordinary fate that had overtaken this very ordinary village? It had fallen to Dymki to become the site of an enormous wood-working plant. Contractors' offices had sprung up next to the log huts, and foundations for two-storied brick buildings were being laid; on the common pasture excavators, rearing their dippers skywards, had begun to dig a huge foundation area. New groups of workers kept arriving from outside – a motley, loudmouthed crew. Even the modest name of Dymki disappeared from common use and was replaced by the grander sounding 'Dymki Project'. And the head of this Project was Dudyrev – an all powerful personality.

For many years the local authorities of the Gustoi Bor district had dreamed of laying a road from the district centre to the railway. Fifty kilometres of hard surface were needed so that vehicles would not break down, and the little town of Gustoi Bor would not be cut off from the rest of the world by the autumn mud. Surveys were carried out, requests for money made, and then nothing was done – it was too big a job. But as soon as Dudyrev came on the scene, he not only got a road made, he also extended the branch railway line, something nobody had even dared dream about. He started a regular bus service from Dymki Project to Gustoi Bor, and from Gustoi Bor to the railway station. He shook up the sleepy life of the district town, and overran it with new people. The secretary of the local Party committee and the chairman of the local soviet treated Dudyrev with respect, while collective-farm chairmen, even the most respected like Donat Borovikov, continually danced attendance on him, trying to do him a service, on the off-chance that some crumbs might fall from the table of the great – a little cement, some nails or sheet metal, which there was no hope of getting through ordinary channels, even if you went down on bended knees to beg for them.

Dudyrev had only just begun. He had yet to send forth narrow-gauge railway lines, like tendrils through the forest. He would cut swathes through the forest. His Project would serve four timber enterprises with very many new lumber

camps scattered around in places where up till now there
had been nothing except one of Teterin's huts. The roar of
great tractors, the whine of electric saws, the hooting of
trucks would frighten away the bears. Simon Teterins'
kingdom would come to an end.

But this would not happen today, nor tomorrow. And in
the meantime Simon Teterin and Dudyrev, with their guns
leaning against the trunk of a birch tree, were resting side
by side, waving away the mosquitoes.

There was nothing to distinguish Simon Teterin from
other men – he was not exactly small or puny, but neither
was he so powerfully built as to attract attention. The skin
on one of his weather-beaten cheekbones was stretched
tight by an ugly scar, and because of this his right eye
looked out at the world with a fierce squint. This scar had
not been caused by a bear, although Simon had killed a
good number of them in his time – forty-three fully grown
ones and about twenty young ones, including cubs. He had
got it during the war: a splinter from a German mine had
caught him while he was putting a bridge across the Desna
with some other sappers.

Dudyrev looked like one of the workers from his Project.
A faded cap was pulled over his forehead, and he wore a
shabby jacket with crumpled lapels, cloth breeches and
rubber boots. He had taken off his new bandolier of yellow
leather, and thrown it under the birch trees near the guns.
He had a large face, square and rugged, a real working
man's face; but his small, deep-set, grey eyes, with their
calm, confident gaze, were a reminder that he was not so
simple after all.

The third person was a neighbour of Simon Teterin's, the
first-aid man, Mityagin.

He was bald, with bags under his eyes, though in the
village, at the first-aid station, he looked imposing enough
in his white overall. The old women, who came in from neighbouring hamlets were afraid of him, and referred to him respectfully even behind his back; they thought he was very
clever. 'What is the use of a woman doctor coming to us
from the town when we've got our Vasily Maximovich? A

young woman is only good for powdering her nose and
putting lipstick on her mouth, and all she thinks of is young
men.' But apart from the old women, no one else had any
respect for Vasily Mityagin. His children ran about the
village in torn trousers, and he was fond of the bottle. It
would have been all right if he had talked sense in his cups,
but as soon as he got drunk, he started bragging: 'We practical men can show all those academic types a thing or
two . . .' He was not to be taken seriously.

For a long time Mityagin had been begging Simon
Teterin to do him a favour, as a neighbour, by taking him
on a bear hunt. He told him he had tried his hand at
shooting in his youth and assured him that he would not
disgrace himself. Simon gave him his old rifle, and said:
'Don't try to get in front, we're not after hares. Just follow
me and listen to every word I say.'

At the moment Mityagin was paying no attention either
to the silence or to the soft murmur of the stream. He did
not share the others' joyous sense of freedom; all his
thoughts were on the exalted company he was keeping, and
he was trying to look both dignified and intelligent; he even
swatted the mosquitoes on his bald head with an air of
importance.

Before long the three men got bored with the silence and
began a slow, easy-going conversation. At first it was about
Kalinka.

'A dog has instincts, or to put it in every-day language,
habits,' Mityagin began to explain pompously, glancing
sideways at Dudyrev. 'She got frightened when she was on
the bridge, in other words the inborn instinct of fear
asserted itself: a Pavlov reflex, that is . . .'

'You mean Kalinka is in the habit of getting scared?
Fancy that!' laughed Simon.

'It's not just a habit, but a special, inborn . . .'

'Well, go on, talk like that if you want. But why does
every hunter for miles around come to me, cap in hand,
begging me to sell them one of Kalinka's pups? Do they
want 'inborn fear' for their money? All Kalinka's litters
have been first-rate – there isn't a braver dog.'

'You're looking at it from the dog's point of view, as it were. I'm talking about it from the point of view of science . . .'

But now Dudyrev spoke up, and Mityagin broke off respectfully.

'Courage . . . Cowardice . . . When you say words like that it's like handing out a prize, or administering a reprimand . . .'

'Exactly,' Mityagin said prudently, to be on the safe side.

Dudyrev was lying on his back, with one hand under his head, while he fended off mosquitoes half-heartedly with the other.

'I remember during the war one of our reconnaissance officers saying that you're less scared of someone actually shooting at you than you are of someone lying in wait for you. You can understand a man who is shooting at you – you know he's just like yourself, he wants to kill you, and is afraid of being killed himself. But someone just waiting for you is a different matter – people are always much more frightened of hidden things which they don't understand. It was because of fear of the unknown that man invented gods and devils.'

'Exactly,' said Mityagin again.

'Tell me,' Dudyrev asked Simon, leaning over to him on his elbow, 'you've been in a tight corner many a time – after all you've brought down sixty bears – have you ever lost your head from fright?'

Simon Teterin thought for a time.

'I have never really lost my head. If I had, I wouldn't be sitting with you now.'

'But you don't mean you've never been afraid?'

'Of course I have, I'm the same as everybody else.'

'Well, tell us . . .'

'What's there to tell? I've been in no end of scrapes. You remember the ugly customer I brought back with me the summer that Klashka got married?'

'Of course I do. He was a unique specimen.'

'I'll say he was. He would have torn me to pieces. I was shooting at him from a hideout in a tree. But it's not easy to

bring down a bear with one shot. I caught him in the
shoulder. I heard him roar as he made off into the forest. I
came down from the tree and went after him. Just like a
game of tag it was! He went crashing through the trees with
such a noise, it sounded like a forest fire. I would have liked
to take my jacket off, but there was no time; all I could do
was loosen my belt to get at my axe. I caught up with him
among some birch trees, and I let him have it from the
second barrel. He reared up on his hind legs. Now, I've seen
some brutes in my time, but this one really gave me a turn.
The birches were just saplings and he was a good deal
higher. I broke the gun, put in a cartridge, but it jammed
and I couldn't shut it again. By now he was almost on top
of me, with his paws stretching out to grab me. I threw my
gun down and pulled the axe from my belt. But what was
the use of an axe when my head only came up to his belly?
He was as big as a house, a walking church-tower, if he fell
on top of me, there'd be nothing left of me underneath. I
waved my axe and yelled blue murder at him – the way you
do if you want to live, using the foulest language I know . . .
And I made such a din, he must have got scared, he dropped
on all fours, and veered away from me. I couldn't believe
my eyes, I was shaking all over and I'd lost the use of my
hands, I couldn't put the axe back into my belt.'

Teterin fell silent. There was a faint smile on his dark,
weather-beaten face, with its badly scarred cheekbone.
Dudyrev and Mityagin were silent too. They could see it all
in their mind's eye: the forest at night, as silent as the
grave, and then Teterin yelling at the top of his voice – a cry
so full of fury that it penetrated the mind of the wounded
bear, a mind clouded with pain, despair and rage. It was
rage against rage, one strong animal pitted against an even
stronger one.

Dudyrev broke the silence:

'And did you kill him after all that?'

'There was nowhere for him to go. I got him by the
Pomyalovsky ravine. This time my gun didn't let me down.
I took him home, skinned him, strung him up from the
roof of the house, and his back paws reached down to the

ground. People couldn't believe their eyes.'

'A unique specimen, I must say,' sighed Mityagin.

3

At this moment they heard the sound of an accordion nearby. Someone's clumsy fingers were picking out a monotonous folk tune. There was something simple and guileless about it, appropriate to the forest, like the sound of the stream in the bushes.

'What are we doing with a musician here?' Simon said with surprise. 'He must be from Pozhnevka.'

A young man appeared at the edge of the forest. He wore a serge suit, unsuitable for the weather, with the clean collar of his open-necked shirt over his coat collar, and his wide trouser bottoms tucked into the tops of his boots; he carried a brightly lacquered accordion in his hands, and his round face shone with sweat.

'Yes, he is from Pozhnevka,' said Simon. 'His father is a foreman at the kolkhoz and he's a tractor driver . . . Say, why are you all dressed up like this? Going to a wedding, or something?'

The young man, who had not expected to run into people here, looked embarrassed for a moment but then regained his composure and slowly hitched up the accordion strap on his shoulder.

'I'm going to Suchkovka, of course.'

'The girls are giving a party, I suppose?'

'What if they are?'

'The things they get up to, these young people. From Pozhnevka to Suchkovka it must be about ten *versts*, perhaps even fifteen. You'll be spending the night with your girl, friend I reckon?'

'How can I? I've got to be back home in the morning to go to work.'

'Well, you're a strong enough young fellow.'

Simon Teterin looked at the young man with undisguised admiration, like a man seeing his own youth again. Mityagin smiled condescendingly, and Dudyrev looked at him not without curiosity. This young man in his best clothes, so unsuitable for the forest, somehow reminded him of a handmade wooden doll, one of those comically prim, crudely painted figures that have become popular with townspeople.

'We're heading for your part of the world,' Simon told the young man.

'I know. My father told me.'

'The bear hasn't been frightened away from his cache, has he?'

'No one has been anywhere near it.'

'Good. You'd better be off, you'll be late if you don't look out,' Simon said kindly.

'I'll be in time. Good luck to you.'

'The same to you.'

The young man hitched up the strap of his accordion again, and walked on. They soon heard him playing his simple tune in the distance.

Simon Teterin got up from the ground.

'Time for us to be going too. The sun is getting low. We'll be there just at the right time.'

The dogs cheerfully leapt to their feet. The hunters sorted out their rifles.

4

Three days previously, Mikhailo Lyskov, the kolkhoz foreman at Pozhnevka, had come to see Teterin, and told him that for two weeks now a bear had been prowling about near their livestock. He had trampled on their oats, frightened their women in the hayfield, and only last night he had killed a year-old heifer. Part of it had been devoured, part hidden, as usual, with turf and moss thrown over it, so that when the meat was high the bear could come back for it and feast to his heart's content.

'Come to the village and I'll show you where he is,' Lyskov had said.

'I don't need anybody to take me to him. Just tell me about him, and I'll figure it out for myself. I know your place as well as my own back-yard.'

Lyskov told him that the bear's cache lay at the end of the ravine, about twenty paces from the edge of the forest, and that the bear could be found either in among the oats or among the raspberry canes that had grown up on a spot where there had been a fire.

'I'll take the dogs,' Simon had decided.

In summer, a bear is usually tackled in one of three ways: with traps, from a platform, or with dogs.

Teterin despised hunting with traps: 'There's no skill in killing a beast when he's got his paw caught in an iron trap. The trap is chained to a log, and he soon gets tired of dragging it after him. Then you go up close and let him have it point blank. That's not hunting.'

It's harder to hunt from a platform. The platform is made of planks in a tree somewhere near the bear's haunts. The hunter hides up on the platform before the sun sets, and waits. But the trouble is that you can't be sure of bringing the animal down with your first shot. If you miss, he'll get clear away. If you merely wound him, you must chase after him. And a wounded bear is dangerous.

Simon Teterin considered that hunting with dogs was simpler than from a platform. With dogs you never lost track, they kept on the scent of the animal, and stopped him getting away. A hunter prizes a well-trained dog more than anything, and Kalinka was altogether beyond price. She was very nearly as famous as Teterin himself.

Simon felt sure that on this very night the bear would come out on the prowl. But confident as he was, he took his time. It was better to get to the place later (the dogs would be able to pick up the scent) than to appear too early and frighten the bear away, which would mean searching blindly for him in the forest and trusting to luck.

Night came on in the forest, creeping upwards, as always, from the roots of the trees. The glow of sunset on the motionless clouds had still not faded, but already one could hardly make out one's own boots on the path below. The darkness thickened; the earth seemed to exude a greasy, black murk from all its pores. In these hours the forest is dead, there is not a cheep from a bird, nor the sound of the wind, and it is as still as the wilderness. Somewhere out in the solitude, there was a huge animal, a powerful, shaggy wild creature. He was not something out of a story, not a figment of the imagination.

Mityagin lagged behind, stumbling over protruding roots; the prickly branches of the fir trees beat on his face. He cursed to himself under his breath, and was already sorry he had talked himself into such a wearisome business.

Dudyrev considered himself an experienced hunter: not only had he shot hare and duck, easy game for anyone who knows one end of a rifle from the other, but he had also taken part in an antelope shoot in the steppes, and in the lakes in the Urals he had brought down wild geese on the wing, and at one time he had even had a licence to hunt the great elk. He had long dreamed of going on a bear hunt, but up till now he had never managed it.

Now he was walking right behind Simon, trying to move silently as a professional bear hunter, but he too was surprised by the hushed forest. It was impossible to tell where they were going, or where the bear was, let alone how they were going to find him in the pitch darkness of this dense thicket. It was impossible to make anything out; you were like a blind man following a guide, completely dependent on another's will.

Often the dogs could be glimpsed in front. They would wait for Simon, and as soon as he came up to them, they seemed to dissolve in the forest again.

Simon stopped. So did Dudyrev. Mityagin stumbled into him from behind and swore out loud.

'Shut up, Maximovich,' Simon ordered sternly in a whisper. 'Not another word.'

'Are we going the right way?' Dudyrev voiced his doubt in a barely audible whisper.

'We're nearly there. Listen for the dogs. As soon as they start barking, follow them and don't get behind.'

Simon moved forward. The other two followed gingerly, and every time a branch snapped underfoot, he looked back angrily.

Suddenly the dark forest ended, and the hunters came out into a field. It was light, quiet and peaceful. It was a field of oats, like a lustreless lake set among dark, steeply rising banks. They were no longer in the savage kingdom of the bears; this was something familiar and human. Mityagin and Dudyrev at once felt more cheerful.

But Simon, who had been moving rapidly up till now, suddenly slowed down. Raising his head, standing up straight with his shoulders well back, he had completely lost his previous stoop. He now looked like a dog approaching reeds where duck are sitting.

They crossed the field and went back into the forest, which was as dark and frightening as ever. An uneven, broken fence separated the field from the trees. Simon stopped by the fence, stretched out his neck, turned his head this way and that, and began to listen intently.

Large, pale stars began to come out in the sky. Far, far away, a corn-crake called wearily and sadly. There was a dank smell from the solid wall of thick firs. The bear hunters listened nervously, but all around there was a dead, sleepy stillness; only the corn-crake cheerlessly performed his evening task.

There was a slight crackle from the forest side, and they all turned round, but it was only the dogs who appeared from behind the fence. They ran up to Simon in a business-like way, and he swore, not troubling to lower his voice.

'What the hell's the matter? Either I've been a fool or Lyskov didn't know what he was talking about . . . We better go and see if there's a cache here at least.'

Simon leapt across the fence and moved into the depths of the forest with his former light and rapid stride. The dogs obediently rushed forward and disappeared in the darkness. Dudyrev caught up with Simon and again asked: 'Have we come to the right place? There was supposed to be a ravine, wasn't there?'

'There it is, there's the ravine,' Simon nodded his head towards it crossly. 'It's overgrown with wild vine. This is where it ends, you can't see the edge even in daylight.'

The dogs began to growl in the thicket. Simon turned

sharply and began to force his way through the branches.

'Get away from that!' he shouted at the dogs.

When Dudyrev and Mityagin fought their way to him through the thicket, they found Simon standing at the edge of a tiny clearing, thoughtfully turning the earth over with his boot.

'This is his cache,' he said.

'But hasn't he been here?'

'Either he's been frightened away or . . .'

'Or?'

'Or he's gorged his fill, son of a bitch. It's not a hungry time. The raspberries are ripening, and the bilberries, and the oats are just coming on. He can eat his fill. He killed the heifer and then forgot about it.'

'How shall we find him now?' asked Dudyrev.

Simon was morosely silent, as he turned the moss over with the toe of his boot. In the damp, clear, fresh air, there was a sickly sweet stench.

'How it stinks. This is what he likes best of all,' said Simon.

'So we're out of luck, are we?' Dudyrev questioned him.

The bear hunter straightened up and adjusted the strap on his shoulder.

'We'll scour the forest. What are you waiting for? Let's go!' he ordered the dogs, and then added more calmly: 'We'll start by combing the raspberry canes.'

Again they plunged into the thicket; fir branches got in their faces; tree trunks, tangled roots, holes in the ground and hummocks made it hard going and there was utter stillness all around. The forest was dank and alien, exactly as it had been half an hour before, but now it was not so forbidding, it did not frighten them. Since the bear was no longer close at hand there was no mystery, the aura had vanished, only the outer trappings remained. Simon now seemed to be hurrying on only out of obstinacy and disappointment. Dudyrev and Mityagin obeyed him from inertia.

The tall forest trees gave way to bushes, it was no longer so dark, but on the other hand at every step there were uprooted tree trunks and pools filled with water. About five years ago there had been a fire here; dead, charred pines lay about, the ground had become marshy, and begun to grow over with alder and raspberry canes.

Suddenly Simon stopped so unexpectedly that Dudyrev stumbled into his broad, stone-hard back.

In the depths of the forest the dogs suddenly began to bark; there were two voices: Kalinka's was harsh and rough while the other dog, Malinka, barked more cheerfully, sometimes breaking off in shrill squeals.

'They must have found his trail,' Simon muttered under his breath, and continued to listen intently, slowly pulling his rifle off his shoulder. 'They've picked up the scent . . . Keep close to me now.'

He set off quickly – not in the direction of the dogs, but somewhere to the side, Dudyrev ran after him, but immediately lost sight of him.

'Where are you?' Simon's voice reached him. 'Keep close to me, damn you.'

Dudyrev moved towards Simon's voice and caught up with him. Branches lashed his face, he stumbled against bushes and rotten tree stumps, and within five minutes he felt very hot, with the blood throbbing at his temples, but he forged ahead, straining to catch the sound of Teterin's footsteps, and he did not fall behind again.

5

Mityagin fell behind immediately. He got on to a fairly broad path, made uneven by ridges of dried mud. Still, it was much easier to run along this than to fight his way through the thickets. As he ran, he heard the dogs barking, but the sound was muffled, as if through a wall. The barking grew more distant, and Mityagin increased his speed, hoping to find Teterin and Dudyrev further on, as they ran straight through the forest.

But branches began to lash his face, and he caught his shoulders on tree trunks. He was again in the thick of the forest, and stopped, panting for breath. His heart-beat seemed to resound through the trees. And suddenly he realised that the thumping of his heart was the only sound in the graveyard stillness. He could no longer hear the dogs barking.

He turned back, sometimes stumbling against birch trunks, or crashing into prickly, wet, unfriendly fir trees, and finally fell rolling over into a shallow gully. He picked himself up and realised he was lost. The path had gradually disappeared under his feet. It was probably a cow track leading straight into the depths of the forest, where it petered out.

It was impossible to see his hand stretched out in front. Above him the wind soughed heedlessly in the tree tops. There he was, all alone in the forest, as vast as the sea. Somewhere, no further than two or three miles away, was the little village of Pozhnevka, surrounded by fields, but where, in what direction? It would be only too easy to miss the village, and then there would be nothing but forest stretching all around for miles, perhaps hundreds of miles. A man lost in the forest is like a fish-lure adrift in a huge lake, you can look for months and never find it again.

The wind sounded in the pines, and in a patch of sky between the tree tops a star twinkled mockingly.

'Si-Simon!' shouted Mityagin.

His voice was weak and pitiful; the damp night swallowed it up. And how could Simon hear him as he plunged after the barking dogs on the bear's trail? How could a human voice penetrate that thick, pitch-black darkness!

'Si-Simon!'

Only the wind sounded above.

Mityagin hurled himself forward blindly, breaking branches, falling, picking himself up.

Suddenly he came across a break in the solid wall of forest, and it seemed lighter ahead. He wondered if he had come full circle. What if he were back in that same field of oats?

But this was only a narrow clearing hemmed in by the forest and overgrown with tall, rough grass. In the middle of it there was a straggly clump of firs bathed in grey mist as thick as pudding. There was an ominous air of abandonment about the place. What particularly frightened Mityagin was the grass – the hay-making was already coming to an end, but no scythe had been at work here: he really was off the beaten track!

And at that very moment he heard a dog barking. Without stopping to think he rushed towards the sound.

The distant barking came nearer. He could already make out the harsh yapping of Kalinka. He ran through wet grass which lashed his knees. Young firs festooned with streamers of mist danced before his eyes.

Suddenly one of the dark fir trees reared up, and lumbered towards him, a great hulking mass. Mityagin was running straight at it, but suddenly realised what it was, and stopped dead in his tracks. It was the bear! He had completely forgotten about him!

The bear appeared to be doing a kind of Caucasian dance, rolling his hind quarters as he approached. Mityagin convulsively began to pull his gun off his shoulder, but he tripped, fell into the grass, and lay there pretending to be dead. Right beside him he could hear the heavy thump of soft paws on the ground and loud breathing.

The barking dogs raced past.

Mityagin felt for his gun in the grass, and got up. First one figure, and then another loomed up suddenly out of the mist. He recognised Simon Teterin by his felt hat. Dudyrev was running about ten paces behind him.

They paid no attention to Mityagin, who looked exactly as if he had sprung out of the ground. Breathing heavily, they chased past noisily. Mityagin threw himself after them. He had learned his lesson and would stay right behind them from now on.

6

All the instincts of their distant forebears had awoken in them. Dudyrev was no longer an ordinary being, but had turned into a wild animal – ferocious, blood-thirsty, capable of endless endurance. The sweat poured into his eyes, branches whipped his face, twigs tore his jacket, and he ran on headlong, feeling neither pain, nor the weight of his rubber boots, leaping over hummocks, fallen tree trunks and stumps. He heard only the barking of the dogs, and had still not seen the bear, but he sensed how close it was and knew it was doomed. He had to keep close to the dogs; sooner or later they would overtake their quarry, and then . . .

They clutched their rifles with sweating hands. Simon was in front. He was straining forward with his whole body so much that he seemed bound to fall any moment. But he did not fall. He ran so fast that he seemed to be almost flying; there was no one faster in the chase. He now noticed Mityagin, who he thought had got far behind, but was all of a sudden very close, nearly stepping on his heels.

The dogs' barks had changed into frantic yelps. Flying over the tall grass, Simon Teterin stumbled, righted himself, and then no longer ran, but moved forward with the leaps of a dancer, his rifle held high above his head. Dudyrev caught his breath and wiped the sweat off his face with his sleeve. He realised that the dogs had finally run the bear down; there they were about to close in for the kill. Their yelping came in sobbing snatches from the far end of the clearing. And although his eyes were completely accustomed to the darkness, Dudyrev could not at first tell the dogs and the bear apart. He could only see a flurry of movement among the trees. There was a young birch tree which, as if in a fairy tale, bowed down to Simon, as he came towards it with his gun. Then Dudyrev made out the backs of the dogs in the grass, and at once the whole picture was clear to him in every detail.

What he had taken at first for a dark patch at the edge of the field, was the bear standing on his hind legs. The yelping dogs were lunging at him, but nevertheless kept a respectful distance. The bear had seized the trunk of the birch tree with both paws and was trying to break it, bending it from side to side, as if using it as a gigantic broom to sweep away the dogs.

Before Dudyrev could reach him, Simon jerked up his

rifle, and stood stock-still for a moment, as if he had suddenly fallen asleep, to take aim. The forest seemed to start at the red flash from the gun barrel and the hard sound of the shot hit their ears and then echoed somewhere far behind their backs. The echo had not yet died away, but was still reverberating near the end of the clearing, when the bear gave a roar of pain – a brief, tormented sound, like someone grunting from effort. The dogs flung themselves at the bear with ear-splitting yelps, but fell back at once.

'Damn you,' Simon shouted with exasperation.

It seemed as if the bear had been swallowed up by the earth. Only the piercing bark of one of the dogs came from the thicket. The half broken birch tree rocked sadly in the air.

Simon, stepping carefully, went right up under the birch tree, dropped on his knees in the grass, and bent down. Dudyrev, running up, saw a dog's body stretched out on the ground.

'She had to get too close, God damn it . . . She wasn't smart enough . . . Kalinka knows better. Look, he's torn her innards out, the bastard. A bad sign that, a very bad sign. Listen,' Simon turned to Dudyrev, 'finish her off so she doesn't suffer. I can't bring myself to do it.'

He leapt up to his feet hurriedly, and moved aside.

When Dudyrev put his gun to the dog's head, she looked up trustingly, and seeing the gleam of her eyes in the darkness, he winced as he hurriedly pressed the trigger, discharging the barrel.

Gunpowder smoke spread out across the wet grass. Simon was no longer close by. Mityagin stood motionless on one side. The broken and twisted birch tree still went on rocking. The depths of the forest echoed with Kalinka's shrill bark. She was on the bear's heels.

The first to move was Mityagin. Dudyrev, not waiting to reload, and with only one cartridge in the breech, rushed off after him. The hunt continued.

7

The bear was wounded and could no longer shake off the
dog. Sometimes the barking would give way to frantic yelps,
followed by a momentary silence. Then again the barking
became louder and even more furious. That was when the
bear tried to get at the dog. But Kalinka always eluded him.

They came to a deep ravine, and started driving the bear
along the edge. Suddenly Kalinka's yelping sounded a note
of fierce triumph, but then trailed away.

'He's rolled down into the ravine . . .' Simon explained,
halting abruptly. 'That's what it is.' He turned to Dudyrev,
breathing hotly straight into his face.

'I'll go along the top of the ravine to head him off. You
go down there. If you hear him coming towards you,
frighten him off. Fire in the air, and keep your distance!
Otherwise, in this darkness, you'll be in trouble. Get going!'

The slopes were thickly covered with alder, and a musty,
rank smell came up from below – it was like a ditch where
last year's potatoes have been stored. However used your
eyes had become to the dark, the pitch black of the ravine
was something all its own – dense and viscous. The ordinary
world had vanished: these were the nether regions. Stones
rattled under Dudyrev's feet and dry twigs poked him in
the face; behind him he could hear the frightened Mityagin
breathing heavily.

'What a place,' he said in a whisper, giving vent to the
eerie feeling it gave him. 'It's like a tomb.'

Quite unexpectedly the dog's barking, hitherto muffled
and distant, suddenly became loud and clear. But in this
dark, rank, nether region there was just no telling whether
the dog was far away or close at hand.

'Shall we shoot?' asked Mityagin in the same frightened
whisper.

Dudyrev did not answer. Perhaps they should. But what
if it was too soon, what if they had merely alerted the bear
without frightening him, and he had got away by crawling
up the side of the ravine? What would Simon think of them
– shooting from a distance because they were afraid to let

him come nearer! Better wait . . .

The barking could be heard very clearly, and again it was impossible to tell whether it was coming nearer. Dudyrev had a job to keep his nerves steady: if the bear were to leap at them unexpectedly, it would hardly be possible to get out of his way – he would savage them to death, wounded and maddened as he was.

Dudyrev remembered that he had only one cartridge in his gun. If he missed, that was the end of him; there would be no fighting it off with the butt of his gun . . . He opened the breech and tried to reach for his cartridges, but the bag he was carrying them in had got twisted round and in the pitch dark he could not unfasten the flap.

At that moment there was a sound of snapping twigs in front of them. This was followed by the hoarse barking of the dog and a growling noise. Here he was, the bear, right on top of them, and his gun was unloaded! He was almost knocked over by Mityagin as he darted past him to get out of the way. Seizing hold of the bushes, his knees digging into the ground, Dudyrev started to crawl up the side of the ravine.

Again he heard branches crackling, then the heavy breathing of the bear, and the frantic barking of Kalinka, now almost hysterical with rage and impotence . . .

Only when Kalinka's bark became fainter did Dudyrev realise what had happened, and he nearly groaned out loud from shame: he had lost his nerve, and let the bear go by – it had not even noticed him!

The breech of his gun was still open; Dudyrev angrily slammed it shut. For so many years he had longed for such a moment – and now this . . . How stupid! What a disgrace! Dudyrev's face worked in the darkness.

'A fat lot of good you are!' Simon shouted angrily. 'You've let him get into the swamp! Now we'll have a fine time, wading around over there. And we had him in our hands! I only asked you to give him a fright, and you bungled it . . . You . . .' he turned on Mityagin, who stood a little way away, looking guilty and frightened. 'What do you think you've got in your hands, a gun or a wooden pole? If you can't shoot when you have to, go home, don't get in my way! And you too,' he said to Dudyrev, 'bragging about all those goats you shot in the steppes. I can see that's all you're good for – shooting goats and rabbits.'

As Simon told them what he thought of them, Dudyrev meekly listened in silence, not attempting to justify himself.

They ran out of the ravine to the edge of the swamp. Here and there, small, stunted fir trees stuck out of mossy mounds. Only the nearest were visible; the rest were hidden by the night. But even so, it looked as though this palisade of wretched trees might stretch for miles. Not even the night could mask the cheerlessness of the swamp.

Somewhere ahead, right in the swamp, they could still hear Kalinka. This small, puny dog, utterly fearless and obstinate to the point of madness, alone continued to harass the huge enraged brute which could easily tear her guts out with a light flick of his paw. Kalinka's piteous bark made Dudyrev feel even worse.

8

By the time they had crossed the swamp, the night had begun to lighten, and the mossy hummocks stood out more clearly.

Kalinka had by now lost her voice and her furious bark changed to something resembling the squeak of an un-greased wheel. Dirty, wet and exhausted the three hunters had to force themselves to go on running. Each of them now felt bitterly resentful towards the bear; he had led them a terrible chase, forcing them to wallow in mud, and making them almost die of shame – no wonder they had a sense of personal grudge far greater than usually felt by hunters.

The bear must also have felt exhausted. He leapt out on to the road, and made off along it, simply because it was easier to run here, heedless of the fact that his pursuers would gain on him more quickly.

This road led to the banks of the forest river, to the plank bridge near which, some five hours ago, the hunters had rested and chatted, waving away the mosquitoes.

Soon they came to the birch tree under which they had stacked their rifles, and the bank sloping steeply down to the river. There, surrounded by bushes was the dead tree, its twisted branches looking like bones in the half light – it was now near dawn. The bear, almost out of his wits, went right up to the bridge – but even if he had had time to get across it could not possibly have held up under his weight; the hunters were close behind. He rose on his haunches and turned back to face them.

In the uncertain light, in front of the spreading bushes, with the branches of the dead birch rising up above them, the bear's outlines were indistinct, which only made him seem all the more terrible and enormous. He moved back up the slope in a shapeless mass. He did not roar and no longer bothered to ward off Kalinka, who leapt up at him, snapping at his haunches and then falling back again. He simply walked silently towards his death.

Three guns pointed at him. Three men put their fingers to the trigger.

At that moment Simon caught the sound of an accordion playing the same silly song as before.

'Don't shoot,' Simon shouted.

But it was too late; two rifles cracked simultaneously. Kalinka gave a hoarse yelp and threw herself at the feet of the bear as he swayed forward. An acrid smell of gunpowder drifted in the slight breeze.

The bear's dark carcass lay slumped on the ground. Kalinka leapt around it in a frenzy. The hollow echo of the shots was dying somewhere far away in the depths of the forest. Dudyrev and Mityagin stood stock-still, holding up their rifles which were still smoking. But there was something missing, something had disappeared from this world, in the dim morning light.

At last the echo of the shots died away, as if it had been stifled. Kalinka stopped her barking, and the murmur of water in the willow bushes could be heard clearly. Simon stretched out his neck and strained to listen; there was nothing except the gentle sound of running water.

Simon threw down his gun and ran towards the bridge.

Over the dark pool formed by the little forest river, three planks lay crookedly on their supports. The sluggish stream, the motionless bushes, the roughly made bridge – nothing could have been more peaceful than this corner of the sleeping forest, rarely visited by men. All was empty and quiet, except for the ceaseless murmur of water in the undergrowth.

Under Simon's weight the planks squeaked protestingly. He looked around and noticed something black in the dark water along which strands of grey mist were now creeping. He dived headfirst from the bridge with a deafening splash, touching the muddy bottom with his hands and feet; then he stood up and, splashing loudly, waded chest-deep in the water straight to the floating black object. He reached out and seized it – it was the accordion.

Holding it above his head, he went on further, trying to keep his balance by digging his boots into the slippery bed of the stream. After a few paces, he was horrified to feel something large and buoyant drifting up against him: it seemed to be touching him shyly and trustingly.

Simon threw the accordion from him and put his hands down under the water. His fingers instantly felt the rough serge cloth. With a faint splash the waters parted to reveal a shoulder, and after it a lifeless head with the hair slicked down on one side.

Holding on to the head, pushing aside the water-lilies in his path, Simon dragged the body to the bank.

9

They laid the young man by the birch tree, almost in the same spot where they had rested before the hunt. Dudyrev bent down over him, then got up hastily, tore off his rifle sling, slipped off his coat and shirt, and began to tear his vest into strips.

'It hit him in the neck,' he said hoarsely.

These were the first words uttered after the shooting.

Mityagin stood on one side, still clutching his empty rifle. Dripping wet, his shoulders hunched, and spreading the cold chill of the river around him, Simon stepped up to him, roughly jerked the gun from his hand, and pushed him towards the young man spread out on the ground. 'I thought you were a first-aid man – do something.'

Mityagin fell on his knees beside the young man, took the torn vest from Dudyrev's hands and set to work, turning the limp head, bending very low, like a short-sighted man, over the wound, and said, 'Wet a piece of cloth – I must wash it.'

His bare shoulders shivering, Dudyrev took a strip of his vest and ran towards the river. Twigs snapped under his feet.

'Oh my God, there's a gaping hole in his neck,' Mityagin moaned. 'Oh my God.'

'Get a move on, and don't snivel,' Simon snarled at him.

'Not even an experienced doctor could help here, so what can I do? They could do nothing even in a hospital.' Dudyrev reappeared and stood behind Mityagin; he was holding a piece of wet cloth in his hands. He was being bitten by mosquitoes on his fleshy chest and shoulders, and he was shivering with cold.

'Have you felt his pulse?' he asked.

Mityagin, dropping the rag, hurriedly seized the young man's hand, and began to feel his wrist.

'My God, my God! I can't feel it . . . my fingers are shaking too much.'

'Feel his heart,' Simon advised.

As obediently as ever, Mityagin snatched his cap off his bald head, and put his ear to the young man's chest.

'Are you in your right mind?' Simon pushed him away angrily. 'How can you hear anything through his jacket?'

With rough but nimble fingers, he tore the wet clothing, and bared the young man's chest.

'Now listen.'

Mityagin's egg-like bald head moved up and down as he searched for the right place and it was quite a while before he found it. Simon, crouching over him, now became completely still – as did Dudyrev who was still holding the wet rag in his hands. Again Mityagin's bald head began to move.

Simon and Dudyrev held their breath as they waited.

'I can't hear anything,' Mityagin said in a faint voice, raising his head.

'Wait a moment,' Simon pushed Mityagin aside, and himself bent down to the young man's chest. He listened for a long time, and then silently stood up.

'Well?' Dudyrev asked hopefully.

'There's nothing – no heartbeat, no breathing.'

'It's the jugular vein – he must have lost a lot of blood in the water, and while he was being got out,' Mityagin muttered.

'What about trying artificial respiration?' Dudyrev asked.

He bent down, and took the young man's outstretched hands. But when he touched them, he could feel how cold they were – almost colder than the wet rag which he had just had between his palms. Dudyrev dropped the hands, and hesitated for a moment, peering into the pale face which looked haggard in the dawn light. He got up with difficulty, shaking from the cold, and, with an effort, bent down to pick up his shirt and coat from the ground. Silently he began to dress.

It was almost morning. The fading stars looked down, tired and uncertain. Over the jagged edge of the tree tops was a dim glow. It was not yet the dawn proper, but rather a faint, turbid precursor. It was still too dark to see the dew on the bushes, although you could feel the weight of their wet leaves, and the birds were not yet awake. It was not so much morning as the slow death of the old, enfeebled night.

In this hesitant pre-dawn light, the young man lay on the grass in his black suit, with his shirt torn open to expose his chest. He looked one-dimensional, as if he had been flattened; only the toes of his boots stuck upwards. It was immediately noticeable that one of his trouser legs was tucked into the top of a boot, while the other had got loose.

The hunters stood with heads bent. Their tired, unshaven faces and sunken cheeks, were pale with the ghostly pallor that comes from uncertain light. Mityagin's elongated bald head glistened with damp. Dudyrev had such a frown on his face that his eyes were invisible under his beetling forehead and looked like dark holes. Simon was all hunched as though his shoulders no longer had the strength to bear the weight of his large hands which dangled helplessly at his sides.

Simon was the first to move.

'Well, we've had our fun and games, now we must pay for them. You, Konstantin,' he turned to Dudyrev, 'go to Gustoi Bor as fast as you can and tell the proper people exactly what happened. And you,' Simon looked sombrely at Mityagin, 'go to Pozhnevka. Tell Mikhailo Lyskov what's happened to his son. I'll stick around here. One of us has to stay here.'

Dudyrev gloomily nodded his head, but Mityagin seemed to cringe.

'You go, Simon, I can't,' he said in a faint voice. 'I can't do it, how can I go to a man and tell him . . .'

Simon put a hand on Mityagin's shoulder and looked sternly into his face.

'A guilty conscience, eh?'

'But I wasn't the only one to shoot.'

'There were two shots. One hit the bear, the other this boy. And the way I reckon: you are not so handy with a gun . . . Get going.' Simon gave Mityagin a slight push – but one that brooked no resistance.

Without picking up his gun or his cartridge bag, his bald head bent down, the first-aid man obediently went off into the forest. Dudyrev gave Simon a grim parting nod, snatched up his double-barrelled gun with its sling, and moved off in the opposite direction.

A growling noise came from the dead bear. Kalinka was standing on the carcass, the hair bristling along her spine. She looked up briefly at Simon with bloodshot, unseeing eyes, and then went back to work. Small and wiry, she was tearing at the bear's neck with concentrated fury, as though triumphing over the fallen enemy, and revenging herself on the dead animal for the death of her daughter.

'Get away!' Simon drove her away angrily. He went up closer and shook his head with amazement.

'God!'

The bear's neck had been torn to shreds and turned into a bloody pulp.

10

One by one the birds began to stir in the bushes and sing, and the top of the old birch began to glow red. The mist over the river rose higher than the bushes. The sun rolled out over the top of the forest, fresh, gentle and warm, ready to serve all living things. There were dewy shadows on the grass.

This tiny green patch of land was beginning its usual morning round, repeated every day at the appointed hour.

The two corpses lying on the ground were foreign and hostile to it. The bear's muzzle was thrust into the grass; he looked like a brown growth on the gentle slope. Dewdrops on his thick fur glistened in the sun. Early flies were already weaving around him. The young man lay spread out in the damp shade, with his head turned to one side.

Beyond the bridge a cuckoo began to call furtively, promising someone a long life.

Slowly, the sun rose higher in the sky. Simon did not bother to dry himself after his soaking. How could he undress, hang out his clothes to dry on the bushes, and fuss about suchlike things after this terrible happening, with a dead man lying there?

'Cu-ckoo, cu-ckoo, cu-ckoo,' the foolish bird repeated.

Simon had often seen men die. He was only six years old when his uncle Vasily Teterin, also a keen bear hunter, had been mauled to death by a she-bear. Simon's father had then killed her – which was not difficult as it turned out that she was already badly wounded. For a hunter to be killed by his prey is a reasonable and even honourable way to die. Men died from illness, from old age, in battle – every day people are killed, but this was the first time Simon had seen such senseless death. The young man had been to see his girl friend and was probably thinking of getting married and starting a family – and then this had to happen. He hadn't been ill, or getting into fights, or hunting bears. In the old

days they would have said it was his fate from birth. What
rubbish! It was just a matter of the queer tricks life plays on
you.

The sun had risen and begun to beat down fiercely. The
cuckoo had either got tired or flown away to another place.
Simon expected the boy's father, Mikhailo Lyskov, to arrive
any minute. He should not have sent Mityagin to alert him
so soon. Until the authorities came the dead man could not
be taken away, but they would not be here for ages. With
the time it would take Dudyrev to reach the district town
and report it to the right people – not to mention the time it
would take them to get here, they could not be expected till
the evening. This meant that Mikhailo might have to sit
here looking at his dead son for hours and hours. It had been
thoughtless to send word to him so quickly . . .

He watched the sun climbing to its zenith, and waited
sadly for the rattle of a cart approaching from the direction
of Pozhnevka.

But in fact it was the district authorities who arrived
first. From across the river Simon suddenly heard the steady
purr of a motor-car; then the motor stopped and he could
make out loud, brisk voices:

'We can't go any further. It's just over here.'

'Let's get out and walk then.'

One by one the new arrivals began to make their way
across the rickety bridge: first came a tall, narrow-shouldered
man, unknown to Simon, in a buttoned-up tunic with
a brief-case under his arm; after him, limping heavily,
prodding the planks with a stout stick, the Prosecutor
Testov himself, hatless, with his shock of curly hair, dark
face and bristling eyebrows; he was dressed in an em-
broidered shirt, and looked for all the world like a visitor
from town who has come to the country for a rest; next
was a young woman in a brightly coloured dress, also
carrying a case; then there was Dudyrev, crumpled and
dirty, without his gun and cartridge bag, but already somehow a changed man – he now seemed quite at ease, as
though nobody could touch him; behind all of them came a
young man in overalls and battered leather boots – evi-

dently the driver who had brought them here.

'You've been quick. I can't think how you did it,' Simon said to Dudyrev.

'I just went to Suchkovka, telephoned the Project and told them to send a car for the Prosecutor immediately. Then I got on to the Prosecutor at once, and asked him to pick me up on the way.'

Simon nodded his head. He had forgotten that it was only in the forest, while hunting, that Dudyrev was so unassuming, and that on his home ground he was a very different person. He only had to pick up the telephone for the Prosecutor himself to drop everything and come running. A far cry from Mityagin. Lyskov must have gone out very early to the hay-making or something, and Mityagin might still be waiting for him.

The Prosecutor, limping in one leg because of a war wound but nevertheless walking briskly with the help of his stick, went straight up to the dead man and stood there a minute in silence, taking everything in with a sharp, appraising glance. He clicked open his cigarette case, lit a cigarette, and wheeled round smartly to Simon on his good leg.

'How did this happen then?'

Simon shrugged his shoulders.

'Scarcely anybody ever comes through here even in daylight, let alone at night – but suddenly he walks right into our line of fire . . .'

'But a man of your experience should have realised in time.'

'I did. But I didn't have time to grab them by the hands. I shouted, but it was too late.'

'You shouted?' The Prosecutor's narrow face, under the thick curly head of hair, took on a wary look. The quick dark eyes became even more penetrating.

'You shouted?'

'Sure I did. I heard the accordion, and I shouted, "Don't shoot!" But by the time they took it in, it was all over.'

The tall man with the brief-case came up as well and stood in front, listening. The Prosecutor exchanged meaning glances with him, and turned to Dudyrev.

'He really shouted something?'

'I seem to remember he did,' replied Dudyrev.

'You heard the accordion too?'

'I didn't hear the accordion. But is that relevant to the case?'

'It is indeed,' the Prosecutor replied grimly. 'It alters the whole aspect of it. If one of you had fore-warning, then the others might have had it, too. In our business we have to stick to the letter of the law. If there was a warning shout, then somebody will have to answer for this in court. Otherwise it would just have been a case of misadventure, as we call it.'

An oppressive silence now set in.

While this conversation had been going on, the cart from Pozhnevka with Mityagin and Lyskov had driven up unnoticed by everyone. There were now eight people altogether: the five who had come by car, Simon Teterin, and the two who had just arrived in the cart. In almost any other place it would not have seemed an excessively large company, but this remote corner of the forest had probably never seen such a throng of people since the beginning of time.

11

In broad daylight, with the sun shining brightly, they began to unravel in every detail the story of what had happened in the dim light between night and morning.

The tall man with the brief-case was the Assistant Prosecutor in charge of the case, and his name was Dityatichev. He took off his uniform tunic, rolled his sleeves right up his thick, hairy arms, and began to ply Simon Teterin and Dudyrev with questions, trying to establish which hunter stood where at the time of the shots.

'So you stood there . . . and Comrade Dudyrev was here . . . Oh, I see, a little further. And the third man – is he here now, the third man?'

'Yes,' said Mityagin, coming forward timidly.

'Good. Now tell me exactly where you were standing. Here? Good!'

Dityatichev at once stood in Mityagin's place, grimacing exactly as if he were squinting at the sights of a gun, and taking aim at the bear huddled on the ground. Beyond the bear the dead birch stuck out of a thicket, its trunk stripped of bark and crooked branches high in the sky.

'Ex-cellent! And the bear, can you remember, did it fall immediately, or did it take a few steps forward? It's important for us to know where it was standing at the time the shots were fired.'

'Almost immediately,' Simon answered.

'Immediately. Good. By the way, we have to establish whether its death took place instantaneously or not. Notice,' Dityatichev said to the Prosecutor, 'that this comrade . . . What's your name? Ah yes, Mityagin . . . that Mityagin was standing a little below Dudyrev, and that Dudyrev is the taller of the two.'

The Prosecutor looked gloomily past the bear to the trunk of the old birch.

'That tree,' he said drily, 'partially blocks one's view of the bridge.'

Dityatichev took the point immediately, and began to click his tongue.

He went back to where Mityagin had stood and looked again. 'But it blocks it less from here.'

'Don't jump to conclusions. Try and establish, as best you can at exactly what spot the young man fell into the water.'

At that moment the woman doctor came up with some forms which she had been filling up near the dead man. The Prosecutor and his assistant bent down to her. The doctor, who was young, with a pretty, pale face untouched by the sun, knitted her thin auburn eyebrows in concentration and began to explain.

'The bullet entered at the left side of the neck, passed through the flesh, and made a lacerated wound at the point of exit. The artery is cut. The vertebrae of the neck are untouched. Death took place within fifteen minutes, if not sooner. It must be borne in mind that the deceased fell into the river and must have swallowed water . . .'

'Obviously,' interrupted the Prosecutor. 'He was already dead when he was taken out of the water. Perhaps you and Dityatichev will kindly have a look at the bear a little later on. I only hope that the bullet is lodged inside him.'

Dityatichev now quickly ran to the bridge, while the Prosecutor stood on the spot from where Dudyrev had shot. They began to shout to each other.

'I'm coming, Alexey Fedorovich!' shouted Dityatichev, hidden by the bushes.

'I can't see you!' replied the Prosecutor.

'And now?'

'I still can't see you.'

'I'm right in the middle of the bridge.'

'I can't see you! You are completely hidden by bushes. From your voice I should judge that you are behind the birch trunk. Find a pole or branch and hold it up so I can see exactly where you are.'

In a minute Dityatichev held up a handkerchief tied to a stick over the bushes. Still standing in the place where Dudyrev had shot, the Prosecutor then shouted:

'Take two steps forward!'

The handkerchief moved above the bushes.

'Another step! Another. Stop! The man could have walked at least two yards from the middle of the bridge without being seen because of the tree.'

'More, Alexey Fedorovich! Three yards!' shouted Dityatichev from behind the bushes.

'Let's see how it looks from the other place.' The Prosecutor went to the spot from which Mityagin had shot.

Again the handkerchief tied to the stick slowly advanced above the bushes.

'I can see you, I can see you,' the Prosecutor called.

'Another four steps and I'll be at the end of the bridge.'

'Stop!'

'I'm only three steps away now. From that angle I'm open to view practically the whole way.'

'Don't let's jump to conclusions. Have a good look at the

planks. Is there any trace of blood on them?' asked the Prosecutor.

The tall Dityatichev – he was no longer all that young – got down on all fours, crawled along the rickety planks, as if he were smelling them, and stopped occasionally to study them closely. In this way he crawled from one end of the bridge to the other, then got up and briskly shook the dust from his knees.

'There are no traces.' He went up to Simon. 'From what spot did you jump into the water?'

'From about the middle. As soon as I saw the accordion, I jumped.'

'Where was the accordion?'

'In the water, of course.'

'I know that. I'm asking you: whereabouts in the water?'

'Near the middle of the bridge, just a little way out.'

'And where did you come across the body?'

'About four steps further on, towards the near bank. There's scarcely any current here, you see – it's a pool. As soon as I stepped forward a couple of paces, he was right there – I felt him drift up against me.'

'Good. It all points to the fact that at the moment when the shots were fired the young man was roughly in the middle of the bridge, and not near either bank.'

'Enough of this clever talk,' the Prosecutor interrupted. 'Let's have a look at the bear – if we find the bullet it will tell us all we want to know.'

They stood round the bear. The doctor sat down by the head; a swarm of buzzing flies rose in the air.

'What's that?' asked the doctor in surprise, pointing to the bear's neck.

'That was the dog,' replied Simon. 'While we were getting the boy out of the water, and doing what we could for him, she started savaging the bear.'

'Why did she go for that place in particular?'

'Who knows? She just liked it, I suppose.'

The doctor, grimacing, carefully began to move the massive, shaggy head of the bear with her thin, white fingers.

'What a nuisance, I don't see where the bullet went in.'

'Go on looking. By all accounts, the bear fell down dead immediately he was shot.'

'Perhaps it's near the heart. Try and turn him over on his back. I'll look at his chest.'

Clutching at the thick fur of the bear's sides and bumping into each other, Simon, Dityatichev, Dudyrev and the driver of the car managed to heave the great carcass over on its back.

Her pretty face creased by a frown of concentration, the young doctor bent over the dead brute's chest, and her small hand went slowly, inch by inch, over the chest, belly and thighs.

'Here it is! There's a wound in the paw! But that's not a dangerous place. He couldn't have died instantly from that.'

'That's where I got him the first time,' Simon hastened to explain, 'when we first came across him in the hayfield near Pozhnevka. I was aiming at his head, and he must have put his paw up at that moment. It took us another three hours to catch up with him here.'

'Well, I just can't make out where the fatal wound can be,' the doctor said uncertainly, continuing slowly to run her hand over the furry carcass.

'Perhaps his heart gave out? I've heard that happens with bears,' the Prosecutor suggested.

'It probably does, but not very often,' the doctor agreed reluctantly. 'I don't much fancy the idea of doing a post mortem in these conditions on a corpse like this with my instruments. We'd better have another look . . .'

'Yes – what we really want to know is whether the bear died from a bullet. If both bullets missed him, and he died of heart failure, then we'll never find out . . .'

'Wait, wait,' the doctor seized the bear's muzzle with both her hands, and with an effort, parted the jaws. 'Yes, there it is. Why didn't I guess before. Look! The bullet went straight into his open mouth – the front teeth were knocked out, see? And it looks as if the bullet went higher than the throat.'

'Cut him open and find the bullet,' the Prosecutor ordered.

The doctor shook her head regretfully.

'Such tremendous bones and sinews, and the instruments I've got with me . . .'

'Look for it!'

Dityatichev squatted down next to the doctor.

The bear lay under the hot sun, and the air was still sultry. The bear's carcass gave off a pungent, unclean animal smell, intermingled with the unpleasant, sickening smell of clotted blood. Everybody walked away and sat down in the shade, only Dityatichev remained near the doctor to help her. The driver walked round, staring at the dead bear with curiosity and amazement.

The Prosecutor, his bad leg stretched out on the grass, was smoking, deep in thought. Dudyrev also seemed calm, but his nervousness was betrayed by the set expression on his hollow-cheeked, unshaven face, the fixed stare of his eyes under his heavy brows, and the way he puffed greedily at a cigarette.

The first-aid man, Mityagin, and the father of the dead man, Mikhailo Lyskov, sat quietly side by side a few paces away from the others. Mityagin was staring listlessly at the ground. Lyskov blinked wearily, looking somewhere past the doctor and Dityatichev as they busied themselves with the bear's carcass. He was a small man with a meek expression on his weather-beaten, deeply-furrowed peasant's face – not the sort who would ever give trouble. All the time he had kept to himself; he did not cry, or shout, or plague anyone with questions, and he had somehow been forgotten.

Simon Teterin, usually so calm and sure of himself, felt deeply upset for once. He was annoyed by all this attention being paid to the bear, and infuriated by the young driver from Dudyrev's car who kept walking round it – he'd obviously never seen anything like this in his life before. Why was he so much more interested in the bear than in the man, young like himself, lying dead nearby? He might at least have the decency not to stare goggle-eyed at the bear like this! Simon was also irritated by the bright sunlight, the smell of the bear, the lanky detective, and the woman doctor. He was deeply aware of the presence of Mikhailo

Lyskov, but was afraid to look at him. Even as a little boy
Simon had never cried. His mother, when she gave him a
thrashing, always used to grumble: 'You can never get a
tear out of the brat.' But now he was so upset, tears were
welling up inside him, with all these people around too.
They wouldn't believe their eyes – Simon the bear hunter,
crying!

Nobody, to be sure, was unaffected – even the Prosecutor
who was here only in his official capacity and had no personal involvement. 'You never know what's going to happen
next,' he said with a sigh, 'what bad luck – it was pure
chance.'

Dudyrev, to whom he had said this, remained silent.

Just then the detective and the doctor got up from the
bear's carcass. Grunting from the effort, the Prosecutor got
to his feet with the aid of his stick and the tree trunk next
to him.

'Well, found anything?'

Dityatichev waved his long arms.

'There's no bullet.'

'Could the bear have swallowed it?'

'It went right through. It must have come out at the
back of the neck – that's why the dog made such a mess of
him there: because of the blood . . .'

'Are you sure the bullet went right through him?'

'The doctor is sure, and I have no reason to disbelieve her.'

'What about looking for it?' the Prosecutor suggested
half-heartedly, but after a glance at the slope overgrown
with rank vegetation along the river-bank, he waved the idea
aside. It was hopeless. They might just as well pack up now
and go home.

The young doctor pulled off her rubber gloves, gathered
up her instruments and went down to the river to wash her
hands. Her face was sweaty and tired.

12

Everybody had business awaiting him at home, even
Mityagin. Only Simon and Mikhailo Lyskov stayed behind

on the bank of the little forest river.

The only reminders of the recent invasion were the trampled grass and the cigarette stubs thrown here and there – and the altered position of the bear. He now lay on his side, and a paw had been placed over his open mouth. The flies were still weaving around.

Simon went up to Mikhailo, who was leading his horse out of the forest.

'Shall I help you take the boy home? It's hard going in places and you might get stuck.'

'Well, if it's not too much trouble.'

They laid the dead man on some hay, and straightened out the head to prevent it lolling awkwardly to one side all the time. Mikhailo picked up the reins, and they set off into the forest, walking by the cart without a word.

But they had not gone twenty paces when Mikhailo suddenly let go the reins, stepped away from the cart and slumped to the ground.

'I don't know what's wrong with me. My legs won't carry me.'

He was short and narrow-shouldered, with a large head; his hands, misshapen and deformed by hard work, were folded on his knees. He had heavy bags under his eyes and his large, fleshy nose drooped mournfully. Simon Teterin felt a lump in his throat at the sight of such irreparable, uncomplaining grief. Again he had the strange feeling of being more upset than he could ever remember. He longed to go away somewhere, to hide in the forest all by himself – not to cry, of course – but just to let himself go. Now he stood awkwardly near Mikhailo with an agonised look on his face, and his eyes tactfully averted.

Mikhailo breathed a deep, tremulous sigh, and began to heave himself to his feet again.

'Go and sit in front,' Simon said. 'And give me the reins.'

'No, I'm all right. I'm better. I'll manage.'

As he picked up the reins again, Mikhailo said quietly:

'My two eldest were killed in the war. This was the last.'

Silent again, they went on; Mikhailo walked with the reins in his hands a little in front; Simon was a couple of paces behind him. He could see Mikhailo's round shoulders with the skinny shoulder blades jutting up under his faded shirt; the neck was dark and weather-beaten, and he plodded along in the same deliberate way as all elderly peasants who have known what it is to walk behind the plough.

He again began to think of the young driver who had been so fascinated by the bear, seemingly quite indifferent to Mikhailo's grief – perhaps he had not even noticed him sitting there quietly on one side. He was far too excited by the sight of this strange new animal to feel pity for a fellow human being. If someone was suffering, the least you could do was to show a little sympathy and understanding, even if you couldn't do anything to help. This was the main thing. Otherwise there was very little you could do about the world's sorrows – they've always been there, and always will be. However much clever people tried to make life easier and happier, there would still always be a lot of tears: children crying because their parents have died, girls because they've been jilted; and there'll still be silly accidents like this, with people getting killed or maimed for no good reason at all. But the worst thing was if nobody cared . . .

Simon did not have the language to express these thoughts – but he felt them keenly nonetheless, churning over inside him, too deep for words.

They reached Pozhnevka without any trouble. Mikhailo Lyskov lived at the far end, and they had to go right through the village.

People came out of the houses; children, old women and young ones followed the cart slowly and in grim silence as it moved towards Mikhailo's cottage.

Mikhailo's wife ran out of the porch, her thin hair dishevelled, the front of her blouse flapping open across her thin chest. She pushed her way through the people crowding round the cart, bent over her son and began to wail, lamenting in traditional peasant fashion:

'My darling treasure, my poor baby! Why have you left me all alone? I should have died instead of you . . .'

The other women joined in, and there were murmurs
among the crowd:

'Did you ever see such hunters?'

'We asked them to help, and now look . . .'

'The damn murderers . . .'

All they could think of in the face of disaster was to look
for scapegoats.

Simon Teterin stood there with bowed head.

13

Unlike the other villagers, however, Mikhailo had no
thought of blaming Simon. He suggested he take the horse
to go and fetch the bear:

'You can't get it home by yourself. You may as well have
it – we shan't feel any better if it just goes to waste.'

Kindness, like anger, is infectious. Immediately the
unfriendly remarks died down, and two young men stepped
forward to offer their help to Simon.

As they went to get the bear, Simon voiced his feeling to
the two young men. Why had he got mixed up with
Mityagin, who had probably never held a gun in his hands
before, despite all his talk . . . Simon had worried that he
might need helping if the bear attacked him, but in the
upshot all the danger came from Mityagin himself. It was
safer to have no truck with people like that . . . It is always
easier to set one's own mind at rest by pointing a finger at
someone else, and as Simon bitterly complained about
Mityagin, putting all the blame on him, the two youths
from Pozhnevka listened sympathetically, and agreed with
every word he said.

Simon usually brought back his trophies in triumph.
Everybody, old and young, would rush out to meet him and
help him drag the dead beast from the cart, prodding it
with their fingers and gasping with awe at the sight of it.
But this time he got back home in the dead of night, and
dumped the carcass in a shed. The two youths said goodbye
and climbed back into the cart. Simon woke up his wife and
had a bite to eat – he had had nothing whatsoever for more

than twenty-four hours – then he fell into bed and slept like
a log.

He got up at his usual early hour, and after quickly
washing his face, went straight to the shed where the dead
animal was lying. Kalinka was on guard at the door, and at
the sight of her master she jumped up and wagged her tail
slightly.

The bear's head had been completely mangled by the
doctor, the skin hung in tatters, and bones were sticking
out through the flesh. Simon decided to start by cutting off
the head, chopping it up into pieces and throwing it out to
Kalinka who, as usual, was sitting at the open door without
so much as a whimper, waiting patiently for her due.

Working with his knife, Simon saw that the top vertebra
– the one that joins the neck to the skull – was smashed. He
poked around a little with the knife and a small dark
object like a pebble suddenly fell out between his knees on
to the sacking he had spread on the floor. Simon picked it
up. It was heavy for its size. It was the bullet – the very
bullet which the doctor had been looking for, a squashed
lead slug of exactly the type that Simon loaded his cartridges with.

Putting down the knife, with the bullet tightly clenched
in his fist, Simon got up, waved Kalinka away, shut the
door and went back to the house.

At the porch he was waylaid by Nastya, Mityagin's wife.
She was thin, with a flat chest, angry, bulging eyes and a
hooked nose of ominous appearance; no wonder that her
nickname in the village was 'the Owl'.

Now she stood barring his way with her scrawny arms
akimbo.

'What do you mean by this?' she screeched in her shrill,
hysterical voice, 'you were all to blame, the whole lot of
you, and now you're trying to fasten it on one person.'

'That's enough,' Simon said, squeezing the bullet in his
hand and trying to get past her.

But the first-aid man's wife would not let him by.

'You daren't look me in the face! You're ashamed to!
And what about these?' She pulled at her skirt, to which

clung the two smallest of the Mityagin children, with their round, dirty faces and bright bulging eyes – just like little owls. 'You want to take their father away, do you? Manslaughter's no laughing matter. You lost your head and got cold feet. And now, you think all the blame can be put on Mityagin, because he's so meek, while you get off scot-free yourselves. And he doesn't say a word, of course. You're just taking advantage of him because he never sticks up for himself. But I won't allow it! I won't al-low it!' Nastya screamed.

The tiny children, used to their mother shouting, continued to stare round-eyed at Simon from behind their mother's skirt. And Simon, knowing well that there was no more hysterical woman in the whole village than Nastya the Owl, stood there uneasily shifting his feet, glowering at her from beneath his brows, and occasionally trying to get in a word:

'What are you so het up about?'

'You can't fool me! You won't answer for it because you didn't shoot, and the other man is too high and mighty. So that leaves my poor fool of a husband, doesn't it?'

'Now, wait a minute . . .'

Suddenly Nastya's voice broke, she poked her nose into a corner of her kerchief, and burst into tears.

'You've got no conscience. I have five children round my neck. We'll all have to go begging. Why am I punished like this? Why did I have to marry that fool? All my life I've had to suffer because of him.'

Nastya's tears, the anguish in her voice, and particularly the vacant stare of the children's bulging eyes, now produced in Simon the same harrowing sense of distress that had come over him while the woman doctor was examining the bear's carcass.

'Stop howling! Nobody is thinking of doing anything to your Vasily,' he said, and pushed past her.

Near the stove Simon found two cast-iron frying pans, one big one, the other smaller. Then he shut himself up in the little room where he kept his guns and the rest of his hunting gear. Putting the squashed bullet on the large frying pan, he began to roll it into shape, pressing down on it with the smaller frying pan.

Simon went on rolling the uneven slug of lead, thinking as he did so that every movement of his arm brought Mityagin nearer to his undoing. The Prosecutor had said yesterday that it was a bad business, and that someone could go to prison for it. Once Simon produced this bullet and testified that it had fallen out of the bear, Mityagin would not stand a chance.

Yesterday, walking by the cart behind Mikhailo, Simon had brooded about how terrible it was if nobody cared about a fellow human being and just abandoned him to his fate. These were good and noble thoughts, and now Mityagin was threatened with disaster, they applied to him as well. It had all happened through blind chance, and nobody was really to blame, but Nastya would be left almost a widow with fatherless children to look after. After his unfriendly reception at Pozhnevka, with people shouting 'murderers', Simon had not thought twice about casting a slur on Mityagin, pointing a finger at him to salve his own conscience. Now he was rolling this bullet into shape, as though nothing but good could come of it . . . He felt sorry for Mityagin.

But he went on with his work all the same; the slug of lead grew rounder, and was no longer bumping under the frying pan.

The Assistant Prosecutor had taken away with him the rifle which Simon had lent Mityagin for the hunt. But Simon's double-barrelled shotgun and Dudyrev's were of the same bore, so he could check the bullet on his own gun. Simon took the gun off the wall, and tried to put the bullet into it – only to be quite taken aback. The bullet would not go into the barrel! Simon could not believe his eyes; he tried again. No, it didn't fit. The bullet that had killed the bear must have come from Mityagin's rifle . . .

Simon sat down on a bench, put the gun between his knees and examined the bullet on the palm of his hand. So it was Dudyrev who had killed the young man. But Simon had no wish to get Dudyrev into trouble either. What should

he do? Hide it? Or throw it away? He couldn't do that – all
the blame would then be put on Mityagin; Dudyrev, on the
other hand, could take care of himself. Better go to him,
show him the bullet, and tell him everything. There could
be no better person to advise him. They could talk it over
and decide on the best thing to do.

Simon put the bullet in his pocket.

Within ten minutes he was striding along the road which
led to the Dymki Project.

14

The Project had not wiped the village of Dymki off the face
of the earth. The village continued to stand in the same
place, consisting of two irregular lines of huts in close
proximity to the river bank. Only now did people notice
how broken down and squalid they were; previously they
had looked like any other peasant houses – dark wooden
huts, weather-beaten and mellowed by time. But by contrast with the new spick and span prefabricated houses
which had sprung up alongside – they had large windows
and were painted a pretty, light-hearted green colour – it
was painfully obvious how wretched the old huts were: a
rickety breed with rotting beams, mossy overgrown roofs
and tiny windows which nobody would even bother to pull
down; they would just be allowed to sink even further into
the ground, until they finally disappeared of their own
accord.

Simon saw a tractor standing by the last hut in the village. It was not the ordinary kind of farm tractor, but a
bulldozer, menacingly lifting a heavy steel blade, with dried
clumps of mud stuck to it, over the wooden house. An old
woman sat outside warming herself. Her tiny face, which
was like a dark, wizened fist, was turned towards the sunlight; Simon recognised her at once. She was about ninety
years old, perhaps more – in any case Simon had never
known her as anything but an old woman. All her life this
old peasant woman, nicknamed 'the Goat' by the other
villagers, had lived in Dymki, getting up at cockcrow, and

going to bed when the hens went to bed; the loudest noise she had ever heard until recent times had been the sound of the ice cracking as the river thawed in the spring. Now, from over the roofs there was incessant roaring and rumbling and the cries of men at work, and this heavy bulldozer had come to tower insolently over her hut.

Out of the hut came a young man with his shirt sleeves rolled up and his coat flung over his shoulders. He was still chewing something as he walked over to the bulldozer. It looked as if he was one of 'the Goat's' grandsons. He noticed Simon and stopped to greet him, still chewing:

'Have you come on business, Simon Ivanovich?'

Like everybody in the district he knew the famous bear hunter by sight.

'Yes, I've come to the Project. How do I get to the office?'

'Which office? There are lots of them. Each section has its own. Which do you want?'

'Goodness me, I feel like a sheep caught in a bush in these parts. I want to see Dudyrev himself.'

The youth whistled.

'Dudyrev? You should have said so. You want the *Director's* office. Get in, and I'll take you over to where they're digging the foundations. They'll tell you where to go.'

Simon clambered awkwardly into the cab. The young man sat at the controls in a practised way. The engine roared deafeningly, and for a moment Simon was a little frightened: what if this roaring beast were to leap forward and trample on the hut and old 'Goat' sunning herself in front? But the bulldozer, like a soldier on parade, smartly turned about and, rattling the heavy blade in front of it, rolled off down the village street, frightening away all the hens as it went.

'The Project will be the end of Dymki,' Simon yelled.

'It sure will,' the young man nodded, looking pleased at the thought.

'Aren't you sorry about it? This is where you've lived all your life, isn't it?'

The young man waved his hand contemptuously, and

then, bending over to shout in Simon's ear:

'As soon as I get an apartment in the new block, I'm going to flatten our old hut with this thing.' He laughed gaily. 'That'll get rid of all the cockroaches!'

'You might wait at least until your grandmother has died,' Simon said with feeling.

Simon understood the old woman only too well. All this building was disturbing even his peace – the natural, inner peace of a man used to the forest, to loneliness and quiet. And for the first time, as well as feeling afraid of the future, Simon thought of himself as an old man – almost a contemporary of old 'Goat'.

He got off the bulldozer at the foundation area, in the very centre of the Project. Dump trucks went past him giving off acrid fumes, and somewhere nearby they slowly discharged whole mountains of sand. One after another they went by, identical, snub-nosed monsters roaring ominously, and heavily laden; there was no end to them. What did they care for marshes, forests, or rivers? Without hesitation they would level them or fill them in. Then there was another monster working in one corner of the foundations. Hampered by lack of space and its own ungainliness, it was moving up and down, digging its huge, jointed steel arm in the ground, while the snub-nosed trucks crowded round it, each waiting its turn. Earth was poured like water from one place to another, and these strange newfangled machines were turning the familiar world inside out. The old fairy tales about wizards, hobgoblins and suchlike creatures living in the forests and marshes were tame stuff compared with these unholy monsters!

'Look where you're going!' somebody shouted at him.

Simon leapt aside. A truck with a trailer carrying concrete beams went past, with a great stench of evil-smelling fumes. Nearby a young lad in a dirty vest, a greasy cap and enormous protective gloves, grinned at him. He was dragging one end of a cable.

'I say,' Simon asked him uncertainly, 'can you tell me how to get to the Director's office, to Dudyrev?'

'Straight ahead, only look where you're going, or there'll be an accident.'

Simon made his way along the path by the road, looking around him on all sides. Past him went more and more roaring machines, carrying either enormous pipes, or great drums of cable, each one as tall as a man, cranes, or cement oozing out of the sides like thick grey cream. Which way should he go? He was an old bear hunter, who knew the forest like the back of his hand, and could find a path through the worst of swamps, but now he was lost and confused, only a stone's throw from the village! Before there used to be a hillocky stretch of pasture here, juniper bushes, a few birch trees mixed with aspens, and crooked little paths used to run to the edge of the forest. It was hard to believe!

Simon suddenly saw himself as he was, in his rust-coloured coat over his old-fashioned Russian shirt, and his peaked cap pulled down over his forehead – small, helpless and unneeded. There were so many machines, so many people, it was like the day of judgement, and at the head of it all stood Dudyrev, the same man who had talked with him so respectfully in the forest, and whom he had angrily told off for his slowness. Now Simon was going to see him, deafened by the roar of machines and squeezing a lead bullet in his fist. It was not going to be an easy conversation.

He couldn't help thinking at this moment about how Kalinka had taken fright as she made her way across the rickety planks of the bridge; at the time Simon had been surprised – he couldn't understand what had come over her. Now he understood.

He marched on obstinately, but Kalinka, looking round anxiously as she stood in the middle of the bridge, never left his mind.

15

Dudyrev got up from his desk to greet Simon with out-stretched hand, and took him over to a sofa.

'Sit down,' he said, looking into his face with his deep-set eyes under heavy brows, 'what's new?'

He was in a light, lock-knit shirt, which was a close fit for his broad chest and powerful shoulders, and he looked as homely as ever, not quite suited to the large room with its huge windows and its furniture – chairs and armchairs, sofa and two tables, one covered with red cloth, the other with green. It was difficult to believe that this familiar Dudyrev, not so very different from what he had seemed in the forest, was the ruler of this strange new world which had so stunned Simon both by its scale and its ferocity.

'Something unpleasant?'

Simon sighed, took the bullet out of his pocket, and passed it to Dudyrev.

'Look at this . . .'

Dudyrev did not understand and rolled the bullet about on his palm.

'I took it out of the bear,' Simon explained. 'This is what the doctor couldn't find.'

'Out of the bear?'

Without looking at Simon, Dudyrev knit his brows and continued to examine the small lump of lead on his palm.

'It had lodged right under the skull.'

Heavy trucks were passing outside the window and rattling the panes. Simon, knees wide apart and his hands resting on them, sat awkwardly on the very edge of the sofa and held his breath as he watched Dudyrev deep in thought.

The telephone rang, startling Dudyrev out of his brown study; he clasped the bullet in his hand, went over to his desk, picked up the receiver and began to talk to somebody in a quiet, commanding voice.

'Yes, I remember . . . Yes, if you want to, but not now, later. Yes, I can guess – it's a question of capital expenditure again. I can't throw away millions of roubles. Come and see me later, I'm busy now . . .'

He put the receiver down, came back to Simon and held out his hand with the bullet in his open palm.

'Whose is it?'

'It doesn't fit your barrel, Konstantin Sergeivich,' Simon answered firmly.

'You've checked it?'

'Yes. Mityagin killed the bear . . .'

None of them spoke for a while. The trucks went past, shaking the windows. Dudyrev rolled the bullet thoughtfully in his palm.

'Konstantin Sergeivich,' Simon started again, 'we must be fair about this – it was as much your fault as Mityagin's. An accident can happen to anyone. I've come to you so we can think what to do.'

Again Dudyrev did not reply, but just looked down at the palm of his hand. Simon waited numbly for his reply.

'Here,' Dudyrev said at last, handing the bullet back to him.

Simon obediently took it.

'You're waiting for my reply?' asked Dudyrev.

'That's why I've come. I can't decide this on my own.'

'But put yourself in my place for a moment. Imagine that someone brings you a bullet, and says: "Here is the evidence that you have killed a man. You are a murderer!" Would you agree with him just like that?'

'So you think Mityagin will have to take all the blame? They're going to be very hard on him, you know. The Prosecutor said that, with the law as it stands, they'd have to send someone to prison.'

'In the eyes of the law, there's no difference between Mityagin and me.'

'In the eyes of the law, but not in the eyes of people. You're not the same as Mityagin, Konstantin Sergeivich. The people who have most say about the law look up to you.'

'Are you suggesting that I should shield Mityagin?'

'I'm not suggesting anything. I've brought you the bullet which killed the bear. It was fired by Mityagin. That means the boy was killed by your bullet. That's all I can tell you. It's up to you to figure out what you ought to do. I don't have your brains.'

Dudyrev got up. Simon noticed a vein pulsing tensely in his forehead.

'Tell the Prosecutor you've found the bullet,' Dudyrev said curtly. 'I can't help either Mityagin or myself.'

Simon left the office. Trucks were still roaring by with their trailers. Bulldozers were crawling at the edge of the foundation area, levelling piles of sand. The excavator's grab was still passing back and forth over the dump trucks, doling out earth. The bullet burnt into Simon's palm – a little slug of lead with a secret. Unless this secret were disclosed, a court of law would send Mityagin to jail. It wasn't fair! If Dudyrev wouldn't do anything to help, then . . . Whether he liked it or not he had to go to the Assistant Prosecutor: Dudyrev would have to take care of himself.

16

The Assistant Prosecutor, Dityatichev, his head, with its prominent ears, tilted to one side, attentively turned the bullet over in his hands for a moment, and then put it on the table.

'You took it out of the bear as round as this?'

'It was squashed. I rolled it into shape to see which barrel it fitted.'

'You rolled it into shape, and now you've brought it here . . .' and then suddenly, looking straight into Simon's eyes, he asked: 'Have you been a neighbour of Mityagin's for long?'

'Neighbour? Yes, for a good ten years, I should think, if not more. He moved next door to us three years after the war.'

'I see. And why did you take him on the hunt with you?'

'Why did I take him on the hunt? He'd been begging me to for a long time.'

'And you couldn't say no?'

'Yes, I did, many times. But it's a bit awkward if someone keeps asking.'

'I see. And you're on good terms with Mityagin? You've never quarrelled with him?'

'Good lord, no,' Simon said in alarm, not understanding what the Assistant Prosecutor was driving at. 'The women occasionally have words, but we never have. We've always got along all right.'

'So, you don't deny that you've always got along well with him?'

'Why should I, if it's the truth?'

'I see,' Dityatichev said, glancing at the bit of lead resting on the ink-stained, cloth-covered top of his desk. 'You've been good neighbours for ten years, and it didn't occur to you that our first thought would be that you made this bullet yourself for the sake of your good friend of ten years' standing? We are bound to think that you are trying to cover up for your guilty friend, and to sink Dudyrev.'

Simon stared at the Assistant Prosecutor in blank amazement.

'You understand what this looks like?' Dityatichev went on calmly. 'False evidence with the aim of perverting the course of justice. Perhaps you didn't realise that you can answer for this sort of thing in Court? You must be very naïve not to understand that it is a criminal offence to fake evidence like this – the bullet is obviously bogus.'

'Listen,' Simon moved angrily in his chair. 'I don't know anything about most things, but that bullet's not a fake. I'm telling you! I took it out of the bear this morning with my own hands. You and the doctor missed it when you were looking . . .'

'You can say that as much as you like! But just think: who is going to believe you? The bear was examined by a professional doctor, not a layman like yourself. Moreover, it was a very thorough examination, as I myself can testify. She failed to find it after a most exhaustive search and had no hesitation in writing out and signing an official report to that effect. She is prepared to stake her word, in writing, that there was no bullet, and now you come along and put this thing on the table in front of me. This bullet of yours is quite smooth, without the slightest deformation—nothing at all to show that it was taken out of a bear's broken vertebra and not from a hunter's pouch. Tell me, why didn't you bring us the bullet in the condition you say you found it in?'

'I wanted to see if it fitted.'

'You wanted to see if it fitted! Really now . . . what im-

patience, just like an inquisitive child! But at least a child
might have had the sense not to destroy such an important
piece of evidence.'

Simon frowned in silence. When he rolled the bullet into
shape, he had been thinking only of Mityagin, and had just
wanted to make sure that it was in fact he who had killed
the youth. Dityatichev had been very far from his thoughts
at that point. Even when he realised that Mityagin was not
responsible, it still didn't occur to him to go to Dityatichev.
His only thought had been to go and see Dudyrev—not to
try and cause trouble for him, but to talk it over with him
as a friend. It had never entered his head that anyone might
find fault with him, and accuse him of destroying evidence. How could he have known he would come such a
cropper?

'What's more,' continued Dityatichev, 'you frankly admit
that you have lived side by side with Mityagin for ten
years, and that during those ten years you never once
quarrelled or fell out with him. In other words you admit
to a long-standing friendship with Mityagin, while you only
met Dudyrev a few days ago. All this goes to show that you
are out to save your friend at any price, even if it means
putting the blame on Dudyrev. This is what it looks like!
Stick to your story, if you like, but I doubt if anyone will
believe you—all the facts are against you.'

The Assistant Prosecutor paused, and Simon Teterin
broke his gloomy silence to ask:

'How can you prove that Mityagin did it? You don't have
all that much to go on, do you?'

'That's what you were banking on,' Dityatichev replied
calmly. 'No, we have no direct evidence against Mityagin,
but there is plenty of circumstantial evidence.'

'So slanted evidence will do, will it?' said Simon, not
understanding the word 'circumstantial'. 'That's a fine
how-do-you-do, I'm bound to say!'

'You don't like our way of doing things, and you're upset
because we are not prepared to save your friend's skin, but
I'd like to ask you one question: did you know that Mityagin had never handled a gun in his life before?'

'He told me he'd done a bit of shooting when he was young, but how should I know? I've never seen him with a gun myself.'

'An hour ago he was here, and admitted that he's never hunted in his life. On the other hand, Dudyrev's been going out hunting for many years.'

'What of it? Even the best of hunters can slip up.'

'I agree – anything can happen, and Dudyrev could have missed the bear. But surely we can't ignore the fact that Mityagin is not a good shot, while Dudyrev is highly experienced?'

'Of course not, you have to take everything into account. Everything. Which means you cannot ignore the bullet either.'

'You saw yourself how carefully we looked for it. Now you come along with this bullet here and expect us to believe it's the one that killed the bear – on no evidence in particular. Now, you were there when we carried out our investigations on the spot. You yourself showed us where Dudyrev and Mityagin stood. Now then, Mityagin stood at a spot where the ground slopes more steeply, a little to one side. He's also shorter than Dudyrev, so from that angle it would have been harder for him to hit the bear. And that's not all. From the place where Dudyrev fired, a good deal of the bridge, the middle of it in fact, was hidden by an old tree. But from Mityagin's place there was a clear view of the whole bridge, right across to the far side. You told us that the boy fell into the river from the centre of the bridge. If Dudyrev had missed the bear, his bullet would have gone straight into the tree trunk. It's ten to one that Mityagin's bullet missed the bear, and . . .'

'But it was his bullet I found in the bear. What you say sounds all very well, but it just wasn't like that.'

Dityatichev shot a sidelong glance at Simon, like a hen about to pick a grain of corn.

'I would be careful what you say. You don't come out of this business all that well yourself. There might be a case against you too.'

'What do you mean? You'll be saying I killed the

boy next! You're so darned clever, you can twist things any way you like.'

'What sort of a case do you think we're bringing? Premeditated murder, or something? No. It's a case of manslaughter owing to negligence. If a driver knocks someone down through negligence, gravely injures or kills him, then, as everyone knows, he is tried and punished. Here it's a matter of negligence on the part of someone who shot at a bear and killed a man. Properly speaking, it's quite true – you are more guilty of negligence than Mityagin.'

'Why?'

'I'll tell you why. Isn't it negligence to take a man hunting if he's never handled a gun in his life before? He's guilty because he persuaded you to let him come, but you're an experienced hunter, aware of all the dangers, all the unpleasant things that may happen with people who are not used to handling firearms. In this sense you are, perhaps, the more guilty. If we condemn careless drivers, careless accountants, careless factory directors, then we cannot make an exception for careless hunters. So bear in mind that you are not innocent yourself!'

The Assistant Prosecutor got up; narrow-shouldered, straight and tall, he stood half a head higher than Simon, who was visibly stooping when he also got up to leave. Pronouncing every word very carefully, Dityatichev concluded:

'Today I did not send for you. This conversation happened by chance, as it were. In a day or two I shall summon you officially as a witness. We shall then come back to what we're talking about now. Goodbye.'

Simon looked silently at Dityatichev, at his long, thin neck, his pale face with its large pores – the face of a man who sits in an office all day long – his large ears, and his flabby mouth, like an old woman's. A moment ago Simon had regarded him as a perfectly ordinary sort of person, only better educated and cleverer than himself. Now he saw that he had some very special quality – a power which enabled him to accuse and deliver judgements. And the Assistant Prosecutor's grey eyes, which had hitherto seemed unremarkable under their wrinkled eyelids, now appeared to be boring straight into him, searching for something vicious. Simon lacked the strength to withstand his gaze; he dropped his eyes, and turned to go.

'Are you leaving this with me?' Dityatichev called him back. He pointed at the bullet which lay on the table.

Simon returned obediently, took the bullet and dropped it into his pocket.

With bowed head, he went out of the Prosecutor's office, away from this man he now found so frightening. At the corner, he turned involuntarily and saw a car drawing up at the steps of the building; out of it stepped Dudyrev.

For the first time Simon felt impotent anger towards Dudyrev and the Assistant Prosecutor. 'They'll put their heads together and take it out on someone . . .'

17

Dudyrev loved calm lakes at sunrise, when they seem to be filled with heavy, liquid metal instead of water, and their quivering reeds are at rest, with still mist clinging to them. He never tired of the thrill he got from knowing that game was close at hand. He loved to follow a fox's trail on skis through the forest over shimmering, almost laughing snow. In short, he loved hunting.

But in every hunt there was always one unpleasant moment for him. It came after he at last saw the quarry he had passionately pursued with might and main – a flock of birds starting up into a sky just touched by a pink dawn, or a fleeting glimpse of a fox's coat hot among cold snow-drifts – after he had put his rifle to his shoulder, after the glorious moment when instinct takes over from reason and the shot had been fired in triumph, and he first saw the sight of blood, and squeamishly took in his hands the corpse, still warm with the life which he had cut short. It was the pain that inevitably went with joy, like brutal prose following poetry. It just had to be endured and forgotten till the next moment of triumph: sleeping lakeside reeds, tracks on the snow, the barrel pointed at a soaring bird . . . Dudyrev loved hunting.

But this last hunt had left very painful memories: first
the death of the dog, which he himself had had to finish off,
her mournful eyes glimmering in the darkness; then the fear
and burning shame he had felt in the ravine, followed by a
terrible sense of personal grievance against the bear –
though he was guilty only of desperately trying to save his
own life. And finally, the way it had all ended: the figure in
the dark suit spread out on the ground in the dim light of
the dying night . . . That was the climax of their frantic
chase through forest and swamps – the grand finale. The
death of the bear had merged with the death of a man. The
one now seemed as monstrous as the other. It was terrible
to think of. He hated himself for it. There could be no
justification.

Dudyrev did not believe it was his shot which had missed
the bear and killed the man. It was bad enough without
having to feel guilty of manslaughter into the bargain. That
would be more than he could stand – it must surely have
been Mityagin's fault. But all the same, he could not rid
himself of an uncanny feeling, which he had experienced
once before, as a very young child. At home they used to
have an old cupboard standing in a dark passage and every
time he went by, he thought someone was lying in wait for
him there, an unknown creature with neither face nor body,
ready to spring out at him. He knew there was no such
thing, that it was only his imagination, but all the same . . .

Now, too, Dudyrev feared something invisible, which he
felt to be lurking nearby. Even stronger than this fear was
a nagging sense of guilt. The Prosecutor and his Assistant
had talked to him in the car on the way back, trying to
console him with the thought that this sort of accident
could happen to anyone. Mityagin, on the other hand, they
simply ignored. There were no soothing words for him, as he
sat huddled in his corner.

Dudyrev was the leading light of the whole district, a
miracle worker who created new roads and got buses
running, shaking the place out of its sleepy stagnation.
What chance did Mityagin stand against him? It would be
so easy to let him be the scapegoat.

But Dudyrev would not try to get out of his own responsibility. However disagreeable it was, whatever the consequences for his future, he would try to be quite impartial, and honestly accept his share of the blame, on equal terms with Mityagin! It would be quite wrong for him to take cover under his own power and authority. Nothing was more important than respect for other human beings.

These noble sentiments were instantly forgotten when Simon Teterin came to see him and put the bullet on the table in front of him. Even before the hunter uttered a word, Dudyrev felt a sudden panic. This was the lurking terror, hitherto faceless and disembodied, but now a creature of flesh and blood speaking with a human voice. Embarrassed, with downcast eyes, Simon Teterin had told him point blank that he was the killer.

There was the little lump of lead on the green cloth before him, carefully rolled into shape, in no way different from other such bullets. But what lent it such fateful distinction was its calibre: it exactly fitted the barrel of the rifle used by Mityagin, but would not go into Dudyrev's double-barrelled gun.

Dudyrev looked at this round slug of lead, and felt the whole of his being angrily rejecting this evidence. How could he be called a killer – he who had worked so devotedly to improve the lot of others. Wherever he appeared, new roads were built, new settlements sprang up, electric cables were strung across the countryside, people were shaken out of their lethargy. For himself Dudyrev wanted very little: a roof over his head, plain food and – his only self-indulgence – a day off once a month, so that he could go out and relax with his gun in the open. Everything else he did was for other people – all those sleepless nights, the exhausting work and perpetual wear and tear on his nerves. And now it was suggested that he should admit to the most terrible of human acts – the killing of a fellow-man!

As long as he lived he would never forget that bleak dawn, the motionless leaves of the bushes weighed down by the dew, the man in the dark suit lying spread out with one trouser leg yanked out of his boot, Mityagin's bald head pressed to the dead man's chest . . . The years might go by, but he would never be able to recall that scene without a shudder. The only saving grace would be the knowledge that he, Dudyrev, was not really guilty but had accepted a share of the blame only in a spirit of chivalry. This would be a secret source of pride – a noble sop to his conscience. Only in this way could he live without tormenting himself.

Now there was this lead bullet, the doleful face of Simon Teterin . . . No, he could not believe it. He would never admit such a thing, never! At least not of his own free will, only if forced, with his back against the wall . . .

Simon went away, taking the accursed bullet with him.

The working day, interrupted by Simon's visit for some fifteen minutes, resumed its accustomed normal course.

Dudyrev answered the telephone, giving orders in his usual firm voice, and waited for his self-confidence to recover from this distressing encounter. But it did not recover.

Then he decided to go and see the Assistant Prosecutor. It was impossible to stand the uncertainty any longer: perhaps he would learn something there. He ordered a car.

18

Dityatichev's voice was respectful and soothing. It was the voice of a doctor talking at the bedside of a seriously ill patient.

'Believe me, we are not just pedants, sticking to the letter of the law. We know that neither you nor Mityagin is really guilty. But put yourself in our place. Imagine if we just covered up this business, and didn't bring it to trial. The dead man's relatives only have to start an outcry, saying that there was a shout of warning and that the accident could certainly have been avoided, and we are immediately in a very difficult position. We shall be accused of covering up criminal negligence.'

'I'm not suggesting that you break the law,' said Dudyrev, 'all I want to say is that in all fairness I should answer as well as Mityagin. I am equally to blame.'

A smile of comprehension flickered in the depths of
Dityatichev's eyes under the dispassionate, half-closed lids.
It did not escape Dudyrev: the Assistant Prosecutor had
sensed his confusion. He would take this sudden visit as a
sign of weakness on the part of the omnipotent Dudyrev.
But to hell with him, he could think what he liked! He must
get things straight, so that he knew how to behave and what
to do. He could not hide behind Mityagin, who was clearly
no more to blame than he was, but neither could he lightly
allow himself to be accused of manslaughter.

'It's too soon to talk of anybody answering for anything,'
replied Dityatichev evasively. 'It's not up to us to pass
sentences, that's the business of the court.'

He was silent for a moment and then added in a confiding
tone: 'I should imagine the court will take a lenient view.'

'Has Simon Teterin been to see you?' Dudyrev asked
point blank.

'He has just gone.'

'What do you think of his discovery?'

'About the bullet?'

'Yes.'

'I think it's an obvious dodge.'

'Why do you think that?'

'He's trying to save his friend. But since he's an honest
man by nature, not good at lying, it looks very clumsy
indeed. The way he figures it is: Dudyrev has a lot of
influence, we'll put the blame on him, and he'll be able to
get out of it. But as soon as I pointed out to him that he
was committing a criminal offence, he backed down straight
away. This only went to confirm my suspicions.'

'Does that really confirm them?'

'Well, you won't deny that Teterin is a determined sort
of fellow – he has to be in his profession. Now, if someone
like this, who is no coward, turns tail and meekly goes off
with his bullet, any misgivings I might have had naturally
disappeared. He does not believe his own story. In other
words . . .'

'You mean the bullet is a fake?' Dudyrev interrupted
gloomily.

'Yes.'

'Teterin is certainly no coward – I couldn't agree more. But don't you know that people who may be quite fearless in battle conditions can get confused in an ordinary peacetime situation, particularly in the presence of an official? I wouldn't jump to the conclusion that he has given up.'

'All right. I'll take this bullet of his into account. Only that may land him in a very nasty mess. If his bullet turns out to be a fake, he will be liable to a charge of producing false evidence with the intention of misleading the investigating authority. Not to mention the fact that it's going to complicate matters for us and confuse the issue.'

'Are you afraid of complications?'

'I think you, too, would prefer a clear-cut situation if you were in my place.'

Dudyrev glanced darkly at Dityatichev who was sitting with his narrow shoulders hunched up to his ears, a model of deference and impartiality, certain of the soundness of his judgement. He was patiently replying to Dudyrev's doubts only out of respect for his person.

'May I tell you an old story?' began Dudyrev.

Dityatichev nodded: 'Certainly.'

'A drunken man is crawling on his knees under a lamppost. Somebody asks him what he's looking for. "I've lost my purse," he says. "Where?" "Over there," he says, pointing at the other side of the street. "But why are you looking here and not there, where you lost it?" "There's more light over here!" '

For the first time in their conversation Dityatichev looked put out.

'In what way do I remind you of that drunkard?'

'Because you're afraid of complications, and prefer to look for the truth where you think it's easier, because there's more light. But that's not the way to find it.'

Dityatichev frowned.

'I don't think your analogy is a very good one,' he replied in a slightly offended manner. 'All the evidence points to that fact that Teterin is trying to confuse the issue and lead us away from the truth, and if he goes on like this, then I don't care what complications I have to face.'

The conversation had not really got him anywhere. Back
in his car, Dudyrev brooded bitterly on it: 'Teterin's bullet
is as bad for me as it is for him. Dityatichev should have
gone at me hammer and tongs over that, but he doesn't
want any trouble with my bosses in the *oblast*.* It's easier
for him to throw Mityagin to the lions. Just like the
drunkard under the lamp post! It's pretty mean. What
should I do? Just keep my mouth shut, or help Dityatichev
to do his dirty work? God, how vile it all is!' Fear and be-
wilderment had given way to anger and indignation. At
least it meant that Dudyrev was now absorbed less in his
own worries.

The car passed through fields. Ahead was a wood, a
pleasant fringe of dense green trees. But as Dudyrev well
knew, it was now only a façade. Only this thin line was left
of what had been a large stretch of woodland, the rest
having been cleared for the Project. In winter and early
spring, when the trees were not clothed in leaves, the lights
of the workers' settlement could be seen between the tree
trunks from this place.

The car sped into the wood and a moment later arrived
in the settlement. Among tree stumps sticking up here and
there, stood huts, all exactly alike, brand new and still not
weathered by the wind, all equally unadorned and built in
rows of a dispiriting regularity. It gave the impression of a
temporary encampment – the whole place had the bleak,
unlovely appearance of army barracks.

A factory was to be built here, and houses would grow up
around it, perhaps well-designed and handsome ones – but
these barracks would still remain next to them. However much they fell into disrepair, someone would most
certainly go on living in them. The reason for this was
simple: the builders who came after Dudyrev would take
these barracks into account in planning future housing
needs. Since they were already there, they would argue,
people might as well stay in them, in spite of the fact that

* Provincial centre.

they were ugly and inconvenient: beggars couldn't be choosers. These builders, like the Assistant Prosecutor Dityatichev, would not want unnecessary complications; they would seek the easy way out.

It was all very well to be indignant with Dityatichev. But what about himself? He had built barracks instead of proper living quarters, for the good reason that it was quick, cheap and simple. His main argument had been that it was so simple – no need to worry about where the necessary funds and labour would come from, no danger of upsetting production targets . . . Wasn't that also like the drunkard looking for his purse under a lamp-post?

The road dipped down to the foundation area, where the earth had been ravaged. It was quiet now, badly wounded, but enjoying a brief respite. Gulls were flying above it, against a crimson sunset.

Dudyrev began to understand something he had, oddly enough, never thought of before, that truth and happiness are inseparable, and that happiness is too serious a thing to be got easily; one is not likely to find it under a lamp-post where it is simpler to look for it.

19

The bullet he had found in the bear became a torment for Simon Teterin. Up till now he had lived quietly, fearing no one, and able to look any man straight in the eye. But now, every time he came out of his house, he had to look out in case he ran into Mityagin or Nastya, and had to face their reproaches or questions. Even the sight of the little Mityagin children, playing all day with shouts and laughter in the lane in front of the house, embarrassed and worried him.

Glashka Popova, with her post bag, was also a bugbear now for Simon, as she ambled on her rounds from village to village. Every time she came through, raising the dust with her boots, Simon's heart sank: would she call at his house, or would she pass by? But when she had passed by, he somehow felt even more upset – it might have been better if she had brought that summons from the Assistant

Prosecutor. Simon remembered Dityatichev's face – the thin, soft lips, the large pale-grey eyes, and the calm, cold look. At the mere thought that this man would fasten his gaze on him again, ask more questions, and try to worm something out of him, Simon already felt himself a criminal. How on earth could he prove that his bullet was the right one? He knew they would think he had an ulterior motive in trying to save Mityagin: unless Mityagin were cleared, he himself could hardly escape blame for taking an inexperienced man on a bear hunt, and they would say it was his negligence that had caused the accident. The fact that the Assistant Prosecutor was so slow to summon him seemed a sign. Was something being hatched up against him behind his back?

For the first few days Simon feared that Mityagin would give him no peace – that he would come round every day and whine. But in fact Mityagin crept out of his house only to go to work. Simon could see him through the window in the morning, shuffling in the direction of the first-aid post, and looking at the ground under his feet, just as if he were looking for something he had dropped. If anyone shouted to him, he would look round in a frightened way, and then hurry on.

Then one day Simon ran right into him. His cheeks had fallen in, the skin on his gristly nose was tightly drawn, his eyes had bags under them and shone unhealthily – he really was in a bad way; almost cringing at the sight of Simon, he blinked and looked away as he spoke:

'What a thing to happen to me . . . you never can tell . . .' he muttered guiltily, avoiding Simon's eyes.

Simon realised now that Mityagin was deliberately keeping out of his way and was going through agonies because he believed that he, Mityagin, was the killer. It was so heart-rending that Simon's first impulse was to tell him about the bullet. But if he mentioned that, Mityagin would start kicking up a fuss straight away and insist that he be cleared. Simon would have been only too glad to get him out of his trouble, but there was no way of by-passing Dityatichev, who would only tie both of them with the same knot.

All Simon could bring himself to say was:

'Look here, now don't upset yourself like that.'

But Mityagin only shook his bald head – with some effort, as though his shirt collar were too tight – and said, with a wave of his hand:

'It's just my luck . . . what can I do?'

With those words they parted.

Simon had a new pastime, which at times made him almost sick. He would hide away from his wife in his own room, spill his whole store of bullets out on to the wooden table and put next to them the one which he had taken out of the bear. Then he would run them through his fingers for a long time, trying to see if he could find any difference. But there wasn't. If he threw the accursed thing in among the others, it would be impossible to pick it out again. Strange how this little round lump of lead, a dead thing, with nothing at all to distinguish it from any other, seemed to cast some kind of evil spell on him. He was bewildered and appalled by it, but there was no getting rid of it. He sometimes thought the best thing would be to push it into the heap of other bullets, so no one would ever know which one had been taken out of the bear's skull. But he knew that if he did that, the next time he saw the little Mityagin children playing in the road outside, he would be tormented by the thought that he had held the truth in his hands, and had done nothing about it out of sheer cowardice. Much as he wanted to, he couldn't bring himself to do it.

Every time Simon put the bullet back in his pocket, he had a panicky feeling that it might be the wrong one. This only heightened his misery – if all the bullets were so exactly alike, then it scarcely mattered which he carried around with him as alleged evidence of the truth. Who would believe it? And if nobody would believe him, then what was the point of keeping the bullet and tormenting himself with it?

Simon kept his secret carefully from his wife. A woman was a woman – long of hair and short of brains, as the saying is. In all likelihood she wouldn't be able to keep her mouth shut, and would go round telling everybody in the village.

It would be better just to tell the whole thing to Mityagin outright. He had to tell someone, if only to be able to discuss it. If he kept it to himself, this accursed bullet might drive him out of his mind.

The most respected man in the village was Donat Borovikov, chairman of the collective farm. He had been elected to the job a long time ago, fifteen years or so. For the first ten years neither he nor his collective farm had in any way distinguished themselves. But then he had somehow got going: he built new piggeries, a cattle pen, a chicken farm and an incubator, and after that he moved forward by leaps and bounds. Before, Donat had been lean and restless, but now he had become portly and deep-voiced, always taking his time. His name appeared in the newspapers, and he was always given a place of honour at local meetings.

Simon had known him for a long time and often called in on him. Donat always brought out a bottle of vodka and they would sit up till midnight, talking about hunting and fishing, although Donat himself did neither.

It was to him that Simon went with his story.

'What a business,' said Donat, drawling his words. He was sitting at the table in his vest, red-faced, well-disposed and mellowed by vodka.

'It's a bad business and no mistake,' Simon agreed. 'You do believe me, don't you?'

'Believe what?'

'That I really got the bullet out of the bear and didn't just make up a story?'

'Yes, I believe that all right. But I'd like to give you one piece of advice: keep that bullet to yourself, and don't go talking about it all over the place.'

'So that's what you think? You want me to hide the truth too?'

Donat settled himself more comfortably at the table, and began to put his point with greater emphasis.

'Truth, you say? And have you ever thought what it is? Now, I've just kicked Gavrila Ushakov out of his job, as overseer of our cattle sheds. He says he's spent half his life on this job, and given all his strength to it; that if ever a

cow had trouble calving, he would be up all night looking
after her and coaxing her. Now, is that the truth? Of course
it is, every word of it. But all the same I took no account of
it. The trouble is that Gavrila's an old man, he's had no
education, and he will go on trying to do everything in the
same old way as his grandfather did before him. We've
bought him all kinds of electric milking machines and suchlike, but he can't handle them. They break down, or stand
idle, just rusting away. I reckon that Gavrila has cost the
kolkhoz about 300,000 roubles in the last two years. So
there were two ways of looking at the truth here. How do
you think I could run this place if I'd seen it Gavrila's
way?'

'What are you driving at, Donat?'

'What I mean, Simon, is that there are two ways of
looking at this as well. I don't know much about the law,
but I'm pretty sure the point is this: if a man has been
killed, someone else has to be punished as a warning to
others. You may say that's damn silly, and I agree. I'd
much rather the other man was let off. But it's not you and
me who make the laws. We just have to face it that someone
will have to answer. Now, suppose you prove that Dudyrev
is guilty, and ought to be sent to prison and kicked out of
his job. Will that make me any happier? No. And why not?
Because I'd be afraid that Dudyrev's place might be taken
by some fellow who would just let the whole thing go to
pieces. Now, what do I stand to gain from that? I can't
wait for the day when the factory over there gets started
and there'll be workers living all around. Last year I had to
feed seventy tons of cabbage to the pigs: there was no one
to sell it to round here. By the time we could get it to the
nearest market, our roads being what they are, it would
have gone up in price so much that no customer would so
much as look at it. But soon I'll have regular customers
right here on the spot. I'll sell them cabbages, tomatoes out
of our greenhouses, and cucumbers – plenty of vitamins, for
the workers and lots of money for us! We'll be able to buy
bicycles and motorcycles in their shops. There isn't a single
man or woman round here who doesn't stand to lose if the

Project breaks down because Dudyrev loses his job. So this find of yours isn't such a good thing after all, if it's going to be the ruin of Dudyrev – we shall all suffer if he goes.'

'But why are you talking like that, Donat? You're making yourself out to be worse than you are . . .'

'That's the way life is, I'm telling you. It's not a bed of roses – you've got to take it as it is.'

'Don't try to fool me. You gave Gavrila another job, so he won't be out of pocket. Your bark is worse than your bite. You should be ashamed of yourself, talking like that.'

Donat frowned, and stared down at his plate with a cucumber which he had already half-eaten.

'Well, why don't you say something?' Simon asked brusquely. 'You're sorry for Mityagin, aren't you?'

'Of course I'm sorry, but . . .'

'Yes, I know there are all sorts of buts, but they shouldn't count with you.'

Donat looked up.

'Everything will be all right. They'll let him off in court.'

'And suppose they don't?'

'Why play guessing games? We'll see what we can do when the time comes . . .'

20

In times of trouble Simon always found refuge in the forest. If things were looking black – whatever the hour – he would leave home with his gun and go off somewhere as far away as possible – to one of the 'Teterin' huts he had built at the far ends of his domain. He slept either in a smoke-filled hut or under an old hayrick, caught fish in the dark lakes, shot duck, cooked them hunter-fashion in the embers of a camp fire, first caking them with clay or mud. He always returned from the forest feeling younger and somehow cleaner inside. It was the forest that washed him clean and gave him strength, and always, after a sojourn there, the next day looked brighter to him. He had no better friend than the forest.

Now once more Simon decided to get away from it all – from the Assistant Prosecutor, Mityagin, the accursed bullet – and escape into the forest.

The walls and roofs of the houses were flushed pink with a soft dawn light. The streets of the village were empty. Only the jackdaws were already chattering along the dusty road: Kalinka frightened them as she ran along in front of her master and they flew up in the air with angry cries. Simon strode briskly through the village and turned off the road by a path running along a rye field to the edge of the forest. It was a familiar path which went first through woods where the women and children from the village went looking for mushrooms and berries, then through fields for about three miles; then again into a wood with occasional clearings used as hayfields, until at last the clearings stopped and the real forest began in earnest.

Simon marched right behind Kalinka, almost treading on her tail as she frisked along in front of him. To hell with Mityagin, Dudyrev, the Assistant Prosecutor, the bullet, and all his worries about them! To hell with the lot of them! The dew glinted frostily on the meadow, the sun was peeping up over the edge of the trees, warming them and sending their long, damp shadows slanting over the ground. The air was so bracingly fresh and buoyant that every breath you took seemed to lift you up. The birds sang, the grasshoppers tried out their powers, and the fog that had settled overnight in the hollows began to lift lazily. He had known this beauty all his life, and had seen it many times, often meeting the sun in the morning, but he still walked along as if seeing it all for the first time, marvelling at it. To hell with them all! He could only pity the man who still slept in his warm bed, not seeing these simple wonders, the lifting fog and the rising sun. How poor in spirit a man must be to miss the birth of the sun, and plunge straight into his daily round of wearisome business, tending a sick cow, quarrelling with the foreman, or worrying about a court summons. They can all go to the devil, Simon thought, as he strode deeper into the forest at a rapid pace.

The sun rose higher, drying the dew; the early morning ended, and the day began. Simon walked on and on, never slackening his pace. He gave no thought to where he was going, as long as he got further away from the village, deeper and deeper into the forest.

The shadows shortened. The leaves which had delighted the eye while still freshly washed by the dew, now lost some of their brightness. The day was well under way and everything fell into place, becoming familiar, ordinary and even a little dull. But Simon forged ahead, afraid of losing his excitement.

At midday he came to a swamp.

There can be no sadder place in the world than a forest swamp at noonday. Night hides its eerie gloom – the moss-covered hummocks and the endless belt of spindly fir trees blighted by the damp. Exactly alike with their thin, rough trunks, you can look right through them, thousands upon thousands of them, stretching as far as the eye can see, until they all dissolve in a rust-coloured blur somewhere far away. Land that gives birth to such pitiful trees must have a curse on it. There is no place where a man is so conscious of loneliness – it is empty even of wild life, apart from the foolish partridges which go there to batten on the black and red bilberries growing on the hummocks.

Simon stopped and suddenly felt tired, conscious of the weight of the gun on his shoulder. Well, here he was in the forest – and now what? Kalinka sat down beside him, and looked up expectantly.

What should he do? Go and find a bear to shoot? But why? It was the first time he had ever asked himself such a question. He had always come to the forest to hunt, as a matter of course, but suddenly he found himself wondering why he should wear himself out roaming the forest in search of prey. What for? For the meat, or the pelts? He had no need of either.

The gun weighed on his shoulder, and his whole body ached. He just wanted to find a dry place to lie down and rest. He had never got tired like this before – he could keep on the move for days on end, chasing through the forest after his quarry, feeling tired only when he halted for sleep.

He was in the middle of a blighted wilderness dotted with miserable fir trees. The air was sultry. No birds sang. Even the grasshoppers were not chirruping. It was quite empty. Only Kalinka was sitting waiting for orders. He was alone.

He had got away from people, but their lives would be going on as before. In the cowsheds the dairymaids must be loading milk churns on the truck that had just driven up, and they must be laughing and joking with the driver, while in the meadows over the river the mowing machines would be whirring and people would be making hayricks. What was so wrong about living the same way as the rest? Was he really better off sitting in some swamp like this, alone with Kalinka? He had to go back – back to the four walls of his house, where he would sit brooding day and night about that accursed bullet, not daring to go out for fear of seeing Mityagin or Nastya, or their little children.

If one thought about it, Simon was no more guilty than Donat Borovikov, who was no doubt sitting at that very moment in his office going through the kolkhoz accounts, and thinking neither of Mityagin nor of the bullet that Simon had shown him yesterday. He could understand Donat, but what about Dudyrev? Could he really be easy in his own mind about it all, and just go on shouting into his telephone? He must have a heart of stone . . .

Simon stood among the hummocks thickly overgrown with bilberry bushes, and clenched his heavy fists. Dudyrev was too high and mighty to be touched; if he had been a lesser man, Simon could have taught him a lesson . . .

Suddenly he felt overwhelmed by bitterness. Neither Donat Borovikov nor Dudyrev seemed all that upset, so why should he, Simon Teterin, want to be better than other people? Who did he think he was, playing the suffering Christ like this? Mityagin was no more his kith and kin than he was Donat's, say. For everybody else all his troubles were like water off a duck's back – they were all quite calm about it. Only he was eating his heart out, taking that bullet

around, first to Dudyrev, then to the Assistant Prosecutor.
They hated this bullet, almost baring their teeth at it, like
Kalinka at the sight of a stick. What a simpleton he was,
Simon told himself, not to have learned at his age that it
was no good resisting like this. Dudyrev and the Assistant
Prosecutor were not bears to be dealt with by the craft he
used in the forest. There was no point in a lap-dog barking
at a wolf. Nor was there any point in his feeling so guilty
and ashamed about Mityagin. You should only help people
when you could – otherwise mind your own business . . . as
for the bullet – to hell with it!

Simon put his hand in his pocket, pulled it out, looked at
it unhappily for the last time, and threw it away. Kalinka,
watching her master closely, rushed to the place where the
bullet had fallen, and sniffed at it; she was confused by all
this; she walked away.

If Simon had changed his mind and started looking for it
there in the thick moss covering the hummocks, he would
have been very unlikely to find it again. The bullet taken
from the bear and the truth hidden in it were now beyond
human ken.

Simon turned and strode back towards the village.

21

Dudyrev hardly knew anything about Mityagin. During
their short acquaintance at the time of the hunt, the man
had made only the vaguest of impressions on him – there
was nothing much to remember about him; he was just not
interesting. He felt sorry for him, but it was a rather
abstract feeling – the sort of impersonal pity one feels for
the victims of a railway accident reported in the newspapers. It was certainly not pity that had made Dudyrev
believe Simon Teterin, impelling him not to rest until the
truth was established. It was simply that he felt it was re-
pugnant to shelter behind someone who was weak and
defenceless. How could he keep his self-respect? What sort
of a life would it be if he despised himself ever afterwards?

He went to see Dityatichev again and told him calmly, in no uncertain terms, why he believed Simon Teterin. If the hunter had simply been out to save his friend and neighbour, he would have gone about it more prudently. He could have left the bullet as it was, instead of rolling it out to look as good as new. He would have taken it not to him, Dudyrev, but straight to the Assistant Prosecutor. Such trust was scarcely consistent with the actions of a man bent on deceit. As regards that dead tree – it did not block off the whole of the bridge from view. Furthermore, there was no sure evidence that the young man had fallen into the water exactly in the middle of the river. It was mere guess-work.

While Dudyrev was putting these points to Dityatichev, the Prosecutor Testov, tapping with his stick, had come into the office; he eased himself into an armchair, stretched out his good leg and gazed at them with his dark eyes narrowed under his shock of dry, curly hair.

Dudyrev was used to respect in the district and to people hanging on his every word. But on this occasion his arguments, however much he pressed them, made no impression. Dityatichev's face was, as usual, politely impassive, but the Prosecutor screwed up his dark eyes with curiosity, and under his bristling eyebrows, his face wore a look of faintly amused condescension. As soon as Dudyrev stopped, Dityatichev began to answer, point by point:

'Your reasoning is not without interest, but to discount the doctor's expert opinion, and welcome with open arms the somewhat doubtful evidence of the hunter, especially as he appears to be an interested party . . . a friend of Mityagin . . .'

At that point the Prosecutor, whose eyes had so far been fixed on Dudyrev, looked away.

They did not agree and they had no intention of agreeing. Dudyrev arguing against himself was to some extent a curious paradox: the eccentric behaviour of a distinguished citizen who was certain of his invulnerability. Dudyrev realised only too well that they felt amused and somewhat embarrassed on his behalf: why, they were thinking to themselves, was he playing this disingenuous game, pretending to be holier than the Pope of Rome?

What made it worse was that Testov, the Prosecutor, had the reputation in the district of being a man of unusual gifts. He was a great book-lover, knew the poetry of Blok and Esenin by heart, and it was said that in his speeches for the Prosecution, he always showed kindness and mercy. How could he, of all people, fail to understand that Dudyrev's attitude was not a pose, but the natural way for him to behave? Why didn't he understand that you cannot possibly keep your self-respect if you stoop to something despicable, even if it's only indirectly, through somebody else? So it was Dudyrev against Dudyrev. He was prepared to disregard his own very high standing in the district. Reputation may be an intangible thing, but it is a powerful one, and it threatened the Prosecutor and his Assistant with 'complications', forcing them to look for an easy way to the truth 'under a lamp-post'. And Dudyrev himself, with all his energy and firmness, trying to stand aside for the moment from his own reputation, seemed powerless to do anything about it.

'But just listen to me,' he said, 'listen, and don't be prejudiced by the fact that I'm putting myself in an awkward position. I would rather take my share of the blame than hide behind someone else's back.'

He spoke these last words with such emphasis that the Prosecutor lifted up his head in surprise, and Dityatichev's impassive face twitched. At last they understood that he really meant what he was saying, and was not just putting on an act.

'All right,' the Prosecutor said, 'we shall see Teterin again, and we assure you we shall be impartial.'

'That is precisely what I want.'

After Dudyrev left, the Prosecutor and his Assistant sat silent for a moment. Only when they heard the sound of Dudyrev's car starting outside did Dityatichev say:

'Damn it all, what a Quixote!'

'More like Nekhlyudov* – another example of that Russian conscience which could drive a man to follow a prostitute to Siberia.'

22

Next day Dityatichev summoned Simon Teterin to come and see him. Trying to make his voice sound as gentle as possible, he asked him to tell how and in what circumstances he had found the bullet. Could he produce witnesses who had seen the bullet before he rolled it into shape?

Simon's weather beaten face grew still darker.

'There is no bullet,' he said in a low voice.

'What do you mean? Did you find a bullet, or didn't you?'

'You can take it I didn't. There isn't one, and that's all there is to say.'

Pressing his lips together firmly, the Assistant Prosecutor looked Simon up and down with contempt. How misleading appearances could be! There he was, sitting in front of him, his powerful shoulders now round and hunched, his stern face full of gloom, and the scar on his cheekbone suggesting a sort of untamed strength . . . It was a guileless, honest face, and yet his eyes were shifty now, and he was cagey and resentful as he denied what he had said previously.

'I must know exactly: did you find a bullet in the bear's carcass after the doctor had examined it, or didn't you?'

Simon was silent for a long time, and at last got out the words:

'No, I did not.'

'That means that last time you were lying to me.'

Again a silence.

'Did you lie, or didn't you?'

'You can take it I lied, if you like.'

Dityatichev was unable to get anything further out of him.

As he walked home, Simon remembered how pleasantly,

* Hero of Tolstoy's *Resurrection*.

almost kindly, the Assistant Prosecutor had started questioning him. Cunning as a fox, he was, trying to get Simon to admit he had found the bullet. It was not difficult to guess his reasons for this – they must have decided to put the blame on Simon as well as Mityagin, on the grounds that there was nothing to choose between them, and they must both be made to answer. What a poor fool they took him for, all these clever people – they thought they'd have him all tied up in knots in no time! But they were wasting their time now: the bullet was buried in the forest and they'd never get it out of him – not even with a pair of tongs! Though even without the bullet, they would try to catch him out somehow and he could end up going on a long journey at government expense to live on bread and water – what a disgrace at his time of life!

From that day onwards it was not the pangs of conscience that tormented Simon, but fear. All the time he felt that something dreadful was secretly being got up against him behind his back – something so obscure that he would never be able to get to grips with it. There was nothing he could do and for the first time in his life he felt as powerless and helpless as a child.

23

The summer had passed, and with the start of the rains, the roads had turned to mud. That autumn there was no afterglow of summer – no golden days with the birch trees gleaming under a sun that was no longer hot, aspens ablaze with crimson foliage and rustling leaves filling up the cart tracks. The forest became bare and the first frosts struck without anybody noticing how it had happened.

All autumn there had been quite a struggle to get the harvest in. Many offices in the district town were closed so that the employees could work on the collective farms. Dudyrev took men off his building site and sent them into the fields.

Because of all this trouble with the harvest, people completely forgot about the accident which had happened during the hunt in the middle of that summer. And if anybody happened to mention it, people just yawned – it was stale news by now.

Mityagin went on living his usual quiet life, only leaving his house to go to work, but he looked older and thinner, as though he had shrivelled somehow. He stopped drinking, spent a lot of time with the children, worked in the garden, and dutifully put up with all Nastya's nagging. There was more peace and quiet in the family than there had been since the beginning of the marriage.

Mityagin and Simon kept out of each other's way, exchanging only a few inconsequential words if they happened to meet face to face and never mentioning the hunt.

Simon, like everybody, helped on the collective farm. He mended the drier, and worked on the threshing floor. He rarely went out into the forest and when he did, he had no luck; all he got was a fox. On one of his fruitless expeditions Kalinka broke a leg and the bone would not knit again – her age was beginning to tell.

Sometimes even Simon forgot about the accident, and for several days did not think of the bullet. But after a few such peaceful days, his fears always returned to haunt him even more. If 'they' were so quiet, it was only because 'they' were lying low for the moment. It was the calm before the storm. But there was no question of the case being dropped. Sooner or later there would be a trial. It was true that the Assistant Prosecutor had not called Simon in again and he had not been asked to sign an undertaking not to leave the district, as Mityagin had. But they knew perfectly well that Simon wouldn't leave anyway, so they didn't have to make him sign a statement. There was bound to be a trial and then they would ask him about the bullet in front of everybody. What an ordeal! But there was no bullet, and that's all there was to it. He was not going to be a scapegoat for anybody!

He continued to think of Dudyrev with hatred. Most of all he resented the fact that everyone was always singing his praises: Dudyrev was going to pull down the barracks and give every family an apartment, he had put a stop to graft

on the site, he was so courteous, he was so kind. Simon
knew how kind he was all right! The way people could be
bought for a tot of vodka!

During the first frosts Glashka Popova came running
into Simon's house and brought him a summons to attend
court . . .

24

Simon was put into an adjoining room all by himself and
told to wait. He sat and tried to listen; all he could hear were
muffled voices through the walls. He imagined Mityagin,
and how everybody would be staring at him, whispering
and pointing. Surely there could be nothing more frightening in the world than to be put in front of people and
covered in shame like this. Simon would rather have tackled
an enraged she-bear with his naked hands than have stood
there in Mityagin's place.

It was true that Dudyrev was sitting there next to him.
However much the Assistant Prosecutor had tried, he could
not completely exonerate Dudyrev from some part in the
killing. But it was clear to everybody that Dudyrev was
there only for appearances' sake. Mityagin was a poor shot
and the evidence about the dead tree behind the bear
would also tell against him. He was the one who was going
to take all the blame. Dudyrev would just sit it out and
might even hear a thing or two that would make him blush.
But he had nothing to fear – he would certainly be found
innocent.

Simon waited for a long time, almost sick with fear. At
last the door was opened.

'Witness Teterin, please!'

Simon stood by the table, sideways to the public, and
managed to see that Donat Borovikov was sitting in the
front row and staring at him with a hard, straitlaced look
on his face. He could not see anyone else, but he felt they
were all looking at him with curiosity as though he were a
stranger.

Simon had often met the People's Judge, Evdokia

Teplyakova and he had once even chatted casually with her on the river bank while waiting for a boat to take him across. He remembered that they had talked about something very trifling – about mushrooms, which had been particularly good that year. Teplyakova was a quiet woman with a large family and lots of worries. Simon looked at her hands, as they lay on some papers in front of her – they were the hands of a housewife, rough with short nails; the sort of hands that did the children's washing, scrubbed floors and dug potatoes. She had no husband, and had a hard time making ends meet.

Teplyakova and all the rest sat close together round a table. They were ordinary sort of people, with nothing bad about them – if need be they would always be ready with a kind word or a helping hand. But not on this occasion: Simon was separated from them by a red-covered table.

Teplyakova glanced around with an impersonal look, and picked up one of the papers in front of her.

'Witness Simon Ivanovich Teterin, born in the year 1904, occupation hunter, place of residence the village of Volok, Gustoi Bor district . . . Witness Teterin, have you been informed that for giving false evidence you are liable under articles . . .'

Evdokia Teplyakova's tone of voice was now very different from the one in which she had discussed mushrooms with Simon.

'Witness Teterin,' she addressed him in a stern, formal manner, 'tell the court what happened during the hunt on the night of July 14th–15th of this year. Try and remember everything.'

Simon coughed timidly into his hand, and began to tell haltingly about how they had chased the bear, how they had driven him to the bridge, how he, Simon, hearing the accordion, had shouted something.

'Witness Teterin, had you ever known the accused, Mityagin, go hunting on any previous occasion?'

Simon's heart fell. They were already trying to trip him up.

'N-no,' he admitted.

'You knew that he did not know how to handle a gun?'

'N-no. He said he'd used a gun a bit before.'

'And you believed him?'

'Yes.'

'Witness Teterin, you brought a bullet to the Assistant Prosecutor which you claimed you got out of the dead bear. You told him that the doctor who searched for this bullet had not found it. Do you confirm this?'

Here it was . . . Simon's palms grew wet; he was silent, stopped and stared gloomily at the floor. Here it was, the moment he had dreaded most of all, living in fear of it for many days and weeks. Everybody waited silently for what he would say. But it was as though he had been struck dumb. Should he confess? Should he tell the truth? But the bullet was lying in the moss, in the middle of a swamp, and the devil himself would not be able to find it now.

'Witness Teterin, do you understand the question?'

'There is no bullet,' Simon said at last with a great effort.

'You say that you did not show a bullet to the Assistant Prosecutor?'

'I do not know of any bullet.'

'Assistant Prosecutor Dityatichev, you confirm that Witness Simon Ivanovich Teterin showed you a bullet, which he said he had taken out of the bear's carcass and which fitted the barrel of the gun used by Mityagin.'

'I confirm that,' Dityatichev answered, rising in his seat.

'On what date was that?'

'On the 16th of July, the day after the event.'

'Witness Teterin, do you still wish to state that you did not bring a bullet to the Assistant Prosecutor?'

'N-no.'

'What does your "no" mean? Did you bring him the bullet or did you not?'

'I brought it.'

'As Witness Dudyrev has stated, you also showed him the bullet?'

'I showed it to him too.'

'According to further evidence, you then denied your

possession of the bullet and that you had taken it out of the bear?'

'I did deny that,' said Simon, bending his head even lower.

'That means that the bullet did not come out of the bear and that you simply showed him some other bullet? Is that the case?'

Simon was silent. He felt completely crushed; his body seemed heavy and no longer obedient to his will; his legs were tired, his knees were trembling. He had really tied himself in knots. If he were to tell the truth and say he had taken the bullet out of the bear, that he had found it right under the skull, lodged in a vertebra at the back of the neck, that he had later rolled it into shape, then they would ask: Why did you deny this earlier? What are we to believe? Why are you trying to mislead the court? Where is the bullet? Why did you throw it away? There would be no end to their questions, but the truth had been buried together with the bullet.

The court waited; he could not be silent for ever, and taking a deep breath he got out the one word: 'Yes,' a lying word, which sounded strangled.

'You did *not* get it out of the bear?' Teplyakova insisted.

'No.'

'You brought it to save Mityagin from punishment?'

Now he had no choice but to go on lying, and he again said with an effort: 'Yes.'

For a moment there was an oppressive silence. Simon stood there with his head bowed.

'Are there any more questions for the Prosecution? For the Defence? No? Witness Teterin, have you anything else to add to your evidence?'

Simon Teterin had nothing more to say; he could hardly stand up.

'Witness Teterin, you are free. You may stay in the courtroom and listen to the proceedings.'

Stumbling, unseeing, Simon made his way towards the public seats. Someone – he did not see who – was sorry for him and gave him a place on a bench. He sat down heavily and stared at the floor until he heard Dudyrev's voice.

In a soft leather jacket, clean shaven, Dudyrev stood firmly, feet apart, in front of the Judge's table, displaying no embarrassment or nervousness. He answered the questions briefly, precisely and calmly. Had he heard Simon Teterin's warning? Yes, he had, but it had been too late and he had fired almost at the same moment. Had he heard the sound of the accordion? No, he had not heard it.

After the usual concluding question: 'Have you anything to add to your evidence?' Dudyrev slightly bowed his large head, and said firmly:

'Yes, I have.'

The public behind Simon Teterin's back, already attentive, became hushed and Simon could hear his own heavy breathing.

'I know,' Dudyrev began deliberately, and calmly as before, 'that the Prosecution has taken into account certain circumstantial evidence which points to Mityagin and makes my own position easier, so I want to state now, in front of the court, that I do not consider myself less guilty. We both fired simultaneously. I am a better shot than Mityagin, but that cannot completely rule out the fact that I may have missed the bear. Mention has been made of the dead tree which hid the middle of the bridge from me. But the dead man only had to take half a step forward, and my bullet only had to miss the tree trunk by half an inch for the Prosecutor's theory to collapse. Witness Teterin now denies that he found the bullet. I do not intend to accuse him of false evidence or to reproach him for his inconsistency. The fact is that the bullet is just not here, and which of us killed the young man is still a mystery to me, as it is to everyone else. We are both guilty – both equally guilty.'

The public buzzed appreciatively.

'But this does not mean that I humbly accept my guilt. I am certain that no one has any intention of accusing either Mityagin or me of premeditated murder. We can only be found guilty of negligence. But is this negligence criminal? We were shooting in a forest, where there are no laws and

no private notices to say that shooting as such is forbidden
or restricted. We could not have imagined that there might
be somebody behind the bushes. The place where we were
shooting is very out of the way and only one or two people
a day ever pass that bridge. Neither I nor Mityagin heard
the accordion. Teterin heard it, but he is a very much more
experienced hunter than either of us. Teterin's shout was
practically simultaneous with our shots, and we simply had
no time to realise what it meant. And I think that no one
would suggest that either of us would have deliberately
pressed the trigger if we had heard the shout in time and
realised its significance. I do not consider myself in any way
a criminal, and, therefore, I do not consider Mityagin a
criminal. But if the court does not agree with my opinion
and nevertheless considers it necessary to pass sentence,
then I must share the blame equally with Mityagin.'

Simon sat listening with a stony, impassive face, his
scarred cheek bone protruding and his eyes almost closed.
Nobody looking at him at that moment would have suspected that this man with the stony face was inwardly
squirming with shame.

25

In his summing-up the Prosecutor did not insist on punishment and the People's Assessors* were not long in coming to
a decision.

The court agreed to exonerate Mityagin, taking into
account the fact that Simon Teterin's warning shout of
danger had been given too late.

Together with everyone else, Simon stood as the verdict
was read out and then he went out of the courtroom with
the crowd murmuring its approval. Only outside in the
road did he pull his cap on to his head.

People were in no hurry to get away and stamped around

* Assistants to the Judge, who in Soviet legal practice have
the right to ask questions during the proceedings and advise in
the passing of sentence, rather like a jury.

on the snow which had just fallen, talking cheerfully among themselves. Everyone felt that something good and fine had taken place. All of them as they stood under the lamppost, on which the lamp was swaying slightly in the wind, were drawn close to each other by a sincere desire to share their joy.

Mityagin came out of the courtroom with his wife, and was at once surrounded. He was patted on the shoulder, and congratulated, and there were simple-minded little jokes:

'Had you already packed your underwear?'

'Bet you're not sorry you didn't have to make the long journey after all . . .'

Mityagin twisted the shabby cap which sat crookedly on his bald head; he was deeply moved and he muttered the same thing over and over again, almost in tears:

'What a terrible thing! What a terrible thing.'

Evidently these words had stuck in his mind during recent weeks.

Nastya, standing next to him, in a warm shawl, held her head high and looked around at the people triumphantly, as much as to say: 'There now, we are not convicts. The truth will out.'

All at once, the talk died away and everybody dispersed.

The Prosecutor and his Assistant came out arm in arm. Dityatichev was tall and straight, the Prosecutor came only up to his shoulder and limped heavily. From the way in which they walked, it was clear that they were not at all upset by the happiness of the people lingering outside the courtroom.

Dudyrev went past, walking briskly, nodding goodbye to right and to left.

Donat Borovikov came out and stopped in front of Mityagin. Strong and stocky, with a swaggering gait, he said condescendingly:

'There, you thought we were going to eat you. But you needn't have worried – people are much kinder than you think. We don't trust each other enough. It's a great thing, trust, isn't it?'

'What a terrible thing. I would never have thought . . .'

Simon, standing on one side, felt cheated. He had had one consolation – one small, uncertain, slightly shameful feeling, which was nevertheless a consolation. He had decided that all men are equally bad, and that someone like Dudyrev was out just to save his skin, and had no conscience. So there had been no point in his trying to be better than other people. But now Dudyrev had stood up for Mityagin, and said he was ready to share his punishment. It was a lesson to Simon not to think ill of others. There was no excuse for him. He should have been the first to rejoice at Mityagin's acquittal. Everybody was happy and filled with goodwill. Everybody except him.

As Simon stood sadly in the cheerful crowd, he suddenly heard a familiar voice. He turned round and saw that it was Mikhailo Lyskov, the father of the boy who had been killed during the hunt. He was standing there shivering in his shabby coat, staring with vacant eyes at the people standing round Mityagin.

'We can't bring Pashka back,' he was saying to a strapping youth in a loose quilted coat. 'There's no sense in spoiling other people's lives. I won't be any happier if someone else is in trouble.'

'Two wrongs don't make a right,' the youth agreed.

Surely Mikhailo should have been angry with everybody! Yet here he was, not at all bitter, behaving like a human being. How much simpler it would have been for Simon not to disgrace himself. But he had lied and betrayed Mityagin. Mikhailo's voice went through him like a knife. He turned away from the crowd and walked off home in the darkness.

26

At this same time Dudyrev was sitting in his car going along the road which stood out black against the snow-covered fields. He was thinking of Simon.

He had denied finding the bullet, but something prevented Dudyrev from believing his denial completely. Whatever it was, whether the hunter had lied just now to the court, or whether he had lied to him earlier when he had

brought him that bullet which was not the one – in either
case, it was an ugly business.

Nobody, it seemed, could have been more a 'man of the
people' than Simon Teterin, the bear hunter. From his
earliest years, Dudyrev had been accustomed to thinking
of the ordinary people with almost religious veneration. He
expected more of someone like Simon Teterin than he did
of himself. Here was an old bear hunter, a man to whom
introspection was unknown, a 'natural' man – it was impossible for a university graduate, an intellectual like
Dudyrev, not to be moved by him. What Dudyrev had forgotten was that, though moved by Teterin, he was himself
building new factories, bringing in new gadgets and whether
he liked it or not – making life much more complicated.
Then he was surprised because someone like Simon, once
he had left the forest with its harsh but simple laws, was
lost and confused, not knowing any longer how he should
behave.

People change more slowly than the life around them.
You build a factory and life is no longer the same in Gustoi
Bor. A Project can be put up in three or four years, but it
takes a score or so of years to form a man's character. It is
not enough to build a factory, to lay roads, and to move the
people into well-designed houses. All this is necessary, but
it is not enough. People must also be taught how to live.

Blind devotion is not love. True love is active.

27

At home Simon's wife was making mash for their cow.
Seeing him coming through the door, she straightened up,
hurriedly wiped her hands on the curtain, and asked in a
worried way:

'Well, what happened? What did you get?'

Simon did not answer, but pulled off his short, worn coat,
patched with army cloth. His wife interpreted his silence in
her own way; she put her bony hand up to her wrinkled
cheek, mournfully shook her head, and began to wail
quietly.

'And who will look after your children, you poor wretch?
The girl is quite out of hand as it is, so what can I do with
her if her father goes away? Oh, my God, you never know
what's going to happen next!'

'Hush,' Simon snapped at her. 'Go off and see Silantikha,'
and seeing that his wife was about to protest, he shouted at
her in a deafening voice: 'Didn't you hear? Quickly.'

His wife obediently put on a shawl.

Silantikha, a solitary old woman, lived three doors away,
in eternal fear of the policeman and the kolkhoz chairman,
Donat Borovikov – she distilled vodka which in times of
need she sold secretly.

Simon went to his own room, and without putting on the
light, sat down at the table with his elbows on it, and
gripped his head with his hands. Outside it was as dark and
quiet as in a cellar. Only on the other side of the passage, in
the shed, he could hear the cow moving about restlessly
because it had not had its feed.

Suddenly the quiet outside was broken by a dog's
anguished howl. It was Kalinka. She knew nothing of her
master's troubles and she was not raising her voice to the
dark sky out of devotion to him: she had her own irreparable
misfortunes. Her paw had not healed, and during the last
hunt she had lost the scent three times. She often had to lie
down to rest. As she understood only too well with her dog's
instinct, her powers were leaving her.

Simon realised that he would not hunt with Kalinka again.
Her time was past, she was finished.

He sat there, gripping his head in his broad hands.

How had this happened? As long as he could remember,
he had never had to blush before people, he had been sure
of his own worth. What had he come to in the last few
months? He felt he had lived the life of a rabbit. How could
this have happened to him. It wouldn't have been so bad if
he had been in real trouble – but he had not been in any
danger at all! What he had thought was a wild beast was
only a scarecrow . . . More than anything he had feared
disgrace, and now here he was – up to his ears in it! It was
a lesson for him. But what good was it to him now? At

seventeen he could have learned it, but he was an old man. In four years he would be sixty. Wasn't that a little late to learn?

Simon clutched his head, and wanted to howl like Kalinka. There is no worse judgement than the judgement of your own conscience.

Under the title *Sud* this story first appeared in *Novy Mir* 3, 1961, pp. 15–60.

Creature of a Day

All Nastya's screaming, all her tears were of no avail. Keshka Gubin, her common-law husband, had already packed his bag; he now threw on a sheepskin coat, jammed his cap on sideways and said with a nod at the door:

'Well, if you won't come it's your own look-out – goodbye and good luck to you. I'm not going to spend the rest of my life wallowing in pig shit, even with you!'

The door clicked open, Keshka's leggings were enveloped in frosty vapour, and in a moment he had disappeared.

She had shouted at the top of her voice, she had implored him and finally she had burst out crying. Now she looked round her at the untidy room – a woollen scarf with a check pattern lay on a bench where Keshka had forgotten it.

With a rustle like the scurrying of mice, Nastya's mother climbed down from the stove on which she had been lying. She stood, bent in two, her sallow face seamed with dry wrinkles. Her eyes had the sad, bleary expression that Nastya remembered from childhood.

'Dear, why don't you go away and leave me? I'm just an old woman who doesn't know how to die, and I'm poisoning your life for you.'

Tearing her hair, Nastya threw herself on the bench and sobbed:

'Oh, why do I never have any luck? Why is there a curse on my life?'

Her mother sat down by her, stroked her heaving shoulders with her skinny hand and repeated:

'You should have gone with him, dear, you really should. I can't last much longer.'

But Nastya had cried her fill. Her face swollen and her hair dishevelled, she rose to her feet and said quietly:

'We'd better go to bed now. I have to be up early tomorrow.'

Walking towards the room in which she and Keshka had slept till the night before in a big bed with nickel-plated knobs, she added:

'After all, we managed well enough before he came along.'

2

Nastya had been five years old when the war broke out. She could still remember clearly how one day her mother had rushed into the cottage, fussing and agitated: how she had hustled Nastya into a warm coat, wound a scarf around her head and cried:

'They're coming, they're coming! Gracious heavens, it may be the last time . . . Oh, hurry up, you silly girl, for mercy's sake hurry!'

Dragging Nastya by the hand, she ran off across the field that lay between the village and the highway. It was an overcast autumn day, and the muddy road was edged with damp stubble. Carts laden with bursting bundles were moving along it, village men straggled behind them wearing waterproofs, quilted jackets or ordinary overcoats. They were on their way from the district call-up office to board the train that was to take them to join the army.

Suddenly Nastya's father, a large red-faced man, broke away from the long line and ran towards them, stumbling over the furrows. He caught Nastya up into his arms and kissed her: his breath smelt of vodka. Then her mother hung about his neck and he began gently and kindly to push her away, looking round at his comrades and saying with an unfamiliar, uncertain kind of defiance: 'Come on, there's nothing to cry about. You know me – I'll come back covered in medals or die in a ditch.'

As he said this, he gazed about him with an expression of bravado. He had never been a drinking man – he was reckoned as one of the quietest in the village.

'Come back covered in medals or die in a ditch. You know me.'

The muddy road stretched on through the wet, dark stubble, under a sky that looked like damp felt. The men plodded along behind the carts, and women sobbed and sighed as the fine rain fell. That was the last time Nastya saw her father – he must have died in a ditch after all.

As the war went on, they took not only the men but the horses away from the village. The women formed themselves into teams of five to do the ploughing, first for one farm and then for another: four would be harnessed and pull the plough, while the fifth guided it from behind. But they were always short of bread, because that was taken for the army. They saved the flour from autumn till spring, when there was heavy work to be done and you couldn't get through it without proper food. In summer Nastya would collect a quantity of grass, which they dried and then pounded to a fine dust: this they scalded twice over with boiling water and mixed with eggs to make a sort of pancake. The cakes were heavy, dark-brown things that looked like cow-pies. With them they ate potatoes which they mixed with milk, browned and covered in amber-coloured butter. They had their own cow, so there was milk and butter to spare. The cakes made their bellies swell up, but no matter how much they ate, they still felt hungry. They also ate dried husks of flax, but at least they were not reduced to eating the bark of trees. There was barley on the farm too, but they used to reap it while it was still green, since you couldn't live on grass for ever.

However, Nastya throve even on a diet of grass, while her mother grew more and more hunched and sickly. She would give up her last scraps of food and make Nastya eat them, and after the day's work on the farm was over she would trudge off to the marshy Kuzkin valley, five miles away, where she would stand all night knee-deep in water, scything away to get fodder for the cow so it would stay alive and Nastya wouldn't starve. During this time a man by the name of Ivan Istomin began to court Nastya's mother: he was one of those who had not 'died in a ditch' but only lost a leg. He walked around on crutches and made felt boots for a living. 'How about you and me getting hitched?' he kept saying. 'Two can pull a cart better than one. It's no use waiting for your Stepan to come back.' Nastya's mother knew very well that Stepan was not coming back, but she turned Ivan down: she was worried about how he might treat Nastya – she wasn't his own flesh and blood after all. She felt she must put Nastya's happiness before her own.

Nastya was growing up: she was not tall, but sturdy and full-bosomed, with good, firm shoulders. She had rosy cheeks that quivered as she walked, and long, sparse eyelashes. While she grew her mother wasted away: for three years now she had not stirred further than the outside of the cottage fence, where she sat in the sun, wearing a cotton dress, with her arms folded in her lap. her face pale and wizened. She could still do housework, light the stove and cook meals, but no longer carry logs from the stack or water from the well. Yet she was only fifty-six, the same age as Mityukova, the village teacher, whom no one ever thought of as a grandmother.

Nastya was much the same as other girls, perhaps better than most, but lately, whenever her mother looked at her she used to sigh: 'Oh dear, that gipsy must have laid a curse on your father all right.'

When Nastya's father was a little boy, he and some of his friends had teased a gipsy who was passing through the village, jumping around him and yelling: 'Gipsy man, gipsy man, sell us your mare – she ain't worth a penny and neither are you!' There were several boys in the group, but for some reason the gipsy with the hooked nose and unkempt beard had pointed his gnarled finger at little Stepan and spat out a curse, as though he was a grown-up:

'You shall never prosper! You shall slip on dry ground and trip on level ground! Your family shall never have happiness, and neither shall your children! They shall be covered in scabs and weep bitter tears, down to the fifth generation!'

The curse had so impressed everybody that for years later, if anything went wrong for Nastya's father, they would say at once, 'You see, the gipsy was right – he slips

on dry ground and trips on level ground.' And in the war
he came to grief, sure enough . . .

Nastya had a young man called Venka – a tractor-driver
earning good wages, a quiet fellow, not given to drink.
When they took him for his military service he had said:
'As soon as I come home I'll come straight to you and we'll
get married.' But he never did come back after his time was
up. They heard he had a good job, operating a power-
excavator somewhere near Cheliabinsk.

Time passed. There weren't many young men in the
village, and every year there was a fresh crop of young girls.
If Nastya wasn't careful, she'd be left on the shelf. Her
mother kept looking at her and sighing: 'It's all that old
devil of a gipsy's fault.'

One day Keshka Gubin, sporting a reindeer cap and a
gold tooth, had turned up from Vorkuta. He had made a
pile there, but had got sick of the north, where there wasn't
a tree to be seen. His sister Pavla was a girl from Dor village
who had married Senka Ponyushin. She and Nastya were
neighbours and friends: they used to borrow leaven from
each other in the mornings, and on twilit evenings they
would sit together gossiping about everyone in the village.
Nastya met Keshka at Pavla's house, and they got on well
from the start. He was over thirty and anxious to settle
down; he had brought his things from one house to the
other and moved in with her, and now this was the result.
'I'm not going to spend the rest of my life wallowing in pig
shit.' He had hankered after town life and kept urging her
to 'chuck everything in and come away'. But how could she
leave her sick mother, who had looked after her when she
was tiny and gone without food for her sake? They wouldn't
be allowed to have her with them in a hostel, and even if
they got an apartment of their own some day, what would
Nastya find to do in town? The only thing she knew anything about was pig-keeping.

'You shall slip on dry ground and trip on level ground,'
the gipsy had said . . .

So off Keshka went, slamming the door. She had done her
best to stop him, with tears, entreaties and arguments – a

quiet life was best, there hadn't been poverty on the farm
for years – but it had been useless. All that was left of him
was the scarf lying on the bench, and the only consolation:
'We managed well enough before he came along.'

3

The pale, watery dawn broke slowly over the dark, jagged
tree-tops. Through the menacing bluish snow which lay
around the hamlet of Utitsy, a path had been beaten which
linked it with the highway, the farm headquarters at
Verkhneye Koshelevo, the district centre of Zagarye, the
whistle-stop station of Yezhegodka and the whole wide
world.

Just outside Utitsy a long, low building stood by itself,
crushed almost to the ground by a heavy blanket of snow.
This was the piggery where Nastya spent her days.

The village was still asleep. Not a single window was
alight, not a single curl of smoke came from the chimneys.
Only a faint sound of cocks crowing could be heard from
inside the timbered barns. Utitsy was asleep – Nastya was
always up and about before anyone else, and now, in a
shabby quilted jacket with a scarf around her head, she
hurried towards the solitary building, crunching the snow
under her big rubber boots – felt ones would have been
soaked through long before she reached the piggery.

The snow squeaked under foot and the cocks crowed; the
air held a threatening bluish tinge, while the dawn continued
to spread feebly from the horizon. The narrow windows of
the piggery winked at her slyly from under their snowy
brows. It had all been the same yesterday and the day before, and it would be the same tomorrow and the day after.
Nastya's life was so familiar that she felt she had been in the
world for centuries, not for twenty-seven years.

In a moment now she would cross the trampled common-
pasture land, lift the heavy padlock off the door and feel
on her face the warm, fermented atmosphere of the pigsty.
She would light the fire under the cooker and, while waiting
for it to boil, she would fill the potato-crusher with small

potatoes from a sack. That was how her working day began.

At nine o'clock she would hear the swish of sledge-runners outside the building and an old man's cracked voice:

'Come on, Cinderella, get a move on! Hey, are you still alive?'

She would fling the door open saying, 'Yes, here I am!' and old Isay Kalachov would lug in his sacks of potatoes with their musty reek of chaff and bran. It was a fairly generous load, but Nastya could not help grumbling:

'How many times have I told you? If the potatoes are frost-bitten, they should give me more. And surely they could spare a cupful of flour, this is nothing but chaff. The pigs won't get fat on this stuff.'

Old Isay, rolling a thick cigarette, would reply with a pompous and knowing air:

'The scientists are now trying to figure out a way to fatten pigs on air. That'll be the day we catch up with the Americans – you mark my words!'

An hour to an hour and a half later, there would be the roar of a large truck, and Zhenka Kruchinin would arrive with cans of whey and skim-milk from the dairy.

'Well, my girl, how are things? It's cold in this cab, you should come and warm me up.'

'I'll give you a clout on the ear if you're not careful – that'll warm you up! Here, give me the cans – you're a cheeky devil, aren't you? I wonder how Glashka ever puts up with you.'

'Well, she doesn't complain – she must like me!'

Glashka was a good match for Zhenka – she had a ready tongue, and would never let a fellow go by without trying her luck with him. They had been married for two years, had two children and seemed to be happy together.

All Nastya wanted was the simplest kind of happiness – like Glashka's, Pavla's and everybody else's, with a husband – even a joker like this one, children and a warm, friendly home where her mother could live out her days in peace. The same sort of happiness that other people enjoyed – they seemed to find it without any trouble, while Nastya ate her heart out. Yet she wasn't pock-marked or a hunch-back,

and by now she was as well paid as almost anybody on the
farm. How easily she and Keshka could have made a real
home together!

The manager of the farm, Artemy Bogdanovich Pegikh,
had said at the last meeting in front of everybody: 'One day
the name of Nastya Syroyegina will be famous throughout
the district – she will be the pride and boast of our kolkhoz!'
Artemy Bogdanovich was fond of high-sounding expres-
sions. And what he said might have come true – he was
always making prophecies of this kind – if it hadn't been for
Artemy Bogdanovich himself . . .

4

Nastya lifted off the heavy padlock, pushed open the door
which had stuck, and – instead of the usual smell of a
healthy pigsty, sharp and biting like that of fermented
liquor, she encountered a sour, stifling, fetid atmosphere
that made her feel dizzy.

She walked past the potato-crusher and the stove, with
the cooker cemented on top, to the part of the building
where the pigs lived. She groped for the wall-switch and
turned on the light. From the far corner she heard the
boar Dandelion, wheezing heavily like an old man. The
pink, corpulent brood-sow known as Goldy rolled to her
feet with an effort: her floppy ears hung forward, and her
little black eyes peered out from under them with a resigned,
intelligent, reproachful expression, as if to say: 'Well, what
trick is this you've played on me?' Her piglets lay about her
feet, squealing feebly. They were about a month old, but
still no bigger than so many mittens: cold, grey miserable
creatures that would not grow, however much one tended
them. Now Nastya saw at once that two of them were
motionless – they lay stretched out stiffly, looking longer
and thinner than the others.

She had been expecting something of the kind. Two days
ago, the piglets had started to scour.

She looked around the familiar piggery. It was not
modern, but it was sturdy enough – it had been built when

the kolkhoz was beginning to make its way successfully. The sties were divided by gratings, not plain ones but pieces of carved metal that had once belonged to the railing round a church. Everyone who first saw the place admired them. Today it looked clean and tidy as usual; the boar was wheezing away in the corner, there was the usual puffing and rustling and squealing – but the air was so bad it took your breath away. Two of the piglets were done for, and what was going to happen to the rest?

She had known it all along – it was Artemy Bogdanovich's fault, but she would get the blame, and for this she had only herself to thank.

Artemy Bogdanovich was a man who sometimes got carried away by grandiose plans. Sitting in his office one day, he had done some figuring on paper and worked things out as follows. The sows farrow twice a year, in spring and summer, just when the barns are empty but the pastures are beginning to be full of grass. This is wasted as far as the piglets are concerned, because they are too small to be turned loose; but if they were farrowed in winter they could feed on the grass and stewed nettles in spring. They could be fattening all through the summer, and by autumn they would be fatter than those farrowed in spring, so there would be a double profit and the farm would be able to increase its quota of pig-meat.

Artemy Bogdanovich had promised Nastya that she would get plenty of cod-liver oil and be able to give the piglets all the vitamins they needed. Unfortunately it turned out that they could not get the oil in bulk: it was only sold at the chemist in small bottles, for which you needed a doctor's prescription, and in any case it would have been ruinous to buy it for the pigs in this way. Artemy Bogdanovich had also promised to provide an extra quantity of sprouting grain, which was said to contain some special vitamin or other. But then a proposal came up to buy two five-ton lorries, and to get the money they had to supply the authorities with an extra quantity of grain against payment. The chance of buying the lorries was too good to miss, and this meant goodbye to Nastya's hopes of getting the

sprouting grain for her piglets. Nonetheless, Artemy Bogdanovich continued to swear by her as the future 'pride and
boast of the kolkhoz'.

It was true what they said about misfortunes never
coming singly. Last night Keshka had walked out on her,
and now in the morning there was this disaster. Nastya
went from one sow to the other, dragging out the dead
piglets from under them. Seven – in a single night! And this
was only the beginning!

She went out into the yard and fetched a wheelbarrow,
threw the dead piglets in and carted them off.

The bluish hue of the snow was lighter now, the air
clearer; a pink glow showed in the sky above the misty
forest, and there was a touch of frost. The piglets lay in a
pile in the dirty wheelbarrow, like so many small logs. Their
snouts were stiff in death, their eyes showed blearily
through half-closed lids, the bristles stood up along their
sharp spines. There you were – once the disease started, it
spread like wild fire and there was no putting it out.

Nastya stood in the frosty air watching the pink glow of
the sky, and felt as if her whole life were falling to pieces. Up
to now she had at least been successful in one thing – her
work. She had been praised unsparingly and given good
wages – last year she had been able to afford a coat with a
lambskin collar, her sick mother wanted for nothing, and in
summer she had been going to buy a motor-cycle for
Keshka. Now everything had fallen in ruins about her ears.
She was bound to be reprimanded and criticised, and they
wouldn't think twice about docking her pay. The girls who
had envied her would soon be giggling about the 'pride of
the kolkhoz'.

But it was no good standing here moaning. The first thing
was to isolate the sick piglets in a pen by themselves; then
she must wash down the floors and walls and partitions
with scalding water and run to the store for disinfectant. It
was like a fire – the only hope was to stop it spreading in
time. Suddenly, from inside, she heard a chorus of squeals –
the healthy pigs wanted to be fed, blast them, so she must
light the fire and start the potato-crusher. Day after day it

was the same thing – feed the pigs and clear out the dung.
'I'm not going to wallow in pig shit . . .' Keshka had said. If
only she had gone away with him and thrown up the whole
cursed business. She would have, if it hadn't been for her
mother.

It was quite light now: the electric bulbs shone faintly
against the ceiling. From outside came the familiar swish
of Isay's sledge.

'Come on, get a move on! Don't keep me waiting
here!'

Isay's straggly beard was curled at the edges with hoar-
frost; his wrinkled cheeks were a purplish colour. He rubbed
them with his mittens, then gestured with his shabby cap
towards the piggery door.

'Got a plague on your hands, have you? A whole barrow-
ful . . .'

The tears stung her eyes once more.

'I'm sick to death of it all. It's all the fault of Artemy
Bogdanovich – he kept at me until I did what he wanted.'

'We all know a willing horse doesn't even need to be
shod.'

'Listen, Isay, are you going to the village? Take me with
you. Take me, and take what's in the barrow there.'

'What for? No one's found a way of bringing pigs back to
life yet, any more than people.'

'I'm going to throw them on his desk in front of his nose
and see how he likes it.'

Isay grunted. 'Well, he'll make sure that somebody else
pays for it. A bad ploughman blames his horse.'

5

Dressed in her old quilted jacket with its smell of pigs, her
rubber boots stained with dung and her scarf askew, her
lips tight-pressed and an angry glitter in her eye, Nastya
pushed her way through the outer office, dragging the filthy
sack behind her. She made straight for Artemy Bogdanovich's door, which she pushed with her toe. Behind her came
old Isay, grinning slyly into his beard, and full of curiosity

to see the boss's face when the piglets were thrown in front
of him.

Nastya pushed the door open.

She was going to let Artemy Bogdanovich have it. Not
only because his idea had been a fiasco which would mean
disgrace and loss of pay for her, but also because of all the
other things that had gone wrong in her life – because
Keshka had left her, because she was tied to her sick
mother. She had to take it out on somebody, and it was
now or never – otherwise people would just go on in the
same old way and never care a damn for her. She'd give him
what for!

Without even saying 'good morning', she turned the sack
out on to the floor. The piglets fell with a thud and lay
there – stiff, skinny and covered in their own filth.

Artemy Bogdanovich was sitting in his office with
Kostya Nespanov, the chairman of the village soviet; they
were having a quiet smoke before starting on the chores of
the day. Kostya was a simple youth with his hair brushed
stiffly back; he had freckles, big ears and light-green eyes.
Jumping up, he stared at the pigs with mouth agape and
then exclaimed:

'What's all this?'

Artemy Bogdanovich had taken everything in at a glance.
He remained sitting behind his desk, a plump, cosy, kindly
figure, his double chin resting on his shirt-collar. He didn't
move a muscle, but a wary glint appeared in his half-closed
eyes.

'Do you see?' Nastya shouted at him. 'And that's only the
beginning. There'll be plenty more to come!'

Artemy Bogdanovich shifted his clasped hands on the
desk-top and shook his head sadly. Kostya Nespanov
looked helplessly from the piglets to Nastya and from her to
Artemy Bogdanovich. The door was still wide open, and old
Isay was enjoying the show, with his head against the
door-post.

'What are you looking like that for? Don't you see what's
happened? Your winter pigs are all dying. They're dying, I
tell you!'

'Well, damn! What have you been doing? Didn't you look after them properly?' said Artemy Bogdanovich in a soft, sorrowful voice, tapping his fingers and shaking his head once more.

'What have *I* been doing? I knew you'd say that. I knew you'd put all the blame on me! Who was it pestered me and made me do it? Didn't I tell you it wouldn't work? And what about all the cod-liver oil and the vitamins? Oh, my God!' Nastya was choking with fury.

Artemy Bogdanovich sat there with a bland expression on his rather flabby face. The double chin, the thinning hair brushed smoothly to one side, the knowing, wary glint in his half-closed eyes, the soft, regretful air – all this was absolutely unshakeable. You could scream and tear your hair, but he would still sit there blinking, tapping his fingers, shaking his head, waiting to hear what you'd say next. Nastya, still gasping for breath, sank on to a chair and buried her face in her hands.

'Well, what do you want me to do?' Artemy Bogdanovich asked in a gentle tone. 'Eh, my dear?'

Nastya turned away from him, wiping her eyes.

'Do you want me to get up this minute and run around the streets shouting "Listen everybody! It wasn't Nastya's fault, it was mine. I'm a scoundrel!" Is that what you want?'

'Oh, I know you'll be in the clear. I'm the one who'll pay, you'll see to that.'

'How can you say such a wicked thing? Tell me, my dear, have I been trying to do you down all this time, or have I been praising you to the skies?'

'Oh, you praised me all right. "The pride of the kolkhoz." '

'There you are. That's what I wanted you to be, and this is my reward – you come and plant these on my doorstep.' Artemy Bogdanovich nodded at the piglets lying on the floor.

'I see. So now I should just dry my eyes and shut up.'

'Oh, cry as much as you like, I won't stop you. Then the others will really know what a mess you've made of things.'

'It's your mess, not mine.'

'Now, now, my girl. You mustn't hide behind other people like that – it's dangerous.'

'But you're in charge, we're supposed to pay attention to what you say. Or are you just a figurehead?'

'I'm in charge, but I'm not a magician. I can't do everybody's thinking for them.'

'Oh, it's no good talking!'

'No, it's not. Listen, the system is the same for me as it is for you. Suppose the corn crop fails on this farm and I run to district headquarters and say "It's your fault, you made me plant the stuff." They'll just say "You made the mistake, you answer for it." And they'll be right – I should have thought things out beforehand. Being wise after the event is the same as being stupid. If you don't use your brains, you pay for it.'

Artemy Bogdanovich stood up. He was a shortish, broad-shouldered man, sturdy in spite of his plumpness. You felt that if he stood like that in the middle of a road, firmly planted on his short legs, a horse and cart would move out of his way. His voice took on a sharper note.

'It's you who are to blame for not sticking to your guns and convincing me at the right time. It's no use crying over spilt milk.'

Nastya grimaced.

'How could I have argued against you? You're the strong one. I'm nobody. You'd only have ridden rough-shod over me.'

'Well, the whole trick in life is how to cope with people who are strong. Any fool can manage the weak ones; with the strong, you must use your wits. "A wise man goes around a mountain, not over it." Just you remember that.'

Kostya Nespanov, who had been listening to the chairman with respectful interest and a subdued, serious air, also now spoke up in a stern voice.

'You've let us down, Nastya. We had great hopes for you. I was going to send a little piece to the district newspaper telling them we had some star performers here, second to none. I even started to make it up in my head – real poetry

... but what can I say now, Nastya?' He sounded aggrieved as well as disappointed: Nastya had not only let them down but had spoilt his lyrical opening.

At this point the aged Isay was heard tittering in the doorway.

'What the hell do you want?' said Artemy Bogdanovich.

'Nothing, nothing,' said Isay. 'A bad ploughman blames his horse ...'

Artemy jerked his head at the heap of filthy piglets and said to Nastya:

'Take your sack and get that lot out of here.'

6

'A wise man goes around a mountain, not over it.' This was Artemy Bogdanovich's favourite proverb.

He had become chairman of the kolkhoz – an agglomeration of straggling, backward farmsteads – at a time when the press, speakers at public meetings and government directives all sang the praises of peat-compost pots. He was already middle-aged and putting on weight; he was an old hand who was already quite experienced as a manager at the district level, but he had burnt his fingers because he swallowed the idea that peat-compost pots were the one thing that would put the kolkhoz on its feet. With the zeal of the newly converted, he had revised the kolkhoz plans, altered the sowing schedule, taken people off their regular jobs and employed retired foremen, accountants and deputy managers in the making of pots. Not only they, but women workers on the farm and children at the local school were provided with potter's wheels and turned pots out by the hundred. The storehouses were full of them, they stood in rows in the village recreation room; in spring, filled with cabbage-sprouts, they adorned the window-sill of Artemy Bogdanovich's office. In short, compost pots were seen as a sure guarantee of future prosperity. The neighbouring kolkhozes, on the other hand, treated them with disdain. They accumulated in frozen heaps in winter, thawed and disintegrated in spring, and their contents were carted off as manure with no more thought.

But Artemy Bogdanovich was undaunted: with curses, entreaties and dazzling promises he persuaded his people to plant out nearly all the pots filled with cabbage-sprouts, little knowing what trouble this was going to land him in.

Yes, pots were the thing all right – the seedlings flourished, and Artemy Bogdanovich was beside himself with delight. 'Let's hope to heaven the frost doesn't get them. Last year a kilogram of cabbages fetched just under two roubles – even if it went down to one rouble, that's still a thousand per ton. If only the frost doesn't get them . . .'

There was no frost that spring, and by autumn the fine, heavy heads had ripened. But disaster was at hand. By this time, more or less everyone had gone over to using the pots; but the district authorities had not built any additional storehouses – they were not provided for in the annual budget. Cabbages became a drug on the market. The village recreation hall was crammed from floor to ceiling with them, and people wrote to the authorities complaining that the place could not be used because of the vegetables rotting there. Then Artemy Bogdanovich had to pay the kolkhoz workers for making the pots, planting the seedlings, walking miles to water them. What was he to pay them with – cabbages? Everybody was sick of eating them. Oh, those accursed pots!

The farm workers were furious and he was in serious danger of being hauled before the district court for allowing hundreds of tons of high-quality vegetables to go to waste. However, a collective farm chairman doesn't have to care too much what his workers think, and Artemy managed to dodge court proceedings; he faced out the reproofs and criticism somehow, and got off with a reprimand. By the time the incident was over he had lost weight and endured much anguish, but he had gained in experience and was no longer a greenhorn in farm management. It was about this time that he adopted the slogan, 'A wise man goes around a mountain, not over it.'

The affair clouded his career for some time, but after all – 'a reprimand isn't TB, you can walk around with it'. When the next campaign began – the formidable one in favour of corn* – Artemy Bogdanovich met it like a seasoned warrior. Fond as he was of eloquence, he did not lag behind his colleagues at district meetings in singing the praises of this new 'queen of the fields'; but in due course he was heard to lament, no less loudly, that his entire corn crop had been suddenly stricken by frost and that, to prevent the fields lying fallow, he had had to sow oats and barley. The district authorities, being hard-hearted men, did not believe his protestations, but demanded to know why his crop was the only one that had suffered in this way; they threatened an investigation and penalties. The inspectors duly came, and right beside the highroad, where no one could fail to see it, they saw a field of corn in the most flourishing condition, such as you wouldn't find for miles around.

'Why did you say your crop was spoilt by frost?' they asked.

Artemy Bogdanovich sighed and threw up his hands. 'This part was all we could save. We did our level best – God knows we tried hard. We set up a special team to look after it.' He did not mention, however, that the 'special team' consisted of one person, Sashka Seleznev, plus the tractor-driver Khokhlov, who brought the manure. 'Try as we might, we could only save five hectares' – here again Artemy Bogdanovich exaggerated slightly: there were not five hectares under corn, only two at the most. He got another reprimand for allowing his crop to get frozen, but 'a reprimand isn't TB, you can walk around with it'. What really mattered was that that autumn they had plenty of bread and could pay the farm workers. Artemy Bogdanovich now took good care never to boast to the authorities, but rather to lament shortages, setbacks and inadequacies of all kinds. They didn't altogether believe him, but at

* This refers to Khrushchev's campaign to introduce corn, even when it was quite unsuitable for cultivation, as a remedy for the Soviet Union's chronic shortage of fodder. In his speeches Khrushchev referred to corn with extravagant epithets such as 'Queen of the Fields'. (Translator's note.)

least they didn't put his farm in the 'front rank' and demand grain deliveries over and above the plan figure. There were threats of another reprimand too, but – 'you can walk around with it. A wise man doesn't go over a mountain.'

Some time after this, the country echoed with the 'Ryazan miracle', an example which all were enjoined to follow: to provide extra meat for purchase by the government they slaughtered not only calves and milch-cows but also cows in calf and stud-bulls. Once again, Artemy Bogdanovich was to the fore at meetings with promises to 'equal and surpass' all rivals, but he was not in a hurry to slaughter his own cattle: the equalling and surpassing was to be achieved in the field of pig-keeping.

At that time, the piggeries on his farm were full of long-snouted, long-legged creatures, with sharp-pointed bristles on their narrow backs; they were extremely lively and had rapacious appetites.

'What are we feeding them for?' Artemy Bogdanovich would ask. 'For pig-meat? No, just to give them energy. These aren't pigs, they're greyhounds – you could use them for chasing hares.' For a long time, he had planned to replace the 'greyhounds' with sedate, indolent pedigree animals which instead of bristles would provide quantities of meat and lard. Now that the time had come to 'equal and surpass', every single one of the 'greyhounds' was slaughtered – boars, sows and sucking pigs alike. Meat was meat, and it looked well in the accounts. All the same, it was not too easy to get by on the 'greyhounds' alone, especially in competition with the neighbouring district of Blintsy, which had set itself the task of becoming a 'second Ryazan'. Once again Artemy Bogdanovich was reprimanded, but – 'it's not TB . . . A wise man goes around a mountain . . .'

It was not long after this that Nastya had been put in charge of the piggery instead of Pelageya Krynkina. It was empty and no longer even smelt of pigs, and there were cobwebs in the corners. One day, a lorry had driven up and Artemy Bogdanovich himself jumped out of the cab: he wore a straw hat pushed back on his neck, his shoulders were squared and his fleshy chest thrust forward. He shouted to Nastya: 'Come on, auntie, your nephews are here!' and from the back of the lorry they took down two large wicker baskets, each containing five travel-weary piglets. The pink, snub-nosed, helpless creatures were tumbled out on to the young grass, warmed by the sun, and began to squeal and clamber over one another. Artemy Bogdanovich poked and prodded them in ecstasy.

'Look at them! Look at their ears – that's where you tell breeding in pigs. The ones with floppy ears are the real aristocrats.' Then he said sternly: 'Now, my girl, you're to bring them up – every single one, do you hear? The eyes of the kolkhoz are upon you.'

Nastya had brought them all up, which was not difficult: they began to thrive in no time, and grew into ten portly sows named Rosy, Goldy, Rowan and so on, and producing a brood of long-eared piglets twice a year. Artemy Bogdanovich never ceased admiring them and saying:

'In the ears – that's where the breeding shows! We'll produce a whole race of long-eared aristocrats.' And, to Nastya: 'You're worth your weight in gold, you are. One of these days we'll be cheering you sky-high.'

And now, as soon as things went wrong, he blamed it all on her.

7

Picking her way home through the snowdrifts, Nastya looked across the fluffy white fields to the half-hidden, blackened huts of the neighbouring villages – Stepakovskaya, Kocheryzhino, Kulichki – and felt a burning mistrust of all who lived there.

Those whom she had trusted the most in life had been faithless to her. Venka was the first person she had ever felt drawn to, openly and without guile. He had a long neck with a prominent Adam's apple, heavy toil-worn hands and narrow shoulders which were further cramped by the tight coat he wore. He had been shy with Nastya, not cheeky like the other boys – how could she have expected that he would deceive her?

Keshka was a different sort – he'd been about the world and known lots of women; he had wanted to settle down and Nastya was at hand, a decent enough looking girl, well thought of by her neighbours. So he had grabbed hold of her in the hall as they were leaving Pavla's house, breathed tobacco over her and said with a flash of his gold tooth: 'Is it OK if I move in with you?' And she had trusted him, and again she had been deceived.

As for Artemy Bogdanovich, he hadn't wanted to be her husband or lover, so what interest had he in deceiving her? Yet he too had left her in the lurch – 'The whole trick is how to cope with people who are strong.' Yes, strong . . .

The whole world was made up of people like Keshka, and she was alone against the lot of them. Before you knew where you were, they had stolen your whole life bit by bit. If only she could rob others in the same way – but she didn't know how to.

The snowy fields stretched out as far as the eye could see. The white expanse was broken only by curls of fragrant smoke from the village chimneys, thickets covered in hoar-frost and ravines full of tangled undergrowth. The whole wide world lay round about her, but where could a lonely creature like her find a hiding-place?

The road led past the piggery, and Nastya turned off towards it. When things had gone wrong with her as a girl, or when she could not bear the sight of her sick mother, she had got into the habit of coming here for refuge and losing herself in her work.

The door which led, beyond the cooker, to the row of pens was wide open. Nastya did not turn on the light, and the pigs did not sense her presence. She smelt the strong odour and heard them puffing, grunting and shuffling about. Here, sheltered from the white world of snow, the pigs lived a life of their own. This was the first time Nastya had caught them unawares: usually her arrival disturbed them, and they began to squeal and jump about.

All was dark, the air was fetid and stuffy, and the boar

Dandelion wheezed ponderously like an old man – 'hunf, hunf'. This was a kind of life all right – they were glad when food was brought, they slept, scratched themselves and reproduced their kind, unaware that the days were passing or even that they were alive. Nastya suddenly shivered at the thought that their life was like a sleep – what was the good of coming into the world if you never saw it?

Dandelion continued to wheeze – a long 'hunf, hunf . . .'

Keshka had wanted her to go away with him and live in towns that were full of lights in the evening, where the streets were crowded and the shop-windows glittered and people from a different world drove about in cars and went to the theatre. All she had to do was to say yes, and she would never again have to hear Dandelion wheezing like an old man or see the snow-bound village of Utitsy; she could laugh at everything that was troubling her now and not care a rap whether Artemy Bogdanovich was pleased or displeased with her. Keshka had never once looked inside the piggery – he had just said, 'Come on, don't spend your life wallowing in pig shit.' All she had to do was say 'Yes'. He had made up his mind, and nothing she said could make him change it – he wasn't tempted by the idea of building a new house or buying a motor-cycle.

There, in the thick, fetid half-light just beyond the doorway, lived carcasses of meat and lard, peaceably, without passion and without thought. Hurriedly, to disturb their life, Nastya groped along the timbered wall for the light-switch.

Aroused by the sudden glare, the pigs began to squeal and move about. Even in that sleepy world there were moments of joy and violence. The piglets jostled one another, crowding towards the partitions.

The diseased sucklings which had been separated from their mothers lay in a heap together under a tarpaulin. One had stretched out apart from the rest, like a dog with its nose along the floor. One whitish eyelid was languidly open, and from it a little black eye peered out with an almost human expression of sadness and resignation. Nastya was cut to the heart by the directness of its gaze and by the pathos of its lonely death, away from its fellows. She took the piglet into her arms and hugged it, saying 'You poor little thing.' Then she picked three others out of the heap and carried them in her skirt as far as the dung-pit, where she threw them in. A dozen or so remained: they were all doomed to die, but Nastya tended them as best she could, gave them some swill and placed them beside their mothers. Then she took the lone one, wrapped it inside her jacket and went home, dragging her feet with weariness.

The room was filled with harsh light from the unshaded bulb that hung from the ceiling. A wooden bowl, covered with a cloth and containing sliced bread, stood on the table. Nastya's mother sat hunched over it, awaiting her return. Her face, as always, was expressionless and, as it were, listening to what was taking place within her, to her own illness.

'There's some cabbage-soup in the oven, and I made a hot-pot with egg in it, but I'm afraid it's been cooking too long. Take whatever you want, dear.' Saying this, for some reason she moved her withered hand, with its swollen joints, off the table and hid it shamefacedly in her lap.

Nastya took the piglet from under her coat and laid it by the door, saying:

'What can I wrap it in? It's going to die, there's no hope of curing it.'

Keshka's check scarf was still lying on the bench. She picked it up and began carefully wrapping it round the filthy animal.

'What on earth are you doing?' said her mother. 'It's brand-new.'

'You don't think I want to benefit by anything of *his*, do you?' Nastya replied crossly. As she said this, she imagined Keshka, with his gold tooth, wearing the scarf and dressed in a cityfied hat and overcoat. At this very moment, perhaps, he was pushing through the crowds in the brightly-lit streets, gazing about him and wondering which shop to visit first. Her mother, just like the piglet by the door, was past curing and was bound to die soon. She would die, so it was all a waste of time, and by then Keshka would have taken up with someone else.

She looked at her mother's pale, dried-up face with the long wrinkles and dull eyes which cared little for what they saw – Nastya, the cottage, the stove or the dying piglet – they were turned inward, she was concerned only with the life still left inside her.

'Take what you want, dear, I feel all funny today somehow. Oh, dearie me, I wish I could die soon. I pray and pray, but nothing happens.'

'It might have been better if you'd prayed sooner,' Nastya burst out. 'It's too late now.'

Yes, it would be just her luck if her mother were to die now – when it was no longer any use her dying, when Keshka had gone away and happiness was lost for ever. And what was the good of her mother having brought her up and fed her on nettles and husks of flax, if all she had lived for was to be a nursemaid to a lot of pigs? For the first time, she felt resentment and anger towards her sick mother – purposely or not, she had robbed Nastya of her chance in life.

'It's too late – you may as well leave off praying.'

'Nastya dear, for heaven's sake, what are you saying?'

'Only that I feel like hanging myself when I think what the rest of my life is going to be like.'

'God have mercy on us!'

'Maybe He will on you. He doesn't seem to care much about me.'

'Well . . . You should have gone away and left me. You shouldn't have stayed on my account.'

'Gone away, gone away – yes, and felt bad about it for the rest of my life. How could I have borne it? Tell me what I've done to deserve all this! Is there any girl in the village who's gone through what I have?'

'I only wish . . .'

'Oh, be quiet! What's the good of wishing? At least you had a little happiness in life, you had a husband for a while, and a family. But what have I got? I suppose I should be glad there's something to put in the cabbage-soup, or that I've a party dress packed away. But who wants to see me in it – who wants me anyway?'

Her mother sat with her head bowed, her clasped hands quivering in her lap. Nastya could no longer control herself – her voice rose to a scream as she went on:

'What is my life for? Tell me! Is it so I can buy one more coat to put away and never wear? I break my back working all day long, what for? Who for? For myself? Goodness me, no, it's for the pigs! There's a fine life for you. Aren't you happy? Doesn't that make you happy?'

Her mother said in a low voice:

'I can't do away with myself. I have prayed, but death doesn't come.'

The apologetic tone of these words brought Nastya to her senses. She sank on to the bench and drew her hard, calloused palm over her face from brow to chin, as if to free herself of a nightmare.

Her mother went on:

'In the old days there used to be homes for people like me. Do they still have them?'

Nastya rubbed her face once more.

'What's the matter with me? I must be out of my mind.'

'Don't think I don't know I'm spoiling your life.'

'Stop it, stop it! I'm going out of my mind, I tell you!'

'It makes my heart bleed to look at you.'

'Oh, forgive me, forgive me for talking like that. Don't say any more! I'll look after you, I'll make you better! How can I get on without you? If it wasn't for you I'd really go mad. All I have to live for is you, mother.'

'You're a good girl, Nastya darling.'

'I'm sorry I lost my temper.'

Her mother nodded towards the door, where the piglet's nose stuck out from under the scarf. 'If you brew some strong tea and make him drink it, it might do him some good.'

'First I behave like a wild animal, and then I feel sorry. I feel sorry for him too.'

'You're a good girl. But it's a pity about the scarf – it was a new one.'

'Well, why shouldn't the poor little wretch have a nice

new scarf?' Nastya went across to the door and knelt in
front of the piglet. 'Poor little Keshka, lie there nice and
quietly. That's a good name for him, the best I can think
of. If he gets better, it'll be something to remember the
other one by – he hasn't left us anything else.'

8

Next morning, she had to throw out five more piglets.
Others besides them had already caught the sickness – it
was spreading like fire.

When Isay came with their feed he told her that Mikhey,
the storekeeper, had only let him have a tiny bit of flour, the
rest was all chaff. Of course, it was clear enough – as long as
she was the 'pride of the kolkhoz' they couldn't do enough
for her, giving her the best and the most of everything, but
once they found there'd been a mistake, it was chaff instead
of flour from then on. If she complained, they would simply
say, 'You're being treated the same as everybody else.
What's special about you?'

Desperately she thought to herself, 'Just you wait and see
if I'm not special after all.' Then she went to Pavla's and
said, 'Give my pigs their feed tonight. I have to go to
Zagarye, and I won't be back till late.'

At home she took out of her trunk the coat she had bought
last year with the lambskin collar, and put a woolly scarf
over her head. Then she walked to the high road and caught
the bus to the district centre.

She could get dried bilberries in the village, but she had
to go to the chemist's for some herbs and a bottle of
germicide and, above all, as much cod-liver oil as possible,
since Artemy Bogdanovich had refused to fork out for it.
There was no point in asking for it at the vet's, since if they
had had any, the farm would have been given some too –
the chief vet and Artemy Bogdanovich were friends. It was
going to cost Nastya a pretty penny, but money didn't
matter so much now – she had only been saving up to get
Keshka a 'Ural' motor-cycle.

She did not go straight to the chemist's, knowing they

wouldn't let her have the stuff without prescriptions and all
kinds of documents, especially as she wanted it in bulk –
treating a whole lot of pigs was a different matter from just
getting medicine for her mother – she'd clean the place
out. So, on getting off the bus she went first to Maruska
Shchekotkina, who came from the same village and was a
second cousin of hers; she was a waitress at the logging
station, and knew everyone in Zagarye.

'You must help me, Maruska, or I'll be done for.'

Maruska was a good soul who didn't forget old friends.
She had helped out before now when sugar was scarce in the
shops – the loggers were well catered for, and the village
people in Utitsy were never short of sugar to put in their
tea.

'Do please help me, Maruska.'

Maruska was a shortish woman with freckles and a ready
tongue. She was the kind of person who falls on her feet –
her husband was a lumberman who didn't drink or run after
women, in fact he was rather afraid of his wife. They had set
up their own house not long ago, and every room had a bed
with springs and a down mattress. When you live on that
scale you can afford to be kind to others, as Maruska was.

Maruska did not actually know anyone at the chemist's
but she did know the local photographer, Isak Kuropevtsev,
who himself knew everyone in the place and never refused
Maruska anything; moreover, being an old man, he was no
doubt a frequent customer of the chemist's.

It turned out, however, that although old and in poor
health, he was not addicted to buying medicines. But he
was able to help them all the same, for he was a good friend
of Vasily Migunov, who had served for many years in the
district health office and, although retired, still had considerable pull there. He turned out indeed to be just the
man they needed. He went round to various doctors and
collected prescriptions ('the chemist's isn't just an ordinary
shop, they have to account for their sales'), and introduced
Nastya to Anna Pavlovna, the pharmaceutist whose
girl-assistant was at present absent on maternity leave,
so that she was in sole charge.

At Migunov's request, Anna Pavlovna readily provided what was necessary. Altogether, Nastya had spent the whole day running from one person to another; but even Artemy Bogdanovich, if he had taken on the job, could hardly have done it quicker, as he would have had to go from one office to another filling in forms and signing them. Indeed he might well not have succeeded in getting everything, as when it comes to forms you often get bogged down completely.

Carrying two heavy bags full of bottles, phials and packages, Nastya said goodbye to Maruska and went off to catch the bus. Maruska was indeed a good soul: she gave Nastya a meal, helped her to pack everything and even added a small present in the shape of half a pound of inexpensive sweets 'to give your mother a treat'.

As she walked along, Nastya was overtaken by a lorry. It stopped, and the driver put his head out of the door.

'Going home, sweetheart?' It was Zhenka Kruchinin, the one who brought her whey and skim-milk. 'Come on, get in – I like having a woman to talk to. You can toss your luggage in the back – it won't come to any harm.'

But Nastya kept the bags on her lap, saying there were bottles inside and they might get broken.

'Bottles? Is it for a wedding-party?'

'The only bridegroom I have to do with is Dandelion, and he's got plenty of wives already.'

'A birthday party then?'

'Or a wake, more likely. I suppose you know my piglets are down with disease. I've been buying cod-liver oil and all kinds of things to keep them from dying.'

'That's not your job, is it? You deserve a medal, you really do.'

'We'll see. I hope at least they'll pay up – I've bought the whole lot out of my own pocket.'

'I wish I had a wife who looked after me the way you look after your pigs.'

'What's wrong with your own? Why don't you trade her in if you're not satisfied?'

'No, I don't want to make a bad bargain, thank you.

Funny how nice girls turn into sour old women, isn't it?'

The lorry skidded at the turns, and the snowflakes, lit up where the headlights caught them, flung themselves furiously against the windows of the cab.

9

Zhenka did not keep Nastya's story to himself. Next day, towards noon, a trap drawn by a smart grey horse bowled along the road to the piggery, and out of it jumped Artemy Bogdanovich, muffled in a black sheepskin coat. His face, lashed by the frosty wind, wore an expression of kindness mingled with embarrassment. Pulling off a fur mitten, he took Nastya's hand in his warm one and said:

'I was coming from Dor village, and I thought I'd drop in and see you. How are things?'

'Do you mean with me or the pigs?' Nastya was bareheaded, tousled, cross-looking and red in the face – she had just been poking at the stove.

'I mean with you, my girl. If you keep well, they'll get better soon enough.'

'Yes, I'm sure they will – thanks to your prayers.'

'My, what a sharp tongue you've got.' He crossed to the window, where the empty phials were standing in a row on the sill, took one and sniffed it, shook his head with a look of concern, took another and finally said:

'All right, my dear, don't be angry. We'll pay you for the medicines. Don't be angry. I sometimes make mistakes too, you know. We all have our ways of doing things. You know me, I always like to be on the safe side – a wise man goes round a mountain . . . but maybe you're one of those who like to charge right over it. Have you lost many since the first lot? Eh?'

Since the first seven which Nastya had thrown on the floor in Artemy Bogdanovich's office, a good many had died and plenty more were certain to – the whole winter farrowing could be written off. But Nastya replied in a firm, disdainful tone:

'One – and that's quite enough.'

Thanks to Artemy Bogdanovich, she knew enough now not to blurt out the truth. As he himself would say, the trustful man gets the kicks and the wily one gets the ha'pence. If he doesn't believe me, she thought, let him look for himself and count those that are left – but for that he'd have to take off his nice soft boots and get on his knees to poke about under the mother sows, and his coat would soon be in a fine state. Yes, let him look for himself!

But Artemy Bogdanovich had no thought of checking her statement. He replied:

'One, eh? By George, you're a great girl, you ought to have been a general. You didn't lose your head and you stopped the rot in time. Splendid! splendid!'

He spoke in a tone of genuine admiration, his face with the wrinkles round the eyes wore a kindly and frank expression, but Nastya couldn't help feeling that he probably wasn't altogether taken in – Artemy Bogdanovich was too clever for that. No, he didn't believe her, but he would go along with the pretence that only one had died, so long as the disease was now stopped from spreading; if Nastya chose to have it that way, she must have some plan for keeping in the clear, and if she hadn't, well, it wasn't Artemy Bogdanovich who would take the blame. So long as the reports and accounts were kept straight, he could escape a reprimand for the outbreak – it wasn't the sort of thing they patted you on the head for, of course. He went on:

'Just you go ahead, Nastya my girl. We'll show them what we're made of. Just clean up this mess, and then we'll break all the records!'

He pressed her hand once again in his warm palm, looked her in the eye and went out. The horse, tethered to the fence, was pawing the snow. Nastya thought to herself: 'Now he's going to be all over me again.' She was quite right.

Kostya Nespanov learnt of Nastya's exploit from none other than Artemy Bogdanovich himself. Next day he came running round to the piggery, his coat collar about his ears and his face turned crimson by the frost, so that his reckles could not be seen. He fished a dog-eared notebook and a fountain pen out of his pocket and said:

'I'd like to write a bit of a story for the district newspaper. You know, a sort of sketch of a typical star worker.'

Kostya was the chairman of the village soviet. At one time this had been a job of some consequence, involving the supervision of several collective farms. The chairman's word was law for the farm managers – he was the local representative of State authority, and woe betide those who disobeyed him. But, some years ago, all these scattered farms had been merged into one big one, and by degrees the kolkhoz chairman became more important than the chairman of the soviet. For instance, if the village recreation hall needed repair, the farm was there to provide timber and labour; if the school needed firewood, the farm had horses and motor transport to deliver it with, and the forests round about belonged to the farm, not the soviet. Without any doubt, Kostya played second fiddle to Artemy Bogdanovich, and if Kostya's roof leaked, it was Artemy that he had to ask politely to get it mended. In fact, Artemy's word was law for Kostya, not the other way about, especially as Kostya was a much younger man and had no ambition to take the lead.

It was not long since Kostya had been addicted to writing love-poems, in imitation of Esenin and Shchipachov.

> Love is a storm in the soul,
> love is eternal troth;
> tell me, fellow-mortals,
> what has life denied me?

Among other things, it had denied him poetic talent, so he turned to writing pieces for the district newspaper; and his ears used to flush with excitement whenever he read in print the words that had so lately issued from his pen, and saw the signature 'K. Nespanov' at the bottom.

When Kostya had decided to write about someone, he immediately began to regard that person with respectful awe. A human being whose name was to appear in print through Kostya's efforts was a being apart: he would no no longer address them to their face as Venka, Sashka or Nastya, as he had done the day before, but would use the ceremonious form with name and patronymic:

'Tell me now, Anastasya Stepanovna' – thus he addressed Nastya – 'what gave you the impetus? What inner impulse? You understand, I am interested from the point of view of life – of psychology . . .'

'Oh, don't be so silly, Kostya! What do I know about life and psychology? All I knew was, the pigs were dying and none of the authorities did a thing to help.'

Kostya solemnly scribbled this in his notebook. At home that evening he sat down and began to write his piece, which began: 'The icy storm-wind swept the highway. A girl battled through the driving snow, braving the furious blast and the treacherous drifts . . .' It went on to describe how the girl, in spite of these obstacles, had brought back medicines for the diseased piglets. Kostya knew quite well that there had been no blizzard that evening and that Nastya had not had to walk home, as she was given a lift in Zhenka Kruchinin's lorry; but it was not for nothing that he had dreamt of being a poet. Next morning he showed his effort to Artemy Bogdanovich, who looked through it, frowned and said:

'Put it away and don't show it to anybody.'

'But why?'

'Because, my dear fellow, you don't wash dirty linen in public. If those people at district headquarters get hold cf this, they'll say: "Ah, you bastards, you have a pig epidemic and you let the pig-keeper pay for medicines out of her own pocket and don't even lend her a horse to go and get them: you don't take any more care of your workers than you do of your pigs." And what will you and I say to that, eh? This sort of stuff has a name, you know, it's called libel. And haven't you laid it on a bit thick about the snowstorm?'

Kostya reacted to criticism of this sort just as he did to praise – his ears reddened. Artemy Bogdanovich went on soothingly:

'Never mind – this one won't do, but next time you'll do better. Just keep watching Nastya – you'll have other chances to write about her, that's for sure. She's on the up and up – and you and I can help her. One of these days, the whole province and the whole country will know about her.'

It was not the first rebuff in Kostya's writing career. He put his article away, but he took Artemy Bogdanovich's words to heart, and began to watch Nastya very attentively indeed.

10

Keshka, the piglet which Nastya had brought home wrapped in her coat when it was at death's door, recovered and began to grow: it grew fat as a drum, and for a long time now had been living in the piggery with the others. But during the time when Nastya had looked after it, feeding it on strong tea, bilberry infusion and cod-liver oil, it had got so used to her that now, whenever it was let out of its pen, it would follow her like a dog, rub itself against her legs and almost swoon with delight if she stretched out a hand to it.

Kostya Nespanov had now taken to visiting the piggery from time to time, and one day she said to him, as Keshka with his sharp back was nosing under her skirt:

'You see, he's only an animal, but he's as faithful as can be. He remembers that I was kind to him. If I threw myself over a cliff, he'd jump after me. You don't get that sort of trust in a human being, do you? With us, it's every man for himself.'

Kostya looked at Keshka's ecstatic expression as Nastya stroked him, and said:

'You mustn't compare people with pigs. Remember what Gorky said – "it is a proud thing to be a human being".'

'Yes, proud – that's just it. All we live for is pride. Animals are more straightforward. Aren't you, Keshka my sweet? There, you see, he's smiling at me!'

'You know, Nastya, you're a first-class worker, but your political education is rather backward. And you're stand-offish with people. Take me, for instance.' Kostya's ears began to flush scarlet. 'I try to be friends with you, and you never say a kind word to me – you keep them all for the pigs. You ought to come half way to meet people sometimes. Now, take me for instance – I know I'm no better than anybody else, but . . .'

He fell silent. Nastya, thoughtfully scratching the delighted Keshka, looked at Kostya with a chilly, appraising glance and said:

'Whether you're better or worse, I don't know. You can do all sorts of things – you write poems and articles and make speeches, but what difference do they make to anybody?'

Kostya's ears flushed angrily. Here was this girl, well on her way to becoming an old maid, with her scraggy shoulders and a temper that even Artemy Bogdanovich was a bit afraid of – and she took no notice of him, treated him as if he didn't exist. And Kostya certainly didn't consider himself the last person in the world . . .

Last winter, Nastya had said to Artemy Bogdanovich 'One – and that's quite enough.' At that time a good many more had died, and since then she had been carrying out others in her skirt to the dung-pit without letting on to anybody. Strangely enough, she felt no fear of being found out.

Every piglet that was born had to be entered in the farm register, the figure in the 'Increase' column being raised by one. If a piglet died, you recorded it and reduced the figure accordingly. All this was done under the supervision of the bookkeeper, Sidor Petrayev – a quiet, henpecked, obliging sort of man, but a stickler for regulations. If you let a single pig die without informing him he confronted you with the book and pointed out the discrepancy. Where was the missing one – had you sold it or made it into soup? It was no use trying to fool him by counting on your fingers. You might not be taken to court to account for the loss, but you'd have to pay for it out of your own pocket.

Yet Nastya had smuggled out a dozen or so. This, you might think, was asking for trouble – dead pigs couldn't be brought back to life. However, 'a wise man goes around a mountain'. What was the way this time? Who could she get to help her?

In spring there would be another farrow, and whatever the plan said and however many figures they wrote in the register, no one could say whether Rowan's litter would consist of five piglets or ten. Whatever figure Nastya gave, they would take her word for it and not rush off to compare the book-entry with the actual state of affairs, as though they suspected her of cheating – any pig-keeper would be astonished and insulted at being checked up on in this way. The office where the returns were registered was four and a half miles from the piggery: they would accept the figure she gave and take no account of any piglets that might have died at birth, so as not to 'complicate the book-keeping' unnecessarily.

In this way, the spring farrow would cover up the deficiency. The number of piglets would be of importance in autumn, when meat contracts had to be arranged with the State authorities. But even then they wouldn't count them by heads, they would only ask why the total quantity of meat was less than average, and plenty of excuses could be found for that. 'Don't forget these are winter piglets – you can't expect full weight, you should be pleased they're as good as they are.' A wise man goes around a mountain . . . There wasn't much risk in it, and as for her conscience – why should it be any more sensitive than Artemy Bogdanovich's? If there was any trouble, he'd take good care that she got the blame.

The winter farrowing was Artemy Bogdanovich's idea, he could answer any questions about that. Nastya had stopped the epidemic and at least saved some of the piglets, while the other women at the piggery had lost not only all theirs but some porkers as well, and some of the sows had been infected. Their pay had been docked in consequence, and they hadn't a good word to say for Artemy Bogdanovich. He for his part praised Nastya to the skies, and whenever the others complained he would reply: 'Why couldn't you do as well as Syroyegina? What do you think she is, a miracle-worker or something? Skill and honest hard work, that's all it takes.' Nastya's photograph was put up on the board of honour, her praises were sung at meetings and admiring articles appeared in the district newspaper. It was clear to everyone that she was being groomed as a star worker of the kolkhoz, and she received special treatment accordingly. On the express orders of Artemy Bogdanovich, Mikhey the storekeeper provided her with the best pig-food and no longer mixed the flour with chaff. Not only was it better in quality but there was more of it, for the dead piglets were still registered as alive, and as they supposedly grew bigger and stronger the ration was raised accordingly.

Thus the winter passed: the snow began to melt here and there, the ravines filled with green stagnant water. The days were longer, and the sun already shone palely by the time Nastya made her way to the farm in the mornings.

The sows did not recover much strength after the winter farrowing, and the spring litters were small. Rowan, the most fertile, produced six instead of her usual eight. There were other troubles too. Although Nastya hardly slept at nights and was continually jumping out of bed, throwing on her jacket and scarf and rushing off to spend hours looking after the mother sows, her care was insufficient. Rosy, a monstrously fat, clumsy old thing, overlay three of her own young, and Turtledove, who had been taken to the boar for the first time and of whom Nastya had high hopes, proved to have a vicious streak: she littered four and devoured them on the spot. Crocodile would have been a better name for her. Then two more piglets came to grief: one was savaged by the boar, and another managed to fall into the dung-pit.

Nastya worked frantically – the expression on her face grew more and more grim, and when she came home her mother lay in bed on top of the stove, out of harm's way, for fear of being snapped at. But Nastya's was still a name to conjure with on the farm. Kostya kept coming around with his notebook; he wrote to the provincial newspaper and waited anxiously for a response, while every now and then Artemy Bogdanovich, busy as he was, would come and stamp about in front of the pens, peer at the brood-sows and say encouragingly: 'Keep it up, Nastya my girl. The whole kolkhoz is looking to you!'

Nastya gave him a piece of her mind about the smallness of the spring litters, but said nothing about the latest losses: she smuggled out Rosy's three in her apron without telling anyone, as before. The question was, should she ascribe all the deaths to the present litter? It would be possible to do so – her own piggery would make a poor showing, but the others were disastrous: the girls had not had extra rations as she had, nor had they got out of bed night after night to look after the sows. She could do this and cover up the previous losses, but then she would get no praise at all, only sour rebukes and, no doubt, chaff instead of flour again. 'What's all this, Nastya? – your figures are way down, as low as Maria Klushina's' – whose pens were empty and covered with cobwebs. No, she couldn't bear to be put on a level with her!

Oh, well, in for a penny, in for a pound. She hadn't been afraid of their checking before, and there was even less reason to fear it now. For appearances' sake, she decided to put two piglets down to Turtledove – just two. The litter was small, but so was the percentage of loss: let them take it or leave it!

Some time after this, out of the blue there appeared a long-nosed youth in a leather jerkin hung about with cameras: he made Nastya drive all the pigs out of doors, set her in the middle among the fat sows and called out stern instructions: 'Keep still a minute! Don't look at the lens!' He clicked away busily, first standing to one side of her. then squatting on the ground, then perched on the fence. By this time Nastya herself and her pet Keshka were famous throughout the province. While she looked shyly to one side, Keshka stood close up against her skirt and stared out from the photograph with an imperious air, having disregarded the long-nosed youth's instruction 'not to look at the lens'.

After the rains, a bus made its way painfully along the slushy road leading to Utitsy, and out of it jumped a party of young farm workers of both sexes from the neighbouring Blintsy district. They all knew Nastya and they took a good look at the piggery and its inmates, asking one question after another: what rations did she give them, when were they fed, would they farrow again next winter? They paid close attention to the answers, hanging on Nastya's every word.

11

Life at home was the same as before – weary and desolate. Her mother hung on to life, getting neither worse nor better, doctoring herself with herbs. Nastya used to find her, as before, sitting on the bench with a fixed expression, her attention absorbed by what was going on deep within herself.

Her mother knew the worth of Nastya's 'success'. If only there had been grandchildren running about, or a well-set-up man smelling of tobacco and coming home from work in a sweat-soaked shirt – then, she thought to herself, her daughter's life would be a human one. All the compliments to her work and photographs in the papers weren't the same thing – an old maid is an old maid, and it's the worst kind of life for a woman. Nastya realised that her mother was thinking this all the time and pitying her inwardly, and for that reason she avoided being at home.

One evening they were sitting at table together: Nastya was having supper and her mother watched her eat, passing her the salt or the bread-knife from time to time. Neither spoke: they had already talked about everything there was to mention. Nastya had fed the pigs, the empty evening stretched before her, and it was a question of how to fill it. Usually she would go round to Pavla's for a chat. Pavla always had some piece of news about Keshka – he was living at Solombal and working in a timber mill, rather at a loose end now he wasn't married – of course, he had always been fond of the bottle, and there was no lack of drinking companions. Pavla related all this with a hint of triumph, as if to say: you may be famous and quite well off, but the men don't seem very keen on you – Keshka writes to us and doesn't even send you his regards. Nastya felt sore about this, but whenever she had a free evening she could not resist going to see Pavla and hear what Keshka was doing. This evening, too, she was about to finish up her soup and go, when they heard the neigh of a horse outside, footsteps on the porch and a well-known voice calling out:

'Is the lady of the house at home?'

It was Artemy Bogdanovich, but not in his usual clothes. He wore a smart blue suit which he normally kept for meetings at provincial level – his ordinary suit was good enough for district ones – white shirt and a tie; his face shone like a coin fresh from the mint. Behind him, slightly to one side, stood Kostya Nespanov, also in a well-pressed suit, with an open-necked shirt and highly polished shoes; his cheeks were red and his eyes looked up at the ceiling. Artemy Bogdanovich spoke.

'I hope you are both well.'

'Yes, we are – if you're not making fun of us,' replied Nastya. As she began to guess what was afoot, she felt a chill down her back and a weak sensation at the knees. 'We'd ask you to have some supper, but we weren't expecting you and we haven't got anything special. You look as if you were going to a birthday party. Are you sure you've come to the right house?'

'Yes, absolutely dead sure – aren't we, Kostya?' said Artemy Bogdanovich. He plumped himself down at the table, and Kostya sat a little way off, at the very edge of the bench. Nastya's mother rose with an effort and was making towards the stove, but Artemy Bogdanovich stopped her, saying:

'No, granny, you stay here. You won't be in the way – on the contrary, we need you more than anybody, don't we, Kostya?'

The old lady's wrinkled face quivered. She sat down again and remained motionless, with an anxious and expectant look.

Artemy Bogdanovich laid his hands on the table, drummed with his fingers, cleared his throat with an embarrassed air and shot a glance at Kostya, who blushed crimson.

'Well now,' Artemy Bogdanovich began, 'I'm a straight-

forward chap, I don't believe in beating about the bush. I
don't know much about the old customs either, but didn't
they use to start off by saying: "You have fine wares to
sell, we have a young lad to buy them"? Wasn't that it,
granny? Nastya, you know what I'm talking about, don't
you?'

Nastya remained speechless, looking sideways at Kostya,
whose face was as red as a beetroot.

'Yes, my dear, I'm playing the match-maker! This
fellow's shyer than a girl himself, so I had to take it on for
the first time in my life. I may not be doing it quite right,
if so you'll have to forgive me. Well, Nastya, what about it?'

'What about what?'

'Good lord, doesn't she understand? Will you marry
Kostya here, or are you waiting for a fairy-tale prince to
come along? There, that's honestly meant, and it's straight
from the shoulder. Well?'

Nastya, still silent, stared at the table, her hands pressed
between her knees. Artemy Bogdanovich cleared his throat
once again.

'Well, don't take all night about it. Have you anything
against him?'

'Perhaps I have.'

Kostya clenched his jaws with a suffering air, raised his
eyes to the ceiling again and whimpered:

'Come on, Artemy Bogdanovich, let's go away from here.
What's the use?'

'How do you mean, go away?' The hollows under Artemy
Bogdanovich's eyes grew dark with anger. 'We'll go away
and hide our heads in shame after we've found out what the
trouble is, but not before. Tell us what you have against
him.'

'Only one thing – he's young. I'm an old maid. I was
twenty-eight the other day, what business have I to be
cradle-snatching?'

'Cradle-snatching? Kostya, do you hear her? Damn it all,
man, get angry with her! Thump the table and let's see the
cups and spoons go flying!'

'No, no, let's go. What's the use?'

'Oh, shut up! If you won't thump the table, I will.' And
Artemy Bogdanovich actually brought down his heavy fist
on the table-top. 'You're twenty-eight, and he'll be twenty-
five this month. Just three years between you. How have
you managed to get so old in those three years that you can
call him a baby? What about Grishka Kukharev – do you
remember how old he was when he married Vera?'

'Yes, I do,' Nastya replied in a low, dull tone. 'And I
know the stories they tell about Grishka too. He chases after
everything in petticoats – if you put a skirt on a goat he'd
run after it sniffing. That's what happened with him and
Vera, and I don't want it happening to me.'

'Don't be silly – this chap's nothing like Grishka. Take a
look at him – can you see him chasing skirts? He's not a
young fellow of that sort, he's as gentle as a lamb.'

'Artemy Bogdanovich!' cried Kostya, jumping to his feet.
His cheeks were blotchy, his green eyes almost melting with
embarrassment; his voice was a hoarse, feeble tenor. 'I don't
want any more – she's said enough. It's no use unless it's for
– for love, and as it's not – well, that's the end of it. I'm
going, Artemy Bogdanovich.'

Artemy Bogdanovich suddenly became quiet and stern.
He said:

'All right, Nastya, tell him to go away. Go on, tell him –
I'm listening.'

'I'm going, Artemy Bogdanovich. I'm going! If she
doesn't want me, if she doesn't feel she can . . . What's the
use?'

'Well, Nastya, I still haven't heard you say anything.
Don't you want to? Well, I'll say something, and it'll be
my last word. You want to put up the price? All right, do –
everyone's got the right to put a good price on himself. But
remember – you may be left with the goods on your hands,
and yours are a kind that spoil quickly. It's like milk – if
you keep it too long, nobody'll give you a penny for it.'

'How can you talk like that about goods and prices?'
wailed Kostya. 'I can't stand it, I won't! If I'd known, I'd
never have . . . Oh, curse it all!'

He turned away abruptly and made for the door. Nastya's

mother, who was still sitting with an air of anxious expectation in her colourless, wrinkled face, sighed and looked down at the table-top.

'Wait a minute, Kostya,' said Nastya quietly.

Kostya paused, with one foot over the threshold. She went on in the same quiet voice, looking intently at him:

'Do you really love me?'

'Not now I don't, I hate you! It's all over – my feelings are burnt out. You have made an enemy of me, Nastya, for the rest of your life.'

Nastya smiled and turned to Artemy Bogdanovich.

'Did you bring anything with you by any chance? You see, I have nothing ready, we weren't expecting such guests as you.'

'Why, yes, we did,' said Artemy Bogdanovich hesitantly. 'Kostya – we left the bottle outside, bring it in, there's a good chap!'

Kostya stood irresolutely for a moment, then went out and returned, grim-faced and avoiding everyone's eyes, with a pint bottle of vodka, which he placed on the table.

12

When Keshka had moved in, he and Nastya had never even registered their marriage, much less had a full-dress wedding. But this time Artemy Bogdanovich himself took matters in hand, and decided that the couple should be married in style.

From time immemorial, Whitsun had been regarded as a special holiday both by the old folk who were still believers and by the godless youth. As Artemy Bogdanovich remarked, it was easier to get rid of God than of His feast-days. Accordingly he now called a meeting of the farm management and, after discussion, issued the following order:

'In the interests of combating religious superstition, the management of the "champion" kolkhoz has decided that:

1. Whitsuntide shall henceforth be abolished.

2. Instead, the kolkhoz will celebrate every year its own socialist festival known as "Welcome to Summer".

3. This year, the "Welcome to Summer" festival will be combined with a joyful celebration of the wedding of Konstantin Nespanov to the farm's champion pig-minder, Anastasya Syroyegina.

4. The management assigns the sum of five hundred roubles for the celebration of the wedding.

5. The wedding celebration will take place on the bank of the Kurchavka river near the former Redkin mill, or, in case of bad weather, in the village recreation hall.

6. All members of the farm are invited to attend.'

Nor was this all. It had always been Artemy Bogdanovich's motto that it was not enough to do a good deed – you must also get the credit for it. He now resolved that not only the district but the province as a whole should be alerted to the kolkhoz wedding. So he went to the stores belonging to the village co-operative, bought up some old shop-worn packages of drawing paper and took them to the office of the district party committee. After he had had a short conversation there, the district printer's office received a message by telephone to say that the chairman of the 'champion' kolkhoz was on his way and should be given all possible help. Soon after this, Artemy Bogdanovich arrived in person, laid the packages of paper on the printer's desk, handed him the text of an invitation, which he had drafted with his own hand, and said: 'Do me a great favour – print it as handsomely as you can.' The invitation read:

'Dear Comrade . . . On the 2nd of June of this year, at Verkhneye Koshelevo village in the Zagarye district, the 'champion' kolkhoz will be celebrating the marriage of its foremost pig-breeder Anastasya Stepanovna Syroyegina to the chairman of the village soviet, Konstantin Ivanovich Nespanov. On behalf of the bridal couple and of the whole kolkhoz we invite you, dear Comrade, to be a welcome guest at the kolkhoz celebration, which will begin at 3 p.m.'

Who could refuse such a favour? So the invitations went round the province: to the secretary of the agricultural commission, the chairman of the soviet executive committee, the chief editor of the provincial newspaper and the head of the agricultural supplies office. The district got its invitations too: they went to Pukhnachov, the first secretary, Kuchin the secretary for propaganda, Gavrilov the chairman of the soviet executive committee, Sivtsov the manager of the district branch of the State Bank (a useful man), Tuzhikov the chairman of the district co-operative (a no less useful man) and one or two more whom Artemy Bogdanovich thought it worth while cultivating. There was no doubt that the guests from district headquarters would come; provincial headquarters were a hundred and twenty miles away, so it was less likely that the high officials would show up from there, nor did Artemy Bogdanovich particularly want them to. The important thing was that they should read the invitation and be reminded of the existence of the 'champion' kolkhoz in the Zagarye district, which – they would conclude – was evidently in a prosperous state if it was able to celebrate the wedding of its best workers in such style.

The invitations went out, and Artemy Bogdanovich, who did not do things by halves, went to work on Tuzhikov, the chairman of the co-operative, and obtained from him whole barrels of salt herring and buckets full of vegetable oil, as well as vodka, red wine and champagne by the crate; while in Stepakovskaya village Anfisa, an aged peasant woman, devoted her skill to brewing large quantities of beer. Excited accounts of the preparations sped from village to village, and everyone awaited the joyful day. The two champion accordion-players Pavel Kleshnyov and Sergey Riukhin, who were eternal rivals – no one could ever decide which of them played better – were given time off work in order to rehearse, with strict injunctions to 'rise to the occasion'.

Nastya made herself a white dress. Kostya came to see her every day before the wedding: he would sit stiffly on the edge of the bench, with his hair sticking up in such a way that she almost wanted to stroke it and say, 'There, there, who's been upsetting you?' Occasionally he would say with a sigh:

'I'm going to give up my job and drive a tractor or go in for animal-breeding.'

'What for?'

'There's no future in my work, no scope somehow. In an active job I could show what I'm made of.'

'At least what you're doing now is clean. If you had to look after animals, your hands would be covered with muck.'

'As though I was frightened of a little dirt! Why, I would give my life for our country's future!'

Nastya looked at the unruly, boyish tuft of hair, the smooth forehead and the indignant green eyes, and thought to herself with womanly compassion: 'Good gracious, he's not three years younger than I am, but a full thirteen. I'm marrying a real babe in arms!'

13

The great day had arrived.

The sky was cloudless: the martins soared upwards into a vault of the deepest blue. The pebbles on the river-bed gave a reddish hue to its dark waters. On its grassy banks, the lush, singing birch-trees of early summer dreamily rustled their leaves, which had not yet lost the freshness of spring.

Beside the river, three trestle tables which had been knocked together for the occasion were arranged to form three sides of a rectangle. The shorter middle section, reserved for the bridal couple and dignitaries, was spread with sheets to form a white cloth; there had not been enough to cover the remaining places. The women who had volunteered as waitresses were busy laying out the first part of the meal. There were slices of cold ham, beef and mutton; herring cut in large pieces, with boiled potatoes, and pickled cabbage doused with vegetable oil; jellied meat, piled on round dishes, which was beginning to dissolve in the heat; cucumbers of last year's salting; and salads of meat, beetroot and vegetables dressed with the same oil from the co-operative. Amongst this rich array were light-coloured bottles of vodka and smarter-looking, darker ones of champagne. Near the places of honour there were glass

decanters of the kind one saw on the farm directors' table
at meetings; these were filled to the brim with dark amber-
coloured home-brewed beer. Further off, the same brew was
served in enamelled teapots of various colours.

The people on the river-bank were as numerous as bees
about to swarm. They shuffled about on the grass and collected in little groups, talking solemnly about the weather
and the spring crops and how a bit of rain would do no
harm – not today of course, heaven forbid, but in the next
week or so. All the men were wearing suits and clean shirts;
one or two even had hats on, and many were so got up that
their neighbours would scarcely have known them: the
moist smell of the river was almost drowned in waves of
naphthalene. The girls wore coloured dresses and wrist-
watches, and each one clutched a clean handkerchief. Old
Isay, in a brand-new pair of boots, grimaced with pain.
Everyone did their best to become absorbed in conversation
in case their eyes should stray towards the table: it would
be unseemly to show impatience.

Eventually the district notables appeared. They came
sauntering towards the party at a leisurely pace: Pukhnachov, a shortish man with close-cropped hair, Kuchin,
who was well built and developing a paunch, the stately
Tuzhikov of the co-operative and the quiet, bespectacled
bank manager. They mingled with the throng and joined in
the conversations about spring crops.

The bridal couple had not yet arrived. It was now four
o'clock, the sun was getting lower in the sky and some of the
men had taken off their worsted jackets. The bride and
bridegroom could not be seen, nor could Artemy Bogdanovich . . . All of a sudden, a shout was heard:

'Make way-y-y!' – and along came an open carriage
drawn by three prancing and neighing horses, with Artemy
Bogdanovich as coachman, leaning backwards and crimson
in the face. He cried again:

'Make way, everybody! Make way for the bride and
groom!'

The bride's white shawl flapped in the breeze. The bridegroom, in his black suit, looked like a starling: his tie was

choking him, and his chin stuck up in the air.

The crowd on the bank became agitated. Those nearest the horses fell back, while others pushed from behind to get a closer view; there was jostling, laughter and shouting:

'Look at old Artemy – you'd think he was the prophet Elijah!'

'He should have stuck on something to make a beard.'

'They ought to have bells; they used to have them in the old days.'

'Oh, bells are out of date.'

'Make way! Make way, good people!'

Then shrill female voices were heard:

'Friends and guests, come to the table, please! Everybody please come! Make yourselves at home!'

The guests didn't wait to be asked twice: they rushed to occupy the benches, rubbing their hands. Long as the tables were, it proved to be a crush, which especially suited the boys with girls next to them. There was laughter and advice:

'Give Nurka a squeeze, she's a juicy one!'

'Just what I'm trying to do!'

'If you don't stop pawing me I'll call Vasily!'

'He can't come, he's sitting on Dashka's lap.'

During the commotion two more guests appeared. They were not noticed until one of them began to jump arouud in front of the bridal couple, aiming his camera at them.

'Who are they?'

It turned out that the provincial authorities had not forgotten: they had sent reporters to write it up with photographs, so everyone would know what festivities went on at the 'champion' kolkhoz.

Kostya was sweating in his black suit; his face wore a distraught expression, his chin was still poking into the air. Nastya was white-faced, overcome with panic and confusion, and looked as if she would hide under the table at any moment. Her mother, next to her, got no peace from Artemy Bogdanovich, who kept twisting about in his seat. The guests of honour sat smiling vaguely, with a touch of embarrassment.

Nastya wore a frilled head-dress and a veil, which reached
to her shoulders and was blown about by the breeze from
the river. The bridal costume was not very becoming to her:
her large round face with its prominent cheekbones looked
like a wooden bowl, and her plump shoulders and breasts
bulged under the thin fabric. Mortally embarrassed by the
gazes she felt on her, she hid her red, pudgy, calloused
hands under the table.

On Artemy Bogdanovich's orders, the kolkhoz foremen
and others in authority were whispering to their neighbours
at table:

'Pass it on – we don't want people filling their glasses too
often, in case there's a shindy while the guests are still
around. See that Yegor Mityukhin's told – he has a nasty
temper when he's had too much. When they've left we'll still
have the beer, we can make up for lost time tonight.'

As each member of the party received this warning, they
nodded wisely as if to say:

'Yes, yes, of course. We invited them, and we must show
them we know how to behave.'

But the formal beginning of the feast sobered them up
more than any admonitions. The first to rise to his feet was
Artemy Bogdanovich, to whom it fell to propose the first
toast. He described how the kolkhoz was flourishing – they
had recently attained a rate of 300 grammes of grain per
work-day – and how those in charge believed in honouring
their best workers. Nastya Syroyegina – he begged pardon
for the mistake, Nastya Nespanova – had once been nothing
and was now everything; people like her were a source of
life to us all; he thanked the honoured guests for their
presence . . . At last, when the hand holding his glass was
practically numb, Artemy Bogdanovich exclaimed:

'To the health of the bride and bridegroom!'

Then Pukhnachov, the first secretary of the district
Party committee, rose to his feet. In ordinary life he was a
simple man who did not waste words, but on this special
occasion brevity and simplicity were out of place. He too
stood for a long time, holding his glass and discoursing on
how the cadres were increasing in numbers, how the

economic and cultural level was improving, how they had here this splendid example of a model pig-breeder . . .

Kuchin, the second secretary in charge of propaganda, made a long speech linking Nastya's wedding with the international situation and the encroachments of imperialism. Once this was over, however, things went faster, as Tuzhikov, the chairman of the co-operative, was not much of a speaker. He had a shot at the international situation but got confused, switched to the country's glorious future but lost the thread once again, and finally, throwing up his hands, roared out the traditional invitation to the couple to kiss each other:

'Bitter! Bitter!'*

The guests took up the cry in unison. Kostya obediently leant over towards Nastya, fumbled with her veil and pecked her cheek. The guests repeated the cry, and he pecked her once again.

The formal proceedings thus being over, everyone was free to clink glasses with whomever they chose.

'Come on, your health!'

'Hey, Pashka, have you forgotten me? Stretch out your glass, you old devil!'

Some tried to make speeches welcoming the visitors, but soon became tongue-tied. However, their healths were drunk with a will.

The two accordions struck up a merry tune; the young people got up and began to dance, but they were outclassed by Zhenka Kruchinin, the lorry driver, and his wife Glashka. Zhenka jumped up and began stamping with his heels; his polished boot-tops flashed, his arms shot out this way and that, his tousled hair flew in all directions. Then with a leap he fell at Glashka's feet and sang an improvised ditty about how he too would like nothing more than to marry a champion pig-breeder.

And Glashka, with her black hair and narrow hips – she might have passed for a bride herself, though she had two

---

* i.e. Our drinks are bitter till you sweeten them with a kiss. (Translator's footnote.)

children – looked at him from under rigid brows, her shoulders swaying in time to the music, and with a wave of her handkerchief replied in kind, urging him to go and marry his pig-breeder and have lots of piglets.

The photographer from the provincial newspaper, squatting in front of them, clicked away like mad.

'Comrades! Citizens! You've forgotten something!' cried Artemy Bogdanovich. 'You've forgotten to drink – '

'No, we haven't!'

'You've forgotten to drink someone's health. Nastya's mother! She who bore her and brought her up to live among us.'

'Three cheers for Anna Yegorovna! Hurrah!'

The old lady, who had been bent over the table, sat up unexpectedly and mumbled something or other. The photographer rushed up. Then Zhenka went on with his antics, his polished boot-tops gleaming in the sun.

The noise and gaiety on the river-bank lasted till nighttime, but the festivities had not yet reached the stage at which old friends quarrel and enemies weep on each other's shoulders. Only old Isay was too much overcome to rise from the table: they laid him to sleep under the nearest bush, after removing his tight boots. And Tuzhikov, the chairman of the co-operative, suddenly remembered that his life wasn't worth living and set off to drown himself in the river. He was dissuaded in time.

Nastya, who had drunk nothing to speak of, sat motionless at the table; Kostya, who had an arm around Artemy Bogdanovich's shoulder, pointed to her and kept saying:

'She's the first person around here; you're the second, and I'm the third!'

Artemy Bogdanovich, whose face was red and sweaty, gave a satisfied grunt and said:

'Maybe, maybe. But, you know, I'm not a proud man, I don't care about rank.'

'No, no, you're the second – I wouldn't dispute it for a moment. She's the first, and I'm the third!'

The party on the river-bank came to an end, but they went on carousing in the villages, where the accordions

played till long after midnight in honour of Nastya Nespanova, *née* Syroyegina. The festivities went on for hours,
with old friends quarrelling and enemies weeping on each
other's shoulders.

14

At dawn every day Nastya rushed to the piggery to light the
stove; then, while the pigs' food was cooking, she rushed
home again to give Kostya his breakfast and send him off
to work.

When she got home, she would hear the radio blaring out
music; Kostya, his eyes fixed on the mirror, would be
making faces as he shaved, and her mother, who seemed to
have taken a fresh lease on life, would be struggling with
the oven-tongs and carrying hot milk to the table.

Kostya was shy, awkward, almost fragile, making Nastya
feel big and strong by comparison. Day by day she felt a
greater sense of motherly responsibility, and whenever he
went out she was anxious in case any harm should come to
him, though she knew perfectly well that he was only going
about his duties at the village soviet as before. Gradually
she came to believe that he had been attracted to her with
good reason, that he would have found life difficult without
her – which meant that he would not fly away, but would
stay with her permanently.

Up to now, all her womanly tenderness had been lavished
on a half-dead piglet – nobody else wanted or needed her
love – who was there to give it to? But now there was
someone, and at night he whispered, stammering in amazement:

'There's as much f-fire in you as in a stove.'

And Nastya spent her time rushing from the cottage to
the piggery and back again, without a moment to rest or to
look around her. This was what life should be like! If she
had tried, she could not have imagined anything better.

For some time past, the newspapers had been printing
one article after another on the forthcoming provincial
conference of livestock breeders. At farm headquarters they

had been busily casting up totals of the animals milked, bred and sold during this or that period of three months. Now, in the district of Gustoi Bor, where Nastya had never been, she had a rival – another 'champion pig-breeder', more eminent than Nastya, since she had been famous in the province for a long time past, had once received a decoration and still bred more pigs than anyone else. Her name was Olga Karpova. Six months ago Nastya would not have dreamt of challenging her – she belonged, as it were, to a higher sphere. But now Artemy Bogdanovich said in plain words: 'You go in and try to beat her – don't be shy.' And he helped Nastya write a letter to the papers about her own achievements. As usual, he did not do things by halves – 'It's not enough to do a good deed, you must also get the credit for it' – and he saw to it that Nastya's letter was published in three papers: in their own at Zagarye, at Gustoi Bor and in the provincial paper.

'Some of our geese are swans too,' said Artemy Bogdanovich, rubbing his hands.

He was doing all he could to push Nastya, though his own motto was that a wise man doesn't go over a mountain. Nastya dimly realised that this was a stratagem of his. It was convenient to send someone else up the mountain, so that if there were any complaints about non-fulfilment of grain quotas or milk deliveries, he could reply, 'Ah, but just you wait, we're outstanding in other ways, you can't do everything at once.' The whole trick was to sit at the foot of the mountain yourself and have someone else plant the flag on top of it. That was the way to get ahead!

Artemy Bogdanovich had done everything for Nastya – he had pushed her forward and made her famous; even found her a husband. She should have thought of him as a father and benefactor, yet somehow she was afraid of him. No matter how far she got, she would never be out of his reach, and if she ever tried to thwart his wishes he would just quietly drop her, and all her fame and glory would vanish. It wasn't all fun having Artemy Bogdanovich as a benefactor.

Feeling this, Nastya worked all the harder at the piggery.

Apart from it, she was just an ordinary farm-girl. If she made a mess of things, Kostya would put up with it for a time and then disappear. After all, he was an educated fellow, he read books and wrote articles and made speeches about 'political issues'.

The summer farrowing took place, and the litters were much bigger than those of spring. Rowan produced eleven piglets, and even Goldy, who had not been much use in the past, farrowed nine beauties – strong, healthy and a joy to look at. This would have been the time to come clean and admit the previous disasters, but it was awkward to do so just before the provincial conference and after challenging Olga Karpova. All the other girls had done well this time: if she alone had setbacks to admit, it would mean a black mark and there would be malicious comments about the 'champion'. No, she could not back out at this stage, when she only needed a few more pigs to beat the record for the province and outdo Olga Karpova. Everyone expected it of her, especially Artemy Bogdanovich. Any time now, the 'pride of the kolkhoz' might become the pride of the whole province. Her piglets were growing up . . .

Every day at dawn she got up sleepily, splashed her face with water and ran off to the piggery. Returning at a slower pace, she found the radio playing cheerful morning marches, while Kostya shaved meticulously at the table, a clean towel over one shoulder.

She was playing with fire, and it made her anxious. The newspapers continued to rhapsodise about the coming conference, at which Nastya was to make a formal appearance. This meant that she would have to hand over her pigs to someone else while she was away. That someone would have to be Pavla, and who knew what might happen then?

Pavla was only a year older than Nastya. She was a big-boned, flat-chested woman, strong but ungainly, with a coarse face and a husky voice; she had not been married so very long, but already had several children. They had tried to persuade her to look after pigs in the past, but she had refused. It was a messy job, you had to stay on the farm all day long and you often had no peace at night either; you neglected your home, and it was a toss-up whether you made any money, which in any case Pavla did not need desperately, thanks to her husband's earnings.

Pavla had used to think herself more fortunate than Nastya, and had been sorry for her because her father had died when she was little, her mother was sick and the man who had promised to marry her was roaming the country somewhere. She had been sorry, and she had thrown Keshka in Nastya's way. But now things were different, and it was Pavla who was glad of a helping hand from Nastya. Of late, Nastya was always being called to district headquarters for meetings that sometimes went on for days, and the pigs could not be left unattended. Pavla was paid a little extra for looking after them from time to time, though not of course enough to buy new dresses or feed her children: she had to go on working in the fields like everyone else.

But it was one thing to let Pavla look after the pigs for a day or an evening, and another to leave her in charge for a week or two. If she had the run of the piggery for a week, she would be sure to discover that there were not only live pigs there but also dead ones. And, once having discovered the secret, she would not keep it to herself – no, Pavla was not a saint, she would not resist the temptation to trip up a 'champion' fellow-worker.

One day Kostya came home from work with his hair bristling even more than usual and a solemn expression on his face. Either he had just been presiding over a meeting and had not had time to relax, or there was some important news – Nastya's photograph in the papers, or perhaps a bonus to be awarded by the management.

'You're being sent on an official tour,' he announced.

'Where to?'

'You've sat long enough in one place, it's time to share your experience with others.'

'You mean I'm to go away?'

'Well, you can't be on a trip and stay at your own fireside.'

'I won't go.'

'Oh, yes, you will. It's a decision by the bureau of the

district Party committee. First of all, you're to go to Gustoi Bor and compare notes with Olga Karpova. Second, the Blintsy people want you to visit them; and I expect there'll be one or two other places for you to go on top of that.'

'But who can I leave in charge of the piggery? It'll go to rack and ruin.'

'We'll find people to look after it all right. We'll guard the honour of the kolkhoz like the apple of our eye.'

It was no use arguing with Kostya: he was as proud as a peacock that his wife had been chosen to go round the neighbouring districts and teach people how to manage things.

She went to bed in a state of agitation. 'Like the apple of our eye.' This was worse than having just Pavla in charge. As soon as anyone with nothing better to do started poking about, the fat would be in the fire. Whereas if it were only Pavla . . . All things considered, perhaps she need not have worried too much about her. Doubtless Pavla already knew each individual pig by the look of its snout as well as she knew each young man in the village; but what she did not know was the entries about the pigs in the farm register, which was kept under lock and key in the office by the bookkeeper, Sidor Petrayev. It was absurd to imagine that Pavla would take it into her head to examine the register, or that she was literate enough to make anything of it if she did. Of course, Sidor knew the contents of his books by heart, and could reel off any figure you cared to ask him; but so far it had not occurred to Pavla to do so, whereas if the whole farm took a hand . . .

Next morning, after feeding the pigs, Nastya went straight to Artemy Bogdanovich and said:

'All right, I'll go, if it's so important. But I must say I'm afraid of what'll happen to the pigs. Pavla's a reliable enough girl, but it's not the same as oneself.'

'Don't you worry,' said Artemy Bogdanovich reassuringly. 'We'll keep an eye on her.'

Nastya was waiting for this. She replied:

'No, what I wanted to ask was that you shouldn't inter-

fere with her. You know what it's like when you're working
and half a dozen others are watching you and bossing you
around. What I want is for you to tell everybody to leave
her alone. I'll tell her what I want her to do and make sure
she's done it when I come back.'

'All right, I'll give orders. No one will interfere with her.'

'And she's to be paid the same as me, do you hear?'

'Yes, she will be, don't worry.'

'And the pigs are to get the same food as if I was here. I
know that storekeeper Mikhey – he'll give flour to one person
and chaff to another.'

The same day, she took Pavla to the piggery and said:

'Listen, dear, you're not to let a soul near the place, or
there'll be trouble with the management. Throw anyone out
who tries to tell you what to do.'

'Don't worry,' said Pavla. 'I won't put up with any
interference.'

The piglet Keshka was, as usual, rubbing himself against
the side of Nastya's boot and squealing for her to stretch
out a hand and scratch his ear. She bent down to him and
said:

'Don't worry, my sweet. I'm not going away for long.
Pavla, you'll be kind to him, won't you? He's got used to
being petted.'

Pavla laughed. 'I'll keep him under my skirt the whole
time.'

'And another thing. If there's any trouble at all, let
Artemy Bogdanovich know and he'll send me a wire at
once.'

'I shouldn't think it'll come to that. Good gracious,
people don't mind leaving their children with neighbours,
but you and your pigs . . .'

Keshka rubbed against her boots, not leaving her for a
single step. Nastya thought sadly that sooner or later she
would have to part with him – for Keshka, as for all pigs,
the end of life was the slaughter-house. 'My God, it hurts
as if I were parting from my own flesh and blood, not just
from a lot of pigs.'

She wore a bright summer dress with little blue flowers on

it, trimmed at the collar, and a dark jacket with padded
shoulders. Over her arm she carried a light-weight fawn
overcoat with a satin lining. Her high-heeled shoes hurt
terribly, but perhaps they would become easier with wear.
She got into the train.

Artemy Bogdanovich had made a point of coming with
Kostya to see her off. They stood on the platform waving
till the train started. Poor silly Kostya looked all upset; on
the way to the station he had kept stealing glances at
Nastya and had said twice: 'Well, you're a real knockout.'
Artemy Bogdanovich grunted and said:

'Watch out she doesn't pick up some young fellow on her
travels. She could easily.'

'Oh, no, she's as faithful as they come.'

Poor, silly Kostya . . .

15

Her journey, after all, was not to the ends of the earth, but
only to the next district. And one district was very much
like another: the same yellowing fields, the same weather-
beaten village roofs as at home, the same roads with their
ruts and pot-holes and rickety bridges. It was all quite
familiar, you'd have thought there was nothing to excite
special interest, yet Nastya was struck by something new at
every step.

As soon as she got off the train, a man had hurried up to
her and said:

'Excuse me, are you Anastasya Stepanovna by any
chance?'

'Yes, that's me.'

'Come this way please, we have a car waiting.'

Three or four times in her life Nastya had been to visit a
cousin of hers who had married a forester and lived some
distance away; but every time she had arrived at a railway
station, whether on the outward or the homeward journey,
she had had to worry about whether she would be in time
for the bus, or be able to catch the fellow who drove passengers on the side for a bit of extra money. And now it was

'Come this way, please, we have a car waiting.' As she moved towards it, a woman came hurrying forward to meet her: her lined face was crinkled still further by a welcoming smile. Yes, it was Olga Karpova herself who had come to meet Nastya! She held out her hand with a touch of shyness and said:

'I'm glad to meet you. I hope you had a good journey.'

So this was the famous Karpova – a shortish, muscular woman with heavy, bony hands, a sun-tanned face and a shy, good-natured smile. Nastya in her best dress and high-heeled shoes must have looked like an actress from the city by comparison – no doubt that was why Karpova felt slightly intimidated.

Everything was new to Nastya, even the guest-room in the district farmers' club. She had never stayed in a hotel room – whenever she was away from home she had been put up by friends or relations. And here she was in a neat, clean, separate little room with a picture of the 'Three Knights'* on the wall and a carafe of water standing on a white cloth on the bedside table. Everything was new, including the polite knock on her door in the morning and the voice that said, 'Excuse me, I've called for you.' It was a young driver who looked like Zhenka Kruchinin: he had the same saucy glint in his eye, and she almost expected him to start singing one of Zhenka's rude songs. But of course it was really a different place, different people altogether. The famous Olga Karpova, the famous consolidated kolkhoz named after the Twentieth Party Congress, its well-known chairman Afanasy Parfenovich Chuyev – a thin man with a big nose and secretive eyes under bushy brows. He stretched out a hand as broad as a spade with the words:

'Take a good look round. Criticise as much as you like.'

Nastya would dearly have liked to get to the bottom of things and discover Olga Karpova's secret. She looked as simple as could be, an ordinary peasant woman rather like Nastya's mother at an earlier age; but could this really be

* Well-known painting by V. Vasnetsov (1848–1926), a regular feature of Soviet hotel rooms.

all there was to the famous Olga Karpova? There was something odd about it: for years she had been looking after large numbers of pigs and getting enormous litters. Nastya had overtaken her, by means that she knew too well, but now Olga was again threatening to beat her. Did she have five or ten pairs of hands instead of one? Nastya worked like a slave at the piggery from dawn to dusk, and her results were good on paper, thanks to the 'dead souls' that didn't need any looking after, but she couldn't wait to see . . . Perhaps everyone else had some kind of trick as well as herself, perhaps it was the usual thing. That would make it all clear enough – certainly you couldn't get on without a bit of cheating. And let Olga Karpova not try to pull the wool over her eyes – she, Nastya, wasn't a mere farm official, she was an old hand too.

'Take a good look round. Criticise as much as you like.' They were now at Olga Karpova's piggery, and Nastya stepped inside. What she saw took her breath away.

Nastya had seen plenty of piggeries in her time: they were mostly dark, stuffy, stinking places, with the floor covered in dirt and slush, with openings in the ceiling for air. She had always been proud of her own, with its cement path, the boiler which filled with water when you pressed a lever, and the ornamented gratings which had been part of the railings round a church. Here, however, there was not an ordinary boiler but a kind of special machine, with nickel-plated handles like the knobs of a bedpost; its sides were painted white and a sort of puffing and bubbling sound came from within, but there was neither smoke nor steam nor smell. Attached to the machine was a sort of conveyor belt, and if you pressed a lever a portion of hot food was carried along it, down a chute with sides, as far as the pigsties, where each animal got exactly the right amount to fatten it up. There was no question of having to lug dirty buckets to and fro; and as regards cleaning the sties – what a lot of time and trouble she always spent on it, and yet the pigs were always rolling in filth. Here you just took a rubber hose and all the filth went down another chute which carried it to a well outside. You put the lid over that and everything was clean, you didn't even need to use a shovel. And the whole piggery was light, airy and painted white inside like a hospital. Anybody could work in a place like this without needing to exert themselves – even an idler could beat all records!

'Take a good look round. Criticise as much as you like.' She had been sent here to share experience, to compare notes on methods. Yes, she could tell them something about methods all right . . .

Ever since Nastya had thrown the dead piglets at Artemy Bogdanovich's feet and he had said to her: 'The whole trick in life is how to cope with people who are strong . . . You must use your wits' – she had done just that and resorted to guile without a qualm of conscience, in the spirit of the saying that 'a simpleton is worse than a thief'. The only thing she had been frightened of was that her deception might be found out. And now here they were saying to her, 'Criticise as much as you like' – for all the world as if she were an honest person, a saint of some kind. Standing there in her best dress and high-heeled shoes – if she herself had come across a pig-breeder in such a get-up, she would have spat with disgust! The dress was a fraud, her show-off voice was a fraud, she had even got herself a husband thanks to fraud. Her whole life and happiness were built on fraud – how could they be lasting? How could she feel any respect for herself? – she was like an imitation stone in an expensive-looking piece of jewellery.

Walking round the spacious piggery with Olga Karpova, Nastya hated her. Olga was a simple peasant, even more backward than herself; she had struck it lucky, that was all. With a set-up like this, she had no need to use tricks and deceive people. Nastya too would have preferred not to use tricks; but her happiness was like a horse with glanders, it looked healthy and arched its neck proudly, but it was rotten inside and only fit to be destroyed. Why? Whose fault was it? Nastya hated Olga.

That evening there was a meeting of all the livestock breeders at the 'Twentieth Party Congress' kolkhoz. Nastya had to make a speech: the high-ups invited her to the rostrum, applauding as she stepped forward. 'Criticise as

much as you like . . .' Nastya realised that it would be wiser
not to criticise; instead, she sang the praises of Olga, her
piggery and its thoroughbred stock.

'I personally have learnt a great deal here, comrades, and
seen many admirable things. I can say in all frankness that
we are a long way behind you . . . Thank you, everybody.'

Her audience looked pleased: Olga Karpova's tanned,
wrinkled face flushed with delight, and even Afanasy Parfenovich Chuyev, a tough, experienced character who could
see right through a brick wall, looked as if he were at a
birthday party. No one is proof against flattery – so Nastya
thought to herself, as she laid it on thick about Olga
Karpova.

They gave her a tremendous send-off.

16

After a roundabout trip through two or three other districts, she returned home. Kostya was at the station. He
looked startled when he saw her and became strangely
subdued, looking at her out of the corner of his eye.

'What is it? Has anything happened?' she asked.

'No, nothing. It's you – you look different somehow.'

She still had on the same dress and jacket, with an overcoat over her arm; but her round face had become more
angular, her cheekbones more prominent. The wrinkles
round her eyes were more noticeable, and the eyes themselves had a restless and anxious expression; there was
something bitter about the curve of her full lips. Yes, she
was different . . .

Kostya himself was just the same as ever: his thick hair
bristled up from his smooth forehead, his big ears flushed in
agitation and his green eyes had a lost, expectant look.

Nastya herself felt that she had changed. Every day had
meant a new step upwards, something fresh to be attained,
but sooner or later the end was bound to come. She had
pretended to be calm and assured, but of late she could not
sleep at night. This had never happened to her before: as a
rule she would lay her head on the pillow and be aware of

nothing more till cock-crow, when it was time to get up.

Would Kostya ever understand? He was a simple fellow, and it was a wonder he had become chairman of the village soviet, even though all the real work was done by Artemy Bogdanovich.

She embraced Kostya, leaning her head against his cheek; then broke away and said with passion:

'Oh, my poor dear, I'm so glad to see you! How have you been without me?'

She saw his eyes grow moist, and thought to herself: fancy that, he does love me – he's glad I'm back, perhaps he even missed me.

'Let's go right away, I want to get home.'

'We can't go home straight away – there's a Party meeting at district headquarters. They want you to make a speech and tell them how you got on.'

'Oh dear, oh dear!'

The pigs, overcome by the heat, were lying in the enclosure outside the piggery. Suddenly one stirred, got on its feet and ran towards her. Keshka – a plump, pink, bouncing creature – nearly knocked Nastya off her feet. He squealed and danced about her with his snout in the air, then nuzzled up against her skirt and wearily closed his eyes with a look of bliss. Nastya felt the tears come into her eyes as she said:

'Look, he knows me! Oh, you sweet darling, you silly little thing!'

She scratched the rough, flaking skin on her pet's back. Keshka swooned in ecstasy.

Pavla, noisily blowing her nose on a corner of her handchief, said:

'Curse the creature! Love is cruel all right. He wouldn't have come up to me like that.'

The sun blazed down, the still air was permeated with familiar smells – the dizzying reek of manure and the tang of the pigs' heated bodies. The fields, the stream hidden by the osier-bed, the woods that seemed to melt in the heat, and the unpeopled village – everything lay in a deep, dreamy peace. Nothing had changed in Nastya's everyday world – it was all just as before.

What Nastya longed for nowadays above all things was
to get up early in the morning, walk the short distance to the
piggery with her face turned to the bright morning sky, roll
up her sleeves and get to work – looking after her animals
with loving care, knowing that not a single day was wasted
but that each one brought some gain in the shape of meat,
lard or money for the kolkhoz; knowing, too, that her own
home and children were waiting for her – sooner or later
there were bound to be children – and that their life would
be a better one than hers. They would not have to eat cakes
made of nettles and flax-husks, hard as rocks and black as
mouldy dung, and they would not have to see their father
go off to war with a bitter joke on his lips: 'I'll come back
covered in medals or die in a ditch.' And there would be
little moments of happiness, little joys like this one today.

Today Kostya was tinkering about with his new motor-
cycle, which Nastya had bought him. It was one with a
sidecar, the kind that was not easy to get: they were
snapped up as soon as they appeared in the shops. But
Tuzhikov at the co-operative had come to the rescue: he
remembered the wedding-party and all the strong drink,
and almost as soon as Nastya had said 'I wonder whether
. . .', the machine was hers. 'Here it is, Kostya, with my
love.' He had his dreams too.

There was nothing Nastya longed for except such a life –
peaceable, joyful, without fame or excitement; aching in the
evening, a sound sleep, a clear conscience. She longed to
start living in this way at once, but was not allowed to.
That evening she had to put on her best dress once again
and go to the other end of the district, to the kolkhoz
named after the Second Five-Year Plan, where she was to
tell them about her work. She was so eminent a pig-breeder
now that she was hardly given a chance to look after her
pigs. Pavla, about whom nothing was written in the newspapers, who was not sent on official trips or received with
honours, had to feed and care for the pigs while Nastya
went about blowing her own trumpet.

Soon, the long-awaited provincial congress would take
place. But for the moment she had to push away the

fawning Keshka and hurry to the village, where Artemy
Bogdanovich was waiting impatiently for a private chat, to
find out what she had seen and heard and how the other
kolkhozes had treated his representative. Well, he could
open his ears all right – she would have something to tell
him . . .

Artemy Bogdanovich was sweating in a dark suit, which
he had put on in honour of the occasion. His hot face
wreathed in smiles, he pressed her hand, clapped her on the
shoulder, moved up a chair and looked into her eyes. But
when they started to talk he became quieter and more
solemn and began to drum on the table with his fingers. He
listened without interrupting while Nastya told him about
Olga Karpova's mechanised piggery.

'Whether you like it or not,' she said, 'we must have one
like that sooner or later. If we don't, we can make as much
fuss as we like, but we won't fool people for long. As long
as they're mechanised and we're not, they're bound to get
ahead of us however hard we try. I can see you're figuring
out the cost. Well, you needn't; I know it's expensive, but I
swear that in a year or two it'll pay for itself with interest.'

Artemy Bogdanovich listened, calculating in silence. She
went on:

'If we are going to make up our minds to do it, it should
be now, so that we can have the new building by spring, or
summer at the latest. Otherwise we'll fall behind.'

'Spring or summer?' repeated Artemy Bogdanovich.
'What would you say, Nastya, if I could get you the new
piggery at the very beginning of winter?'

'That would be much better, of course. If I had it then I
might even risk another winter farrowing.'

'Well, why shouldn't we?' said Artemy Bogdanovich,
screwing up his eyes with increasing excitement. 'You know
we were going to build a new stockyard, we'd even laid the
foundations. We were going to put in a water system with
wells, and room for manure storage underneath. But we
made a mistake in choosing the site: the cattle would have
to be driven out to pasture across the sown fields, so that
we'd either have to make a path or they'd trample every-

thing. Why don't we scrap the stockyard and build a model piggery instead, before it's too late?'

'It would pay off quicker, too. Our pigs breed well, while the cows around here just turn fodder into dung.'

'Yes, it would pay off . . . All right, we'll think about it. But you'd have to walk four or five miles to work: how about that?'

'I could have my house moved closer to the piggery. You'd help me, wouldn't you?'

'Of course I would. All right, I'll put it to the management board.'

To all intents and purposes, this meant that the matter was settled. Once Artemy Bogdanovich raised the question, the board was not going to say no.

17

The provincial Theatre of Comedy and Drama was ablaze with light. It was a building with columns which had been altered several times since its erection in the nineteenth century. Architects and builders had done their best to ensure that all who entered it felt they were taking part in a festive occasion. There were carpeted floors, sparkling chandeliers and marble walls with huge mirrors.

Today the foyer indeed wore a festive air: it was crowded and bustling, there were colourful stands covered with books and pamphlets, and reporters darted about amid the throng as if possessed. The occasion was not a holiday, however, but a conference about practical matters; there was in fact little to be festive about.

At one time, the region had been famous throughout Russia for its lush meadows and its special breed of cows, whose butter, meat and hides earned millions for the local merchants. Then the province had gone over to grain production: the country needed bread, as much land as possible had to be brought under the plough. The lush meadows were ploughed up. Then, when it was too late, they found that the fields became marshy and overgrown with shrubs. The thoroughbred herds grew sickly and were replaced in the kolkhozes by a smaller, tougher breed which could be fed on coarse hay from the forest glades. But by now these had begun to get covered with undergrowth, and it was time to sound the alarm. The conference had not been called to celebrate victory – some people were going to get it in the neck.

However, Nastya was not there to be reprimanded or criticised: on the contrary, even before the conference opened she was being sought after on every hand. 'Please come and visit the provincial department of agriculture; please look in on the veterinary course.' At the Party's provincial headquarters the First Secretary himself had spoken to her; newspaper and radio correspondents lay in wait outside her hotel room, which was a special one with a bath and telephone, a handsome writing-table and a view of the main square. Artemy Bogdanovich shared the next room with Pukhnachov, the secretary of the district Party committee; he looked after Nastya assiduously and even talked to the reporters on her behalf so that she should not get overtired.

At the conference, Nastya was chosen to be a member of the presiding committee. She walked right through the auditorium up to the stage, with everyone looking at her – Anastasya Nespanova, *née* Syroyegina, from the Zagarye district, no less. Beside her, at the table covered with red cloth, sat a grey-haired man in glasses who was a professor at the local Institute – even Nastya, who, it must be admitted, had not had much education, had read pamphlets of his on fodder rationing, and now here she was sitting beside him in a place of honour. Hundreds of faces looked up from the darkened hall below; somewhere among them were those of Artemy Bogdanovich and Pukhnachov and many other chairmen of kolkhozes and secretaries of district Party committees, while she sat up there above them all. The chairman mentioned her name several times with respect, and when there was a break in the proceedings and she went down the steps into the auditorium, the grey-haired professor took her politely by the arm and said, 'Be careful, don't fall.' Then he added: 'I've heard a lot about you; I'm glad we've met.' They went out together into the foyer with its blazing chandeliers, and were assailed by photographers: 'Just a minute! Just a minute! We won't keep you!' Next morning Artemy Bogdanovich brought her the paper with the words: 'A union of practice and theory, you might say', and there were the two celebrities, hand in hand.

Next day she was asked to make the first speech. 'No, no excuses – we can't go on till you've spoken.' So she advanced under bright lights to the rostrum, clutching the notes of her speech in a sweaty hand. The many-headed, many-faced audience gazed at her with its hundreds of eyes out of a mysterious, frightening twilight. This was a different matter from talking to her fellow-kolkhoz workers: her knees almost gave way with fright. However, she managed to say her piece:

'We, the livestock breeders of the "champion" kolkhoz in the Zagarye district, solemnly vow to continue our efforts . . .'

The audience applauded, and Nastya realised that they needed her – needed her badly, more than they needed Artemy Bogdanovich or Pukhnachov or anyone else, even Olga Karpova. Olga was ancient history, she had been famous too long: to go on mentioning her was like confessing that none of the younger ones could come up to her, that they were marking time. But here there was a young rival at last – the province could not be in such a bad way if such reliable, capable younger people were coming into the field.

'We, the livestock breeders of the "champion" kolkhoz in the Zagarye district, solemnly vow to continue our efforts.'

The ordinary pig-breeder who spoke these words was the one they had just seen in the newspaper, arm in arm with the celebrated professor. A union of practice and theory – if that was the sort of thing they could do, the province would soon be on its feet again.

Up till now, Nastya had felt fear and suspicion of other people: at any moment they might turn and tear her apart. She was a fraud, an interloper, an imitation jewel in a necklace. But now she suddenly realised, not only with her

mind but with all her being, that people needed and wanted
to believe in her. If you have no real jewels, you make do
with imitation ones. Keeping up people's courage was an
important service, and it was what everyone in the audience
needed, as they needed her, Nastya. As for Artemy Bogdanovich, he would do everything he could to keep her
riding the crest of the wave. She had imagined that she was
alone, surrounded by enemies – but now she found she was
not alone and had nothing to fear. They were going to build
a new piggery, like Olga Karpova's or perhaps even better,
and there Nastya could really show what she was capable
of: she would breed huge litters which would sooner or later
make up for the 'dead souls', and then her conscience
would be clear and she would be as if reborn – in the whole
world there would not be a more honourable person than
Nastya Nespanova!

'A wise man goes around a mountain . . .' But now that
she had risen to this height, what terrors could even the
steepest mountains hold for her?

'We, the livestock breeders of the "champion" kolkhoz in
the Zagarye district, solemnly vow . . .' The hall rang with
applause. They believed her, they trusted her. And she
too trusted herself – she would fulfil every duty, she would
not let them down. She would give all her strength to benefit
those who depended on her. Her eyes filled with tears –
tears of happiness and gratitude towards those who needed
her.

18

The dawn broke timidly, as it always did, through the flimsy
clouds over the dark strip of forest on the horizon, and lit up
the dark windows of the sleeping cottages. Nastya was still
the first person in Utitsy to be up and about. Junketing was
all very well in its way, but she had had enough of meetings
and triumphs: it was a relief to cast off her high-heeled shoes
and get back into her rubber boots and shabby quilted
jacket. Back to the uncertain dawn over the forest, the
well-trodden path, the stove under the cooker and the drum

of the potato-crushing machine.

As of old, she heard the rattle of wheels and old Isay's voice calling 'Hey, Cinderella, are you still alive?' Nowadays they brought her the best pig-food and as much of it as she asked for – woe betide anyone who refused.

Under Pavla's care, which after all wasn't the same as her own, the pigs had begun to look a little peaked; so Nastya fed them up and gave them even more attention than before. Her pet Keshka grew bigger and fatter, but was still as lively and affectionate as ever. He was the first to squeal when Nastya opened the door, rousing the whole piggery; he had learnt to push up the bar that closed the entrance to his own sty with his snout, and would jump out and get under her feet, pushing and wriggling.

Meanwhile, on the outskirts of the village, the construction of the new model piggery was in full swing. The underground manure pit was being lined with bricks, the walls were already built and the rafters were going into place. Artemy Bogdanovich was in a frenzy of activity: every day he rushed off to district or provincial headquarters, while telephone calls came pouring in from all directions. All his unofficial sources of supply, such as Tuzhikov, were mobilised: Artemy Bogdanovich had such contacts by the dozen, and he needed them too, for it was no easy matter to get hold of all the necessary water-pipes, cast-iron sewer lids, electric motors and swill-boilers. But Artemy Bogdanovich used Nastya's name to put the fear of God into all of them, and if there was any sign of reluctance or delay he would shout: 'You ought to be ashamed of yourselves! It's for our champion pig-breeder, the pride of the whole province!' Consequently the piggery was going up in record time: the pipes and electric cables were already laid, and now the rafters were going on.

It looked as if, by the time the first frosts came, Nastya would already be able to say goodbye to Utitsy and set up house near the new piggery. They were going to move the old cottage bodily, at the same time touching it up and enlarging it a bit: they would probably give it an iron roof and strengthen the walls with boards. But as Nastya was an

interested party she preferred not to use her own authority
to secure favours over this, but to let Kostya arrange it with
Artemy Bogdanovich.

Kostya had got himself a leather helmet with big goggles,
and instead of rushing off to work on foot every morning he
now roared off on his motor-cycle. Every Sunday he would
tinker with the machine, taking it to pieces and re-assemb-
ling it, oiling it and running the engine. It stank and made a
deafening noise, but Kostya listened to it like music, saying
contentedly:

'Ah, the twentieth century's a great thing. Technical
progress – that's what counts!'

Kostya's voice had begun to sound deeper lately; he had
adopted an imposing manner like that of Artemy Bogdanovich, and was beginning to know people at district
headquarters. Much to his fury, Zhenka Kruchinin had
composed a ditty about a man who had done very well for
himself by marrying a woman pig-keeper.

Otherwise, life continued as usual. The harvest was early
and they had a fine autumn, which became drier, sunnier
and more golden as winter approached. The stubble was
covered with gossamer that looked like hoarfrost. In the
evenings, crowds of rooks flew around over the roofs and
fir-trees.

One sunny, windy day, Nastya had washed out the skim-
milk cans and hung them on the fence. She looked across
the fields to the highway to see if Kostya would come
rattling along it on his motor-cycle, as it was dinner-time.
Suddenly a well-built man emerged from a dip in the road
and came walking towards the piggery, swinging his
shoulders. From his walk and the tilt of his head she knew
at once that it was Keshka. Her heart missed a beat from
surprise; she tucked up her hair under her scarf, turned
towards him and waited. Still some way off, he paused and
said:

'Hallo, Nastya.'

'Hallo.'

He came up and stood there in his heavy boots, with his
feet apart. His brow was puckered under the peaked cap,

and his gold tooth flashed as he nibbled on a blade of grass. He looked a little the worse for wear in his shapeless cap and shabby leather coat; his face wore a dull expression, and the lines on his cheeks were deeper: the last time she had seen him, he had seemed more dashing. But he was still sturdy enough, with a bear-like strength of the sort that Kostya lacked.

'I thought you were so far up in the world, you might not want to know me.'

'Oh, I'm still wallowing in pig shit, as you can see.'

Keshka evidently recognised his farewell words: he grunted unhappily and fell silent.

'Are you spending long here?' Nastya asked.

'Only a night. I was passing through and thought I'd stop by. Not much point in staying longer – nobody's fond of me here anyway.'

'If you look, you might find someone. There are kind people here the same as anywhere else.'

He grunted again, looked at her wryly and said:

'Anyway, you haven't forgotten me?'

'No, how could I?' She turned towards the open door of the piggery and called out, 'Hi, Keshka!' The clatter of an upturned bucket was heard, and out jumped Keshka – the other, fat, pink one she knew so well. He rushed at Nastya's feet and nearly knocked her over.

'Look out, you clumsy thing! You see, I used to have a man and now I have a pig – it's like a change in a fairy story. Oh, yes, I remember you all right.'

At that moment the roar of Kostya's motor-cycle was heard, and he came bumping along the road in his helmet and goggles, his face lashed by the wind. He stopped, pushed up his goggles and looked at them with startled green eyes. Keshka, still chewing the blade of grass, surveyed Kostya and the motor-cycle with calm interest and said:

'It's a "Ural", isn't it? Have you done many miles?'

'No, only about two thousand,' replied Kostya, slightly confused.

'They're a good make. I always meant to buy one, but

they're not for the likes of me. Well, I'll be seeing you some time.'

He turned and began to walk away, swinging his sloping shoulders; then took another glance at the motor-cycle and said without envy: 'Yes, it's a good make.'

'Keshka! Back to your sty, you little wretch! Go away, damn you!' exclaimed Nastya to the pig, which was pushing at her legs. The other Keshka turned round, shaking his head.

'What did he want?' said Kostya. His green eyes, edged by watery-coloured, flickering eyelashes, were aflame with jealousy.

'Nothing,' said Nastya sadly. 'He's wandering about looking for someone to be fond of him. Let's go and have dinner, Kostya.'

The sight of the footloose Keshka had reminded Nastya that it was not only fame that kept her warm and happy. She had everything that a human being could possibly wish for.

19

The new piggery was nearly complete, and Nastya stepped inside it. She was accompanied by Artemy Bogdanovich, muffled in a sheepskin winter coat; the senior carpenter, Yegor Pomelov; the mechanic in charge of the equipment, a lanky youth in a round fur cap, who came from the neighbouring town; and Senka Slavin, the electrician.

The shimmering daylight poured in through the wide, low windows with their double frames and shining new glass. The walls still smelt a little of damp plaster; the paved flooring was of a coppery yellow colour; the cement path and the chutes were strewn with curly shavings. The long rows of pens, divided by gratings, stretched into the distance. All that remained to be done was to install the conveyor, connect the electric motors and add a final coat of paint; the water was already laid on.

'You should celebrate, Nastya. The boys have worked hard,' said Yegor with a wink of his red eye. Nastya said nothing.

'She can do that when you've moved her house,' replied Artemy Bogdanovich.

'If you put the whole lot of us on the job, we can do it in a week. It doesn't take long when you know how.'

Artemy Bogdanovich screwed up his eyes like a cat that has just been fed. He walked about feeling the partitions and touching the damp plaster with his nails – not saying anything, but purring inwardly with satisfaction.

'Well, Nastya, now you can really let yourself go. Pavla can take over your old piggery – take up where you left off, so to speak.'

Nastya still said nothing as she looked at the empty, echoing building. She felt the old, half-forgotten fear clutching at her throat.

Artemy Bogdanovich was waving his hand this way and that.

'The porkers will be here, the brood-sows here, and these are the sties for the ones that have just farrowed. This one here is for piglets that have just been weaned. All nicely divided up, just like a post office. As soon as you've increased the numbers a bit, you stop there and have some of them breeding while others are slaughtered. It's a sort of one-man factory – you'll be turning out meat by the hundredweight. Everything nicely cut and dried, all checked and counted . . . Well, don't you like it? Why don't you say anything?'

Indeed Nastya liked it, but – all checked and counted, that was the trouble. Suddenly she realised! It was she herself who had insisted that they should build the new piggery as soon as possible – and now she saw that it would be her ruin. Porkers, brood-sows, sucklings, a factory with everything cut and dried . . . In her old dark, stuffy, crowded piggery, no one could possibly tell how many pigs there were, but now, with everything 'checked and counted', it would soon be seen that some of the sties were empty. And then not only Artemy Bogdanovich, not only the members of the auditing commission and Kostya Nespanov, the chairman of the village soviet, but anyone who cared to take a look, even if it was only Yegor the carpenter, would see that the 'champion pig-breeder' had made a first-class mess of things. It would be all cut and dried, like a factory or a post office – where then were the missing animals, what had become of part of her stock? Had they got lost on the way? Be so good as to report, my girl! And they would start to cast up accounts: so many pigs missing, so many hundredweight of meat – theft, fraud, embezzlement. There would be no way of covering things up or of squaring the accounts, and her disgrace would be more resounding than her fame had been.

She had brought it on herself. She had thought that life would go on just the same under a new roof – she had insisted on the new building, and in so doing had dug a pit under her own feet.

The cement path cluttered with shavings from end to end, the gullies leading to the manure pit – yes, everything was first-class, it was as fine a piggery as could be found in the district or even the whole province. Artemy Bogdanovich was purring like a cat that has just swallowed some cream.

'Are you sure there's nothing wrong with it?' asked Yegor. 'Don't be afraid to say if there is. We don't mind criticism here – we're a responsible firm!'

'No, it's all very nice – very nice indeed.'

'That's good. And don't worry about your house, we'll have that here in no time. It'll be as smart as a new pin, you won't recognise it. You'll just have time to spend a night or two at your relations', and we'll be along to tell you it's ready and you can have a house-warming!'

The lanky engineer and Senka the electrician moved from one wall to another discussing additional wiring. Somewhere water was dripping from a tap that had not been turned off properly.

'Next week as ever is you'll be able to move in here with all your tribe,' said Artemy Bogdanovich.

'Next week as ever is . . .'

20

It was night. She looked out of the window at the fields,

snowless but stiff with cold under the full moon. Kostya's head rested on her arm: his comfortable, heavy breathing sounded close to her ear. Nastya's eyes were wide open. Staring at the moonlit night, she remembered another night, the happiest she was likely to know in all her life.

Like other August nights, that one had been warm and fragrant. The river, and the sedge on its banks, gave off a fresh smell. The stream – black as pitch, viscous and still – lay under the sky as if paralysed. Not a ripple was to be seen in its waters; not a blade of grass stirred on its banks. Somewhere beyond the forests heavy, rain-swollen clouds hung close above the earth; but overhead the sky was clear, and a sharp-edged moon poured light on a spellbound world. The only sound that broke the stillness was the creaking of oars in dry rowlocks, like the cry of a wounded bird.

It might have been a night just like all other August nights . . . The oarsman was Nastya's old sweetheart Venka; his shirt was wide open at the neck, his eyes mysterious and frightening under his tousled hair. Nastya had on a new spotted dress, and over her shoulders a scarf with pale pink roses. She felt that she was looking beautiful. Venka's eyes disturbed and frightened her a little. The oars creaked in anguish once more as the boat cut through the smooth, oily waters.

A night like any other in early August – but no! All of a sudden, the still moonlit air above the sleeping river was full of white whirling flakes, like a snowstorm. They surrounded the boat as it moved on, and reached as far as the nearer bank. Only the cold, angry moon pierced through the cloud of white foam, touching the downy flakes with light.

Venka lifted the oars out of the water and was still for a moment: they heard a dry rustling sound, scarcely audible yet with something feverish and ominous about it. It was the beating of the tiny, featherlight wings of thousands of diaphanous white insects, dancing in the still air by moonlight. There were myriads of them, too many for the broad surface of the sleeping river: they flew up into the air to mate, to enjoy a moment's pleasure and – to die.

Such was the dumb, frenzied snowstorm of that warm August night – a numberless crowd, a swarm of tiny moth-like creatures. Some were spinning in rapture; others, their revels ended, fell into the boat, stuck to Nastya's face or got caught in her hair, with the exhaustion of death on them: the whole river was sprinkled with their tiny forms. They were ephemerids, insects which live only for one day.

The boat glided on through the storm of tiny creatures, over the oily river. The oars creaked, Venka's eyes shone, and the insects whose lives were ended fluttered down to earth, while the moon with its sharp outline glittered overhead.

The fairy-like storm made Nastya feel joyful. Venka was close to her; the insects came down in showers, and she believed that her life would be long and happy. No one had ever yet been false to her. What could have been so happy as that moonlit night?

Tonight the moon again shone brightly. Nastya stared at it, wide-eyed. The moonlight crouched on the doormat; it crept along the floorboards, lighting up every knot in the wood, leapt on to the nickel-plated knobs of the bedpost and then sat, like a snub-nosed animal, in a corner of the window, staring at Nastya and shining on the back of Kostya's neck as he lay there breathing comfortably, with his head on her arm.

Kostya's neck was white, firm and covered with a tender, curly down, like a boy's . . . She bit her lips to keep from groaning aloud. There he lay beside her, warm and trustful, breathing peacefully, his head on her arm. She gazed at the down on his neck and felt her heart melt with tenderness and helpless sorrow.

Soon he would know the whole story. Oh, Kostya, Kostya! Let everybody else know, let them laugh and point at her and make up cruel rhymes – if only there could be some miracle so that Kostya wouldn't have to know too! Miracles – there weren't any nowadays, they had disappeared with the saints. Oh, Kostya, Kostya! She would never again see the down on his neck or feel his breath close to her ear. Just

a short week from now! Biting her lips, she found them salty
with tears.

She saw again that happy night with the fairy-tale storm
of insects. The sort of night that happens once in a lifetime.
Once – but surely it could happen again. The winter would
pass, there would be other warm, moonlit summer nights,
and the same swarms of insects – creatures of a single day.
It could all happen again, if only . . . But now she had only
a week to live.

Thinking of her sentence, her heart wrung by the sight
of Kostya's head on her arm, she began wildly to devise
plans of escape.

Supposing she said to the management: 'I'll take just a
few brood-sows and start all over again in the new piggery –
after all, I began before with only ten sucklings. All the
others can stay where they are, in the old place.'

Hope sprang up for a moment, and expired. She would be
handing over the old piggery to Pavla, who would naturally
want an inventory to be made, and then everything would
come to light.

Suppose she said someone else could take over the new
place? After she had insisted on it and pestered them to get
it ready in time? No, they would smell a rat, and everything
would be found out.

Suppose she and Kostya simply ran away somewhere?
Ran away? Where to, silly girl? And how to explain to
Kostya? She'd have to make a clean breast of it all to him.
And what about her sick mother? And what would they do
in a strange place, and how could she hide anyway? They
might easily get the police to track her down.

However she tortured herself, there was no answer. She
lay in the moonlight and gazed at the curly, childlike down
on Kostya's neck, and her heart bled with tenderness. She
was in a witch's circle, and there was no way out. For the
time being she still had Kostya lying by her side. For just
one week more.

There it was, the new piggery, the hope of the kolkhoz –
well built, everything in apple-pie order. The new piggery
for the champion pig-breeder, 'the pride of the kolkhoz'.

She felt an urge to touch Kostya's neck with her free hand. There it lay in the moonlight too – a strong, working-woman's hand. 'I feel part of you, my sweet, I can't go on without you. If you knew what I'm suffering, you'd forgive me – you're so kind, I know you are.' Why didn't she wake him, and tell him the whole story and say: 'Forgive me if you can, for your own happiness' sake – we are part of each other. If you forgive me, I promise I'll care for you my whole life long. I'll slave for you and love you till my very last breath.'

Her hand dropped. Even if he forgave her now, he might think better of it afterwards. It wasn't only she who would have to put up with bitterness and spite, it was Kostya as well. No, the noose was drawn as tight as it could be – and she had tied it round her own neck.

Was there no way out? Yes, one – and a very simple one.

What was there to live for if everything collapsed around her? They would throw her out of her job, her husband would disown her – why should she live, to be covered in shame? Yes, indeed there was a simple way out.

The tears dried in her eyes; she felt as if a cold stone had been laid on her breast.

All she had to do was to free her arm cautiously from under Kostya's head, get up and go into the hallway, where some rope was hanging on a peg – it had been used during the summer to tie up bundles of hay. Then she would take it straight to the attic . . . Perhaps she would stop just a minute to look at the sky. There was a sharp frost, and the moon's disc had a ring round it. One last look at the moon, and the earth where there was no place for her. One last chance to remember that warm night with its storm of insects, the happiest there could ever be. The curls of down on Kostya's neck. For the last time . . .

She no longer felt tearful: her resolution grew stronger. But Kostya clutched her more tightly, his breathing became more agitated, and she was afraid of waking him. Well, there was no hurry – there would always be time for what she meant to do.

Dawn was breaking. The moon paled, and the sun pushed

its way up from behind the forests. Its rays darted out, and
the old cottage began to creak in the frosty air.

No, she would wait for a while.

Kostya had not woken up; she now had both arms about
him. Soon he would be getting out of bed, fresh-faced, with
his light, freckled cheeks . . .

No, she would wait. There was still a week's grace: she
might as well make use of it. Bare-legged and without a
scarf, she went out across the frosty yard to fetch firewood.
Returning with an armful of logs, which were chilly and
heavy as lead, she found that her mother had got down from
her sleeping-place on top of the stove.

'Take care of your own work, Nastya dear, I'll look after
things here. I had a dream last night about your father,
God rest his soul: we were walking along the shoals at
Klimovskoye, and there were some fish in the dream –
perch, all of them. A golden fish – that's a sign of good
fortune.'

Nastya washed and put on her boots, and then hurried
back to the bed to catch a glimpse of Kostya as he lay
still sleeping. Clumsily, she trod on a squeaky board
and he woke up. He raised his dishevelled head with
a dazed, sleepy expression. She smoothed his hair with
her rough palm and said – quickly, so as to disguise the
pain she felt – 'It's morning, my sweetest.' Then she went
out.

When she was half way to the piggery, she saw Zhenka
Kruchinin's truck tearing along the highway towards the
village. Could it be something for her at this hour?

Apparently it was. Zhenka pulled up beside her, poked his
cheeky face out of the cab window and said:

'Thinking of burning the place down, your ladyship?'

'What do you mean, burning the place down?'

'Well, why have they made me race over here at the
crack of dawn – Artemy Bogdanovich's orders, he told me
yesterday I was to get all your stuff out of here right away
and not keep your ladyship waiting a moment longer. Be
sure you tell him how punctual I'm being.' He yawned
luxuriously. 'The carpenters are on their way already. Yes,

just as if you were going to burn the place down or something.'

'What does Artemy Bogdanovich think he's doing? . . . Kostya's still only half awake.'

'Would you like me to wait at the doorstep, your ladyship?'

'Since you're here, you can go and wake Kostya up. I've got my own work to do.'

She walked on towards the piggery. Clearly she wasn't going to be allowed any peace, even in her last short week.

As always, Keshka was the first to scent her arrival: he pushed up the bar with his snout and rushed towards her, breathless and joyful, making little whimpering noises and trembling with impatience to be caressed. This happened every morning. Afterwards Keshka would squeal loudly, the others would wake up, hungry after sleep, and the place would echo with their cries demanding food.

Usually she pushed away the importunate Keshka – 'Get out and don't pester me, you silly little beast!' – but today his joyful devotion cut her to the heart; she felt quite dazed by it.

She had been drunk on fame and admiration, and now what was left of it all? There was one single living being that loved her and would not shy away from her or cast her off. Even her mother, her own mother would condemn her. The one solitary soul that would stick by her was the little pig Keshka. He was fond of her, she could trust him, he was the only one who would not betray her.

She felt a stab of self-pity which made her legs give way under her. Sitting on the ground, she embraced Keshka's snout and rubbed her forehead against his rough, bristly ear, exclaiming: 'Oh, my faithful sweetheart!' It was the cry of a hunted animal – a cry of reproach to human kind.

Yegor Pomelov and his team of carpenters worked hard all day. By evening Nastya's cottage had disappeared: instead, she saw a pile of logs and the lonely stove, the front door leaning against it, its familiar staple and bolt hanging loose.

A light, dry snow was falling; the stovepipe pointed up at

the sky. The old house was demolished; her mother and
Kostya had moved into Kostya's house in the village,
where his mother lived with her daughter and son-in-law.
The walls were gone, and everything else would be dis-
mantled tomorrow. It was like looking at the scene of a
fire . . .

All day long, since she had burst into tears over Keshka,
Nastya had had savage thoughts about people – they were
all her enemies, every single one. For the time being, they
were still doing things for her: it was for her sake that they
had taken her home to pieces, reducing it to these piles of
logs and the bare, chilly stove pointing heavenwards. This
was the beginning of the end: a scene of desolation, like that
after a fire. Nastya stood looking at it, and felt a cold thrill
run down her back. Catching her breath, she realised that
she had found a way of freeing her head from the noose. It
was a perilous way – but what had she to lose now?

21

As arranged, she spent the night at Pavla's, while Kostya
and her mother remained at his house in the village: it was
better for her to stay in Utitsy than have to walk miles in
the morning to the piggery.

That night, like the previous one, she did not sleep, but
lay awake thinking.

At dawn she went as usual to the piggery. She lit the
stove, cleaned the place out and distributed the bucketfuls
of swill. In a corner, under a small table, there was a gallon
bottle of kerosene, which she used to splash on the wood
when it was damp and would not burn properly. The can,
which had stood there for a long time, was dusty and almost
full. She placed it carefully close by the stove.

Before dinner she said to Pavla:

'I have to go to Zagarye – I've an awful lot to do there. I
have to see Pukhnachov and look in at the bank about
mother's pension. If I don't get finished by the end of the
day, I'll stay the night with Maruska. Mind you feed the
pigs well, tonight and tomorrow morning if I'm not back.'

'Don't worry,' Pavla replied. 'I'll look after them – I've done it before.'

Kostya rode up on his motor-cycle across the fresh snow – he had come to see how Nastya was getting on without him. She told him too that she was going to Zagarye.

All their goods and chattels had been moved, including Nastya's coat with the lambskin collar. She could not go to the district centre in the shabby quilted jacket in which she looked after the pigs; so Pavla lent her a sheepskin coat and a woollen scarf, and she rode to the bus-stop on the pillion of Kostya's machine.

'Why stay overnight in a strange place?' said Kostya. 'When you've finished there, come and stop the night in the village, then I can take you to Utitsy in the morning.'

'All right,' said Nastya. 'If I'm not too late, I'll do that.'

Seeing her in a borrowed sheepskin coat, with light felt boots and galoshes, Kostya felt as if Nastya were somehow a stranger . . . When she got to Zagarye, Maruska was delighted that she hadn't forgotten her old friend. The last time, Nastya had been desperate because her pigs were dying, and had come for help. In those days she was just an ordinary farm-hand, but now she was as famous as anyone in the district, and yet here she was calling on Maruska just like old times.

'Maruska dear, I've so many things to do here – I've got to go to the bank and then see the district committee people, it'll take me all day. It looks as if I'll have to stay the night with you.'

'But of course, dear, why not? We're only too pleased to have you whenever you like.'

Maruska was a good soul . . . The house was her own property, and every bed in it was nickel-plated and had a feather mattress.

'But I may not be finished till after midnight. You know what it is with these meetings and discussions, they go on till all hours.'

'Come at any time you like – just knock at the window and I'll let you in. I'll make up a clean bed for you in the evening.'

'I am giving you a lot of trouble, aren't I?'

'No trouble at all. What an idea! We're old friends, after all.'

The early winter's day was a short one – what with her journey and stopping to talk to Maruska, it was already dusk: the street lamps were alight outside the post office and district committee headquarters. She popped into the bank and knocked at Sivtsov's office. He was glad to see her and ready to help over her mother's pension, but he would have to make enquiries of the social welfare department and the military. Sivtsov crooked the fingers of his bony hands and looked kindly at Nastya through his thick spectacles, but there was a touch of severity in his courteous tone: 'Yes, I know you're a celebrity, but even celebrities have to obey the rules.'

'It looks as if I'll have to spend the night here,' said Nastya with a sigh of resignation. 'I won't get everything done today.'

She did not linger in the bank, but went straight to the district committee. There she found that both Pukhnachov and Kuchin were away in the countryside for the day, chasing up belated grain deliveries. Instead of them she saw Lapshov, one of the supervisors, and said: 'I'll be staying the night here. I'll come in first thing in the morning.'

Having done this, she did not make for Maruska's but went straight to the bus-stop. As she walked along she wrapped the shawl more tightly around her and turned up her coat-collar so that her nose could not be seen, only her eyes. This was a natural enough thing to do: it was frosty, and the light, dry snow was coming down again.

As she had calculated, the bus had not yet left – otherwise she would have had at least two hours to wait.

She sat in the bus, muffled up to her eyes, and pretended to be asleep. Almost everyone in the district knew her by sight; and there, two rows in front of her, was the lanky youth who had installed the machinery in the new piggery. He had not recognised her, muffled up and wearing a strange coat as she was; he sat there hunched in an untidy attitude, reading a book, and got out at the village stop.

Nastya went three stops further, to where a side-road led off straight across the fields to Utitsy.

There was not a soul on the road – no one was likely to leave their house on such a dark, cold night as this. She clasped the shawl round her and half-ran as far as Utitsy. Lights were still burning in a few cottages, where people were sitting around the samovar drinking a late-night cup of tea. One of the windows at Pavla's was alight, though she was not expecting Nastya to return from Zagarye. But there was no light at Nastya's own place – no light, no windows and no cottage: all that was left of it was a pile of wooden beams and the big, freezing stove.

Faster and faster she went along the path – its every bump and pot-hole were known to her, she could have followed it blindfold without stumbling. The scattered lights of Utitsy were behind her now – her own native place where she could no longer live, where her cottage had been turned into a pile of logs.

The door of the piggery was fastened with a heavy padlock, and that day she had handed the key to Pavla – a key on a piece of string, duly and properly handed over . . . She pulled off one of her mittens: in the palm of her hand she had, for some hours past, been clutching another key exactly like it. No one knew the duplicate existed – she used to keep it out of sight on a shelf near the stove, above the wooden table.

The heavy lock fell open, and she pushed the door. Through the scarf she felt on her face the warm air and the rank smell which marked the beginning of every working day.

She pulled the door shut behind her, but did not turn on the light. She stood for a moment, imagining the scene. The boar Dandelion was snorting, asleep in his sty; the thick air was alive with puffing and rustling noises. The life that went on here was sheltered from the great world: it consisted of sleeping and feeding, carcasses of meat and lard growing heavier day by day. Now this sleeping life was about to be cut short, overtaken by calamity . . .

Suddenly her heart gave a jump – she remembered

Keshka: faithful, loving Keshka . . .

She got out a box of matches, and tore the stifling scarf from her face. The matches broke in her trembling fingers.

'Oh, my God! Oh, curse it, curse it all!'

At last there was a flash of light. She hurriedly screened it with her hand in case it should be seen through the window, and looked about her. A bundle of kindling wood under the stove; beside it, a bundle of straw; a bench or two, the rickety table, some empty buckets, a spade. Where was the kerosene bottle? – ah, there it was!

The match went out. It was dark and quiet, here in the room next door to those lives which Nastya had fostered, day in day out, with her own hands. Rosy, Rowan and Goldy were all as big as mountains now, but there had been a time when she held them in her lap and fed them from bottles – when she was miserable if they pined and did not eat, and full of joy if they ate and frisked about. Each of the piglets had been her own child – she had tended them, petted them and spoken words of love to them. And now she was about to strike a match, and disaster would overcome them. One little match would bring death to Rosy, Rowan, Goldy and Keshka. Keshka too!

She held the box in her hand. Suppose she did not strike it after all? They might simply try her as a criminal – she wouldn't mind that, it wasn't the sentence, perhaps they would be lenient or even pardon her. No, it was the shame, the lifelong shame – everyone would spit when they saw her, her husband would have nothing more to do with her, her mother would die of sorrow; and she hadn't even a home left, only a heap of logs. She loved the pigs and was sorry for them, but if she spared them, she would die herself. Which was dearer, the pigs or her own life?

With trembling hands Nastya groped for the bottle, which was plugged with a piece of rag. She pulled this out and heard the cheerful gurgling of the kerosene as it splashed to her feet, filling the place with its sharp fumes.

The piggery was old and solidly built. Its walls were timbered, and its roof was of planking with birch bark between, so that the rain would not get in even if the planks rotted. Roofs of that sort lasted for dozens of years . . .

The smell of the kerosene. Just a match put to the straw . . .

'Thinking of burning the place down, your ladyship?' Well, why shouldn't she? She had a good alibi. She had been at Zagarye, where Maruska had seen her, as well as Sivtsov at the bank and Lapshov at the district Party committee, and she had told every one of them that she was staying the night there – and what was more, she was going to do just that. In a little over an hour the bus would be coming along and she would get in, with her face covered by a scarf and a stranger's coat on. She would get to Maruska's – 'Oh, my dear, I've been simply run off my feet!' – and find a feather bed with clean sheets all ready and waiting. Then in the morning:

'Nastya! Heavens above – there's been an accident at your place!'

An accident! She would be distraught, she would rush off home without a thought for her mother's affairs or for Pukhnachov, whom she had been so anxious to see the day before. An accident! Oh, heavens! That careless wretch of a Pavla! I only have to go away for one night, and look what happens!

Of course she was sorry for the pigs – she had nursed them and brought them up, she wasn't a monster, her heart bled for them. But it was them or her this time, and pity must go to the wall. For the sake of her husband, her home, her whole life – if she were not to lose all these, she must light that match.

But wait a moment. It was not for nothing that she had lain awake all night making her plans. The piggery was completely airtight, and the fire might go out. She felt her way to the window and, with her elbow clad in the sheepskin coat, pushed out first one pane and then another. A gentle frosty breeze mingled with the reek of kerosene.

Just one match . . . She still hesitated, shifting from one foot to another; then she made up her mind. She pushed open the inner door and called softly: 'Keshka!'

Even he was asleep, the silly little thing – he had not noticed that she was there . . . Then she heard him stirring some way off. All the pigs were shut up in their sties, and he was the only one who knew how to push up the bar with his snout. Everyone in the kolkhoz knew this trick of his – he was as much of a celebrity as Nastya herself. Nobody would be surprised if Keshka were the only one to escape from the fire.

'Keshka! Come here!'

Out he jumped, squealing and pushing at her knees, delighted by her unexpected presence. Holding the outer door ajar, she shoved him into the yard, saying: 'Run along, my pet! Quick!'

That was that. Now the match!

It spluttered and flamed; the beams of the walls were lit with a fever-red glow. Dandelion, suspecting no harm, heaved and sighed in his pen at the far end. Nastya dashed to the door and opened it wide. She looked back just once at the walls on which the light danced merrily, then sprang out, re-fastened the padlock as well as her shaking hands would let her, and turned the key.

The road was empty; the snow came drifting down. It was dark, and there was not a soul about. Behind her a few windows glowed, where her friends and neighbours were getting ready for bed. Not a soul on the road – who would leave their warm cottages so late on a night like this? There was no need to hurry – the bus would not come for some time yet – but her feet somehow rushed her along. When it came, she would sit in it in Pavla's coat, with the scarf covering her face, and she would doze all the way to Zagarye. 'Oh, Maruska, my dear, I've been simply run off my feet' – and there would be the feather bed with the clean sheets, and in the morning: 'Nastya! Nastya! Heavens above – there's been an accident at your place!'

Not a soul on the road! Suddenly she gave a start – from behind she heard a sound of heavy breathing, as though someone were chasing her. 'Oh, you silly little thing, what a fright you gave me! I nearly collapsed!' It was Keshka running after her, faithful Keshka whom she had saved from the fire. Everybody would think how clever he had been to escape . . .

Keshka nestled against her knees in his usual fashion.

'Shoo! Go away, there's a good boy! Go and live by yourself for a while. Perhaps I'll see you tomorrow.'

She pushed Keshka out of her way and ran on. How lucky there was nobody on the road – some fool might have come along and then she would be in trouble.

Keshka was still at her heels – he was running too, and was now squealing with fear. And suddenly it dawned on Nastya that he would not leave her side – he would follow her all the way to the bus. The road was empty, but at the bus-stop there would be people waiting. And even if there weren't at this time of night, the passengers in the bus were sure to see a woman and a pig on the highway, and wonder what was up. And then they would recognise Nastya, and that would be the end of her!

'Go away, curse you! Go away, you devil!'

As she turned, he ran full tilt into her skirts.

'Go away!' She hit him between the eyes with her mittened fist. He gave a short squeal and jumped backwards. Nastya continued to run. But the panting noise still pursued her. She felt a chill under the warm coat – disaster had caught her unawares, it was death at her heels. And she herself had let the animal go free, had taken pity on him – once more she was being made to pay the price for taking pity on another creature.

'You wretch, you cursed little monster!' Her hands were trembling; cold shivers ran up and down her back, which was sweating under the sheepskin coat. She swerved out of Keshka's path, fell on her knees and began feverishly digging in the snow with her mittened hands – if only she could find a stone, the bigger the better, to drive away the devil that was chasing her! But all she could find under the layer of snow were lumps of frozen earth. She threw some at him. 'Get away from me, you accursed beast! Get away, do you hear?'

Keshka was squealing; his shadow loomed as he trotted

round her in the dark. Still on her knees, she crawled
forward, gulping down her tears.

'If I'd known – my God, if I'd known! You wretch, you
fiend, what wouldn't I have done to you!'

At last – a big, heavy clod of frozen earth, caked with
snow! Clutching it in both hands, she rose to her feet.
Keshka, frightened now and mistrustful, was keeping his
distance. She called to him:

'Keshka, come here, my beauty, my darling! Come here,
you silly thing.' Her coaxing tone was strangled by tears.
'Come here, damn you – come here, I say!'

Keshka came sidling up; she brought the heavy stone
down on his snout, and a blood-curdling scream echoed
over the field. He disappeared into the night, which re-
sounded with his piteous, heart-rending cry of injury and
sorrow.

Then an extraordinary thing happened. It was as if
Keshka's scream had awakened Nastya, and she now saw
herself clearly and pitilessly as if through another's eyes, as
she stood there in the desolate snowy field in the thick
darkness. She saw herself as a criminal hiding from her
fellow-men – hiding because she was no longer one of them.
Everyone but her repaid affection with kindness – she had
answered it by casting a stone. People had admired and
honoured her – her answer was to light a match, to burn
what had been her sacred trust, to consign it to the flames.
Even now the pigs would be screaming in the terror of their
death-agony. Death by fire to all her labours, to her past
joys and sorrows, to every living thing that her hands had
created! The pigs were screaming as she stood there under
the lightly falling snow – the languid flakes that reminded
her now of the dying insects of that happy August night: the
boat on the river, Venka, her own youth . . . She felt horror
and repulsion towards herself – a monstrous outcast, alone
in the dark field. The pigs were screaming . . .

She remained still for a minute only – just as long as it
took for Keshka's cry of pain to die down. Then she set off
back at full speed towards the village – where her fellow-
villagers were, where the fire was burning and the pigs were

wailing – back, back to the things and people that were hers.

Sweat poured into her eyes. Without stopping, she pulled of the woollen scarf and flung it away. Breathless and stumbling, she tore at the buttons of the heavy coat and cast it off likewise. Bare-headed and wearing only her dress, she ran on, heedless of the cold, panting hoarsely, tripping and picking herself up again . . .

In the village, a single midnight window was still alight. No glow from the fire could be seen. She ran past the place where her own cottage had been, the stove and the pile of beams, her own private plot – along the tracks made by her own footsteps. She would, she must reach the piggery in time! There it was in the distance, dark and sleepy, the roof lightly coated at one end with snow. Nothing seemed to be the matter – could she have imagined it all?

But before she reached the building she heard the pigs' desperate cries, muffled by its walls. The sound spurred her on.

She stood at the door nearest the cooker. There was the padlock. Then her blood ran cold. She did not have the key – it was in the pocket of the coat that she had thrown away. Through the door she heard the pigs' shrill tumult and a kind of crazy, stamping dance. There was the padlock, but no key. The gate at the other end was barred on the inside.

She rushed along the side of the building, trying one window after another; but they were narrow, with strong frames, and there was no hope of forcing them except with an axe. When she got to the corner she gasped in horror. The side that faced the village was dark and sleepy, but behind it the snow was suffused by a pink glow. Fierce, greedy flames and eddies of black smoke were pouring out of the window. The flames were licking at the walls, part of which had turned to a bright golden colour that hurt the eyes. Suddenly an impish flame appeared, flickering and dancing, at a single spot on the roof. She heard the hoarse bellowing of the pigs, now mad with terror, and could do nothing. She wrung her hands and screamed:

'Help! He-e-elp!'

Still screaming, she ran to the village, to the first cottage with a light in the window. She hammered at it with all her strength, crying 'Help! He-e-elp!' Then to the next one: 'Help! He-e-elp!'

One after another, doors were flung open; men shouted hoarsely, women gasped and screamed. The glow around the piggery could be seen clearly now: it was a dull purplish colour, like embers in a dying stove.

The doors banged open, and above all the din rose the sound of Nastya's desperate, imploring wail:

'Help, he-elp! Save them, save them!'

Save them, good people – and save Nastya!

Under the title *Podyonka-Vek Korotkii* this story was published in *Novy Mir* 5, 1965, pp. 95-141.